THE BLACKTHORN
CONSPIRACY

A NOVEL OF INTRIGUE, DECEPTION, GUILT, INNOCENCE, POWER, EXPLOITATION, GREED, SEX, AND POLITICAL DENIAL, ALL ON THE BRINK OF GLOBAL ECONOMIC AND MILITARY WAR.

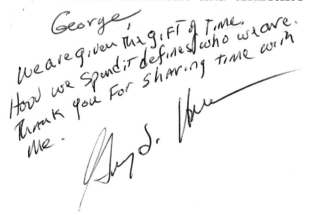

George,
We are given this gift of Time.
How we spend it defines who we are.
Thank you For sharing time with
me.

THE BLACKTHORN CONSPIRACY

T.T. BROTHERS

BRYCE
CULLEN
PUBLISHING

PO Box 731
Alpine, NJ 07620
brycecullen.com

Cover design by Tracey Polson

ISBN 978-1-935752-13-4

Library of Congress Control Number: 2011942675

Printed in the United States of America

10 9 8 7 6 5 4 3 2 1

CONTENTS

PROLOGUE

FOR the past century, the nations of the world have experienced the radical changes of six major wars, many revolutions, military skirmishes too numerous to count, and natural disasters resulting in staggering amounts of damage. The dynamic changes in governments—peaceful but sometimes violent—have produced both good and bad results for countries around the globe. Regrettably, some dictators and international leaders have imposed their malignant philosophies on the majority of peoples in parts of the world. Changes in leadership or entire governments have served as vehicles for creating the best and worst conditions on Earth. Advancements in science, medicine, and technology, as well as the information revolution, have sparked positive changes that have benefited the masses enormously. However, with the positive accomplishments have come the negative, exposing an expansion of greed, prejudice, theft, persecution, terrorism, and exploitation of peoples unable to defend themselves. For example, with the advent of advanced thinking and the expansion of technological thought, talented intellectuals and business entrepreneurs have brought to the world the hybrid automobile, micro-mass production techniques, the use of robotics, the airplane, and rockets able to deliver destructive payloads long distances from the point of launch to faraway places, as well as propel man into space. With all these creations has come the ambitious quest for resources to fuel these innovations. That pursuit has propelled the world into a dangerous encampment of opposing ideologies bent on controlling the supply of valuable resources.

The twentieth century might well be known by several names. First, it was the age of mass production and locomotion. Second, it became known as the jet age as advances were made to pierce the sound barrier with a capability of moving objects from place to place in record time, reducing the size of the Earth not by miles, but by hours of travel. Third, it was an age of exploration as discoveries were made to conquer diseases, transplant organs to prolong life, conquer space by landing a man on the Moon, propel a telescope into space to view the cosmos, and send crafts to distant planets in hope of discovering other signs of life. The exploration of Earth, particularly life under the ocean, made huge advances. Fourth, the peoples of the Earth were propelled into an electronics age that expanded man's ability to store, control societal infrastructure, and transmit information, which again reduced the size of the Earth into minutes. Indeed, we have discovered ways to accelerate as well as disable and cripple elements of a nation's infrastructure in lieu of invading them. If we accept the reformation as an age of enlightenment, then during the twentieth century a second reformation—or an information age—occurred, which now exponentially expands yearly.

Sadly, repeated missed opportunities to right the wrongs of generations have found the United States and its neighbors increasingly driven by events that have occurred apparently outside the control of any power or nation. Rather, mankind has been required to react to events instead of shaping them, not unlike a knee-jerk reaction. This has been nowhere more prevalent than in the Middle East, where subversive elements and governments of that region have influenced their people to believe that great nations with strong economic and military power lack the resolve to fight for interests of other nations as well as their own, abhorring economic and financial pain. In spite of this attitude, the revolutions and civil wars in the Middle East in the 2010 to 2011 time frame seem to have the theme of doing away with despots, dictators, and repressive governments, in favor of an emphasis on the desires and needs of the people. This is admirable, and indeed what the United States has advocated and stood for in the last two hundred years, but continued assault on US and allied motives has led many around the world to doubt the resolve of the United States and its allies. Many nations have come to believe that the United States has become one of those faux powers. In spite of US accomplishments to successfully seek out and kill Osama bin Ladin, we are still regarded as ineffective and inefficient. Bin Ladin is now regarded as a martyr for the Islamist terrorist community.

A belief has come to persist in many nations of the world that the United States resists making the sacrifices needed to stand up to interests that are inimical to its own objectives, such as being negligent in advocating its own security. Various internal political policies and financial imperatives over the years have been opposed to strong military preparedness, causing some to believe that the United States has failed to support and defend the principals of its own Constitution.

Foreign nations have come to believe we hold our laws so inviolate, to the point where we will support and defend the rights of foreigners to come to the United States—foreigners who then take our wealth without paying for it or offering any exchange in kind. The reaction to the actions by fundamentalists such as Adolf Hitler, Mao Tse Tung, Nikita Khrushchev, Ho Chi Mihn, Saddam Hussein, Osama bin Laden, and Muammar Gaddafi have led some to decide that the United States will not react to the activities of international despots until it is too late. They believe that when it comes, our response will be overreaction and a commitment of our national treasure and blood to fix what is broken—at the expense of our own independence.

Hopefully the foregoing will cause the reader to better understand the events that will be presented in *The Blackthorn Conspiracy*.

1

THE THREE AMIGOS
TUALATIN

Into each person's life, if they are so fortunate, come three good friends. Good friends are those people who are with you, stay with you, and support you through thick and thin.

LEE Grady, PhD, criminologist, widower, and federal agency consultant, glanced in the rearview mirror, signaled, and then slowly steered his 2017 maroon Corvette into the far right-hand lane. Debussy's "Clare de Lune" was playing serenely on the Sirius Satellite radio channel on the Corvette's Bose stereo system. It was one of those clear, warm, amber Oregon October days in 2016. He was about to meet up with his two oldest friends after twenty-five years. His cell phone rang. "Hello, this is Lee Grady."

"Hi Eag, this is Jerry. Where are you?"

Years ago in their college days, everyone referred to Lee Grady and Jerry Mayhew as the "Eagles" because of their friendship, their independence, and their strong attitudes about both serious and frivolous things—women, clothes, military service, university policies, and authority in general. Today they still refer to one another as "Eag," short for Eagle.

"At this moment I am at the Tualatin exit and almost to Dave's Famous Ribs restaurant. Where are you?"

"I'm almost there too. I'll see you in a few. John called a moment ago and informed me that he will be a little late. He's fighting the traffic trying to get onto I-5."

After arriving at the restaurant, Lee stepped out of his car and looked back and smiled admiringly. He then made his way towards the entrance. Inside, the hostess greeted him. She was young but mature, shapely and very much in control of her domain. "Hi, are you here for lunch?"

"Yes, but I have two friends joining me. I'll go sit down. They'll find me when they get here. I'm the only guy in here that looks like me."

A few moments later, Jerry approached the table, a big grin etched on his face. "Is there a doctor in the house?"

Rising to greet his old friend, Lee extended his hand. "What's all this formality bullshit, Eag? Nobody refers to me as Doctor except students."

"You don't say? Well, we've both come a long way since an incident involving an old Model A Ford during a snowstorm on the Willamette U campus. Perhaps you also recall that night before finals when a gallon of red wine was consumed in the fraternity house before we took that trip across the quad in your Model A? We made a pretty good mess of the quad with those figure eights, right?"

"Right, now however, how are you, Eag? How's your prostate, your colon, and your heart? At our age you know, we tend to narrow down our concerns to what's really important."

"I'm fine and they are fine. Life has been really good to you, too."

"Well, it hasn't all been a bed of roses, but I take care of myself, watch what I eat and drink, and stay in shape."

"Yeah, we really do have a lot of catching up to do."

"So, what have you been doing all of these years, Jerry?"

"Well, I retired from the Air Force as a colonel, and then I went to work for the CIA."

"I'm sure you remember Connie. She and I didn't make it. She met and remarried a retired Air Force general. She's much better off than she would have been with me, but before the split, she gave me two wonderful daughters."

"My next wife, like yours, died of cancer after some really great years. Near the end it was very painful for her. I'm sure you know what I mean."

Now I'm married to Joy. Someday I'll retire and disappear to the Galapagos Islands and no one will ever find me."

Lee chuckled, "That would be ideal."

A waitress appeared at the table. She was in her mid-thirties and had short blonde hair and sparkling blue eyes. She offered, "What will it be, boys? Are you here for some ribs? Would you like to start off with something to drink?"

Lee nodded eagerly, "Yes we are. There is another person joining us. Why don't you just bring us a couple of beers to start?"

The waitress smiled, nodded, and started to depart. Turning back towards them, she offered, "My name is Debbie. I will be your waitress, so when your friend arrives, just give me the high sign, and I'll take your orders."

Lee nodded, "That's terrific, Debbie. You sound like you might be from the South."

Debbie smiled. "Yes, that would be Florida. I'll be back in a moment with your beers."

"Debbie, why don't you make it three beers? Our friend will be here in just a moment."

"Debbie nodded. "Three beers coming up."

Moments later, with their beers in front of them, Lee and Jerry heard a husky voice from behind them say with authority, "I see you have ordered for me as well. I really appreciate that. You don't know how thirsty I am. John extended his hand and reached around Jerry's shoulder to give a bear hug that only longtime friends can offer. John turned towards Lee and extended his hand and both embraced in a similar, masculine bear hug.

Jerry chuckled. "I'm not going to be long on ceremony, John. Slide your ass in here beside us and join in as we catch up." Jerry turned towards the bar and extended his arm, denoting that one more beer was needed.

"Well, Lee, what are you waiting for? What have you been doing?"

Lee looked at the table for a moment, gathering his thoughts for what he had to offer. Looking at John, he asked, "Did you know about my Sandy?"

John nodded affirmatively.

"Well after many years of a great marriage she died of cancer. She put up a valiant effort, but the disease was just too much for her. I don't need to tell either of you. You both know what an insidious disease cancer is. But let's not dwell on the sadness of life. Let's talk about drives and putts. My handicap on good days for eighteen holes is a six registered with my club."

John couldn't contain himself, offering, "Holy shit. Your handicap is right where mine is. We should team up sometime in a tournament."

Jerry then said, "Count me out of golf tournaments unless you need someone with a maximum handicap. Lee, just for curiosity's sake before we get too far away from events of the recent past, how was it, working professionally with Sandy and the federal prosecutor's office, if it isn't too painful to talk about?"

"Well, I had nothing to do with her legal case involving the prosecution of Trish Knight/Anatolia, a.k.a. Pat Brown. I was intentionally kept out of the loop so that Trish would testify against her father. We all also agreed that we needed to avoid possible allegations of conflict of interest because my activities indirectly supported Sandy. I had previously known Trish when I was at Naval OCS. I met her as Trish Knight but was told that her original family name was Anatolia."

"Yeah, yeah, I know all about the Anatolia Enterprises connection."

"Well, her father concocted a story about her demise to throw me and legal investigators off her trail. After Trish's supposed death she moved to the West Coast as the wife of Vinnie Trabogo. Sandy tracked her down and found that her husband had disappeared under mysterious circumstances. She was able to gain Trish's confidence and proceed with her case against elements of the Anatolia family. After Sandy died, I met with Trish at the insistence of my daughters to clear up the mystery. For your information, I am seeing Trish now when she's in town. She travels a lot. She is starting some kind of new operation in McMinnville. The long and short of it is that after my service in the US Navy, I got my PhD in Criminology and used my degree to teach and do investigative work for the federal prosecutors office, Sandy, and occasionally for the FBI and the CIA. I guess you could say that I'm sometimes retired and sometimes a freelance investigator."

Interrupting, Jerry looked at John and offered, "Lee is too modest. You have to know that the bureau and the agency like using Lee for ongoing cases and investigations both in the US and overseas because he is thorough, meticulous, observant, and tenacious when on a case."

Lee nodded affirmatively. "The tasks have usually not been dangerous, but on occasion, I've found myself in some potentially compromising and precarious situations. Jerry, it makes me shiver sometimes to think how close I came to a tragic, but unexplained termination. Even though it was authorized and I was trained to shoot it, I never carried a concealed weapon for self-defense. I guess I always knew that if I ever drew it, I'd have to use it. I'm not sure I could snuff out the life of another person dispassionately." Pausing for a moment, Lee continued, "I'm sorry to have dominated the conversation."

The waitress approached cautiously, inquiring, "Would you gentlemen care for another round? On second thought, are you ready to order some of our famous ribs?"

Lee nodded. "Yes, Debbie, why don't you bring us another round, and I think that eighteen bones should just about do it. We can fight over who gets the most. At a buck a bone, it could turn out to be a real free-for-all."

Jerry chuckled, offering, "That sounds great."

John echoed, "Count me in!"

"Okay then, gentlemen. I'll be right back with the order."

John then said, "Well, now I believe that it is time for me to share."

He began, in his usual casual and conservative manner, by talking about where he'd been and what he'd done in the last twenty or so years. "Most recently I have been the deputy ambassador to Egypt for the past two years. Last week I received reassignment orders to Iran. I have to report for indoctrination in four days, but I don't take the post until June. I am not sure exactly what I will do about the situation there. If you read the papers, you know what I mean."

Jerry nodded. "John, from what I know about you, I think your judgment in this case is perfect. I'd also say that there are some great things that have been said about you in the quiet halls of government. Just between us girls, you are held in high esteem by national security officials as well as diplomats in all levels of our government."

John smiled and then jokingly said, "Aw shucks, guys, I'm just a poor bandage binder trying to get by."

All three laughed at John's uncharacteristic country-boy modesty.

"Well, I think that we all agree that not being 'in the know' is completely foreign to your nature, John. In the past years both in medicine and politics, you have been a man always well prepared with information before you ever begin working toward a goal."

"You're exactly right, Jerry. Politics and international relations in that region of the world are still strained. The current US ambassador to Iran has worked hard to stabilize relations between our two countries, but progress has been slow. We do, however, now have an embassy in Tehran, and I'll be moving into it in late spring."

Lee interjected, "John, before your retirement five years ago from practicing medicine here in Oregon, you were an ophthalmic surgeon with a great reputation. I know you are a dedicated medical practitioner, as well as a dedicated political scientist. Thankfully for you, in forty-five years of marriage to Rosemary, she has always given you encouragement and assistance."

"Yes, she has been really super about being dragged all over the world—and she is my closest diplomatic advisor. Well, you both know that after I completed my medical studies years ago—and after completing a tour with the US Air Force as a flight surgeon in Vietnam—I followed my heart into medical missionary work, feeling that physical healing and intellectual understandings were concepts that were inextricably intertwined. So, I was inspired to return to school to earn a PhD in political science. While practicing medicine I also practiced a bit of diplomacy by quietly speaking to heads of state, prime ministers, foreign secretaries, and many military generals and admirals, offering my unsolicited diagnoses on the medical and political status of their nations."

"I have heard that your opinions in both fields have been quietly solicited by not only the leaders of nations around the world, but by presidents and congressional leaders in the United States.

"Jerry, you are too kind. All I know is that it is time for us to wrap up this bullshit session and get down to the serious matter of enjoying these ribs." John paused for a moment and then continued, "Jerry, when are you headed back to DC?"

"I leave tomorrow, but before we leave here today, I want us to all promise to meet again, sooner rather than later."

The three amigos all shook their heads in unison, as if programmed to do so. They all quietly laughed knowing full well the future was tenuous and indefinite.

2

THE INAUGURATION
THE BEGINNING OF CHANGE

A beginning, a bridge to the past, is sometimes heralded as a fresh start while at other times merely a continuation. When the need for change is proclaimed, hope springs eternal that this new beginning will accomplish all that is necessary. Not unlike any widely anticipated event, the excitement is electric.

CELL phone time indicators, computer time indicators, and all other time pieces synchronized with the official time of the day registered 7:22 a.m. (EST), January 20, 2017. This was a special day, a special moment. Long awaited, the much anticipated event was but four hours and thirty-eight minutes away. With hope and excitement viewers were glued to their TV sets, any display broadcast in the streets or any other broadcasting venue across the United States, as well as the rest of the globe. The eagerly anticipated event, Inauguration Day, was about to unfold in the United States of America.

The sun had just broken the horizon over the Chesapeake Bay, the first rays of light streaming across the eastern shore over Annapolis, over Suitland, over Fort Meade, racing toward Washington, DC, where the biggest twenty-four-hour party in the history of the nation was about to play out, with the temperature expected to reach a windy high of thirty degrees Fahrenheit at noon under a crystal-clear blue sky.

In contrast, three thousand miles away on the other side of the country, in a small, rural community in the Pacific Northwest, most people were still asleep. Those who were awake had only a casual interest in the events in Washington, DC, at that moment. Those up and about were doing their best to deal with the impact of an unusually severe winter storm. McMinnville, Oregon, most often identified as the home of Linfield College, Evergreen Aviation, and the new home for the famous Spruce Goose, was not unlike most other places across the nation. *Good Morning America*, *The Today Show*, Fox News, MSNBC, and others were already busy with the endless details necessary to provide the in-depth televised coverage of this special event, which was so widely and enthusiastically anticipated. In two hours or so, children would be preparing to go to school. Those workers not granted the day off readied themselves for another day at the office or plant.

In a small neighborhood housing development located off South End Road in Oregon City, Lee Grady's eyes danced with excitement. From his perch on the couch in his Faircrest Drive living room, he watched as his flat screen, high-definition Toshiba clearly transmitted the historical events unfolding in Washington, DC. Beside him, still dressed in a nightgown and robe, was a very attractive blonde whose hair was a tangled mess as a result of an on-and-off night's sleep. Even so, she still looked great for that time of the morning.

Lee Grady had never been seen with a shabby looking woman, at any time of day.

Lee's voice, an intended aside and barely audible above the din of the TV, proclaimed, "It's about time! The time for this to happen in our country is long overdue. This is truly a day to celebrate. We broke the ice first with JFK and then with Obama. But today is really special because we transcend both religion and race all at once."

Trish's blue eyes flashed defiantly, a quick jerk of her head backward indicating less-than-passive disagreement. Accompanied by a disgusted stabbing wave of her left hand—not intended as a reprimand to the transmission of the events unfolding—it served as a nonverbal rebuttal of Lee's nearly inaudible remark. Gathering herself, she rebutted, "Only if you are an Independent...that would be an Independent who has no idea of the consequences of electing that liberal so-and-so." She paused for a moment to consider what she had said and then continued, "Personally, I doubt that it really matters who the president is anymore. Everything is so fucked up in this country it's a wonder that the entire nation hasn't revolted. Well, I for one have no intention of sitting around and watching the US turn into a socialist state and walk away from our responsibilities in the Middle East. I think that what this country needs is a wakeup call to get us focused on what we need to do."

"I doubt that we'll ever see eye to eye politically, but the least you can do is give the new president a chance before you pass judgment."

"Like you did with W? Come on, Lee. For an intelligent man who at times seems to have so much insight—a man who seems to know where we need to go—I can't believe that you can celebrate at a time like this."

As was his habit when a discussion started to turn into an argument, Lee turned back towards the TV, smiled, and shrugged his shoulders in resignation. This wasn't a battle he was going to win, and winning would not turn out to be a victory in this rekindled relationship with Trish. Chuckling, he teased, "You are looking particularly attractive at this early hour. I guess all that sleep we got last night agrees with you."

Trish snorted. Nodding, she offered mild rebuttal, purring, "Nice job! As usual, you avoid a confrontation when it gets too hot in the kitchen." Pausing to reflect on his efforts to redirect the conversation, she shrugged and countered, "I suppose that if you call trying to ward off an oversexed zealot all night your definition of sleeping, then I would say that, yes, it does agree with me. Now that you have brought it up, don't you think that we can leave this video offering to those who really care and go back to bed? I think that I feel a need for some more of what you just referred to as sleep."

"Hmm, that's an intriguing thought." Pausing to reflect, he continued, "You know, I think that the time has come for me to come clean and tell my daughters about us."

"Us you say?" Smiling, Trish placed her hand on his lap. "I thought that your daughters already knew about us."

"They know about you from what Sandy told them before she died, but they don't know that we have been spending a lot of time together."

"Is that what it is? Hmm, I thought that we were doing a lot more than spending time. Anyway, there isn't a rush to confess all of your sins to your daughters, because I have to return to Seattle tomorrow. I have some unfinished business up there to complete."

Lee stared at her a moment and then inquired, "So, just what are your plans? Do you plan to just go back and forth between here and Seattle, or do you still think that you'll move down here as you suggested that you contemplated doing the last time this topic arose?"

"I'll know more after my trip to Seattle." Grinning, she teased, "Enough talk. I think that we have some unfinished business to complete in the bedroom."

* * *

In DC, Jerry Mayhew gazed at his TV with indifferent approval. Not unlike the event surrounding Barack Obama's ascendency to the presidency, this was the climax—the apex of excitement that exploded onto the American scene on election night. A scant eight weeks previously, Sally Marie Chenoa (her Indian name meaning Bird of Peace) became the first Native American woman to be elected as president of the United States of America. Then, as now, faces etched with hope or stained with tears displayed smiles of joy and anticipation as the clocks across the nation slowly ticked away the moments before the great event's arrival. The nation was captivated with another first. First there was JFK, the first Catholic to be elected as president. Next Barack Obama became the first African American to be elected president, and now Sally Marie Chenoa, the first woman and the first Native American to be elected president.

JFK had his skeptics who believed he would look to Rome for political guidance to lead this country. The political pundits and speculators turned out to be wrong. Obama also had his critics and those skeptical of how he would serve. Many feared that a Muslim had been elected to the highest office in the land and that United States' policies would lean towards the Islamic faith and away from Christianity. Again the political pundits and speculators turned out to be wrong. Now the nation waited to see if the pundits would again be proven incorrect with their prediction that President Chenoa's leadership would usher in an era of racial inequality and social unrest. Would they see, as some cynics had predicted, her use of the bully pulpit to call upon years of history to mete out revenge for the way her people were treated as the white man carved out a nation, disrupting and displacing her people? It was an historical event to be captured on tape, in print, and photographs, as well as transmitted via TV, radio, the Internet, and other devices employing the use of cyberspace. The time of a long-awaited change was about to arrive.

"Those poor, overzealous bastards probably don't even feel the cold. Christ, if a person were stupid enough to stand on the highest promontory point in this city, they could see the small wisps of steam coming from all the chimneys and ventilation pipes on the roofs of every building. And why not, it's only eighteen degrees outside. I hope they are smart enough to realize that excited or not about Chenoa's election, no matter how brave they are, they are going to need multiple layers of clothing to stay warm and avoid frostbite."

"What was that you said, Jerry?" Joy, his wife, only halfheartedly sought clarification of what he had said. She too was mesmerized by the events unfolding on the screen.

"No matter. I'm just intrigued by the fact that on an ordinary day, there would be many cars laboriously making their way into Washington."

He was right. They normally would be headed south from the Beltway down the George Washington Parkway past the CIA and Roslyn, north on I-95 through the Springfield Interchange and past Franconia and Landmark, west from Maryland toward the new Woodrow Wilson Bridge that now spans the Potomac River to points west past Alexandria. Still, others would be headed east on I-66 from Front Royale and Winchester through Marshall, Haymarket, Gainesville, and Manassas, and past Fairfax. They would normally be headed into the city to greet another day of business as usual at federal agencies, in the commercial industry, at international corporations, and at special interest organizations. What they all had in common was that they would arrive at their destinations with a mild case of road rage and would need coffee, tea, or soda drinks to soothe them before they could objectively begin their work. Others among the commuters would normally be on the Metro Rail systems in subway cars packed with unenthused bureaucrats, anxious military officers, and enlisted personnel wondering what crisis awaited them on this day. There would be lobbyists, service workers, cleaning men and women, computer geeks, lawyers, students, congressional staffers and aides, and many who were special for what they knew and did, and of course, many who thought they were special but were really not. Most would appear to be zombies, reading *The Washington Post*, *The Washington Times*, *USA Today*, *The New York Times*, or *The Wall Street Journal*, looking for some news or clue that might guide their day's activities, or merely trying to be left alone in their own private world with their own private thoughts. Normally trying very hard to avoid eye contact with anyone, they only wanted to make it to their office desks without a confrontation.

This day was different. All of the usual commuters who were headed into town by car, commuter bus, Metro Rail, or car pools were uncharacteristically happy, talkative, engaging—and even excited. To top it off, they had abandoned their normal modes of transportation outside the Beltway since all routes leading into the city were closed for security purposes. These commuters were traveling into the center of the city on public transportation systems, with special tickets in their pockets that afforded them a small seat to sit on or a square piece of land to stand on, no larger than one page of a newspaper. Nearly one and a half million of these men, women, and children—yes children—were on their way to see the inauguration of the forty-sixth president of the United States.

"You know, Joy, the most astounding thing about today is that they began streaming into the city before 4:00 a.m. to stake their territorial claims. Giddy with excitement, they are engaging strangers they have only just bumped up against moments before. This is indeed a remarkable day."

Joy smiled. "Thanks for all of the information, honey. You don't know how much better I feel after learning all of those facts."

The television commentator who Joy intently listened to, but who only occasionally captured Jerry's attention, reported, "At 7:50

a.m. outgoing President Barack Hussein Obama, known by historians and humorists alike as '44,' is seated in the backseat of the new presidential limousine, a 2017 Cadillac stretch, specially equipped, bulletproof version of a 'rolling underground bunker.' The presidential limousine will drive less than one hundred yards to the front of the Blair House across the street from the White House, to meet incoming President-elect Sally Marie Chenoa. President-elect Chenoa will be known by the same historians and humorists as '45' and will soon become known as 'POTUS,' president of the United States, or by a one-word code name of her choosing. It is interesting and relevant to know that the new president—the first Native American president in the nation's 240-year history—and her predecessor, at this moment are the man and woman who represent the most powerful nation on earth. They will display, as is the custom, a completely peaceful transfer of power. They are on their way to St. John's Episcopal Church, which is a mere one hundred fifty yards from the White House. Orchestrated, but willingly electing to sit together and pray together, they and their spouses will share a mid-morning coffee before leaving for Capitol Hill. There they will demonstrate what is so rare in politics across the globe: a peaceful transfer of power from one national leader to the other at exactly high noon. High noon is usually thought of as the appointed time for two gunslingers to face off, but not on this day. Today will be welcoming and a farewell to two people from completely different backgrounds."

The commentator's co-anchor offered, "The campaign leading to this moment has been lengthy and vitriolic. President Obama has served during troubled times, trying to shed an inheritance of two wars, other international crises, and an economy that hovered on the brink of a drastic depression. Many saw him as a man who was not a citizen of the United States, aligning his political strategy with the Muslims, and a president who, along with the citizenry, faced a huge national debt that our children and grandchildren can't possibly avoid suffering the consequences of for their entire lives. He was criticized for signing a national health bill that critics chose to label 'ObamaCare.'"

The lead anchor fired back, "Yes, but President-elect Chenoa has taken her fair share of direct hits as well. Even though she served a four-year term as the governor of Idaho and was renowned as a superlative administrator, she has been broadly characterized as inexperienced, naive, never for or against anything, lacking in strategic planning skills, predicting change without ever saying what it was, and lacking any knowledge of what she will do if the international call for help comes by way of that dreaded 3:00 a.m. phone call. Considered excessive also are the continued national debt problems, as well as unemployment. Terrorism is still an issue even though Osama bin Laden and his successors are gone. Saber rattling between Pakistan and India, and the perilous situation in the Middle East, North Africa, and Korea causes continued concern about our national security."

"Chet, the amazing thing about our system is that President Obama and President–elect Chenoa are treating each other with respect, consideration, and admiration, which hasn't always been the case in the past. For example, I cite how President Herbert Hoover and President-elect Franklin D. Roosevelt reportedly rode to Capitol Hill for the inauguration in icy silence. More recently, the ride President Harry S. Truman and President-elect Dwight D. Eisenhower took where President-elect Eisenhower is purported to have only asked who recalled his son, Colonel John Eisenhower, to the United States from the war in Korea. President Truman supposedly admitted that he had done so because he thought a son should see his father be celebrated for a rare achievement. Not impressed, President-elect Eisenhower let it be known that he believed his son belonged on the warfront with his troops."

Jerry, noting the commentary on the screen, remarked, "Time

will record the event. Yes, Chenoa will become the forty-fifth President of the United States in exactly one minute on this cold but beautiful day on the twentieth of January, but I have problems cheering for the outlined agenda that she proposes to solve here and abroad. I just hope that she heeds the words of warning the vice-presidential nominee, Governor Smith, offered during the campaign."

"Yes, love, I know your passion for the opposite side, but what exactly was Mr. Smith's warning?"

Jerry replied, "He said that it will not be long after Chenoa has assumed responsibility for the office, that some nation, some foreign power, or some contrary terrorist group will economically and militarily confront her."

"That sounds strangely familiar. Hmm, do you think that Smith will be proven right?"

"I really don't know, but I suppose that when all of the euphoria of today and tonight comes to an end, the new administration will find out what reality is all about. I pray to God that it is up to the task."

Mayhew continued to sit in front of the TV, staring, but it's doubtful anything registered. His steel-blue eyes were glazed over, his jaw set defiantly. His usual smile was replaced by grim, pursed lips, hiding that toothy grin that had for so long been a trademark. Mayhew was deep in thought.

With the arrival of sunrise tomorrow, it's probably going to be a chilly January twenty-first. The White House staff will probably be euphoric, almost giddy. Their woman won and they'll believe that the dawn brought hope and promise. Needless to say, they'll also be elated that the "old rascals" are now gone.

Jerry sighed. "Yes, the West Wing staff will be looking forward to and set on making the campaign promises come true. Even with all of the euphoria, a number of them will hopefully come to realize that the implementation will not be a simple process…especially in

Washington, DC."

Mayhew looked away from the TV, glancing at his wife. He smiled, offering, "You know, Joy, for an old broad, you are still damn good looking."

Joy frowned. "Hmm, so I'm an old broad, am I?"

"It's just a term of endearment."

Joy smiled at her husband. "I know that you did not favor Chenoa's election to the presidency, but as you've always done before, I know that you will give your undying support. Like it or not, we're all in this together."

3

PEACEFUL BUT VIGILANT

Optimism is traditionally a boundless, endless characteristic,
but it sometimes has to be tempered with a sense of reality.

WITH the arrival of sunrise the next chilly morning, January 21, 2017, the White House staff was indeed euphoric. The mantle of power and responsibility had now officially been passed to them. All the members of this new administration would, from this point forward, share equally in the successes as well as the failures of the president.

The starting points for President Chenoa and her new administration were many, and so were the issues facing the nation and the world. The country was faced with the immediacy of confronting the financial system's problems, including the mortgage crisis, the volatility of the stock market, the cleanup of the lingering Middle East situation, and the need for improvement to national healthcare reform. Those were just a few of the most urgent issues.

In the bowels of the Pentagon in the offices of the Joint Chiefs of Staff National Military Command Center (the NMCC), all events, domestic and foreign, that could have impact on the national sovereignty and interests of the United States were being monitored. Data from phenomenologically different sources was being received with uninterrupted regularity and continuity. Multisource intelligence data was being fused into bins and categories of importance. The information was being forced to computer monitors arranged in several semi-circular rows of positions situated on three dais levels. Highly trained and experienced Army, Navy, Air Force, and Coast Guard—and even Canadian military officers—as well as enlisted personnel and civil service analysts stared at the computer monitors to which overhead satellite imagery and worldwide commercial network television were being funneled. Digital displays were collocated next to each monitor to allow the personnel to call up force-level, headcount, or historical and real-time information to be viewed and assessed for determination of intent or damage assessment.

An eerie glow was cast over the entire room, half the size of a standard basketball court. The glow emanated from the floor-to-ceiling, wall-to-wall segmented screens showing foreign vessels cruising at sea, space-based imagery of international troop movements and training maneuvers, and real-time imagery from cruising and circling fully armed Predator and Reaper unmanned aerial vehicles (UAVs). Other screen segments showed large civil demonstrations going on in another part of the world, special data feeds from the National Security Agency, the Central Intelligence Agency, and the National Geospatial Intelligence Agency, and selected overhead satellite reports from National Reconnaissance Office space-based platform sources. An equivalent, almost duplicate command center was located in the North American Aerospace Defense Command (NORAD) Cheyenne Mountain Complex in Colorado Springs, Colorado, and another similar center was located at Air Force Strategic Command (STRATCOM) at Offutt Air Force Base in Omaha, Nebraska. While the Pentagon center focused on worldwide events and deployment of most Allied forces, the NORAD center focused on worldwide events and Allied and foreign space activities. The Offutt center focused on worldwide events and Allied and foreign strategic-strike activities. Together, the command centers can (and do) observe, report on, and recommend a variety of retaliatory options if the situation requires it.

Activities around the world were generally peaceful. In the United States there was the traditional happy transition of power that takes place in the greatest and most powerful nation in the world. Everything was as it should be in these combat operations centers. The military forces of the United States of America awaited a command from the commander in chief to remain vigilant or deploy for potential conflict. Relative general peace prevailed in nearly all regions of the globe. In places where peace was difficult to find, US military forces were at least temporarily in control.

Beneath all the anticipation of meeting new challenges was the nagging feeling on the parts of some senior administration and military officers that the nation's new president was soon going to be tested by some foreign force. Where would it occur? Why did it need to happen at all? And of course, who would do it?

4

ELSEWHERE IN THE WORLD

Beware the Trojan horse or the diplomat bearing false promises.

HALFWAY around the world in Western China, high in the Santsung Mountain range near the city of Shangri-La—that mythical utopia where love and peace were thought to prevail—a meeting was taking place in a secluded Chinese government winter resort. Love and peace, however, were not on the minds of the attendees. For twenty-five miles in all directions from the center of the resort, security was so tight that anything moving in or around the exterior and interior perimeters of the compound was seen with day-night infrared vision cameras, motion detectors, and vibrometry sensors that could see and identify animals as small as chipmunks or humans as small as three-year-old toddlers. Magnetometer devices were also integrated into the surveillance and detection system to detect metal weaponry or munitions as small as a 9mm Beretta pistol or a hand grenade. To assure nothing avoided detection, an advanced-phased-array air surveillance radar was secluded in a stand of trees five miles from the elaborate great hall and lavishly furnished guest quarters and meeting rooms.

This facility was located near the route flown in the Second World War by Allied forces supporting the Chinese military forces commanded by Generalissimo Chiang Kai-shek on their way to the city of Perpetual Spring, a.k.a. Kunming. In World War II the war in the China-Burma-India Theater had taken a turn for the worse for the joint US-UK-Chinese armies fighting against the Imperial forces of Japan. The mountain range was affectionately called "The Hump." To supply beleaguered Allied forces, US aircrews flew the route through monsoon-strength storms, hellacious winds, and gut wrenching turbulence. Many valiant airmen lost their lives flying The Hump.

Now this plush, highly secure winter resort, Shangri-La north-west of Kunming, is used by very high-ranking Beijing government officials to host high-level, secret strategy planning sessions, foreign policy development meetings, strategic and tactical military-force-employment scenario development, and economic-expansion planning activities. All the meetings are closed. Communications facilities into and out of the "resort" are encrypted. All the visitors are thoroughly screened and cleared three to four months before meetings take place. To avoid the appearance of the facility being a military garrison and to evade the prying eyes of imaging satellites of the US, Russia, France, and Israel, all assigned personnel wear civilian clothing and vehicles appear to be standard, commercially made sedans, but are in fact armored limousines. Underground subway systems connect the facility to the nearest airport twenty-five miles away near Shangri-La.

On this day, the minister of economics and a dozen carefully chosen key staff members, the vice chairman of the Ministry of Military Defense, a four-star army general and his staff members, and selected members of the Ministry of Finance were meeting in lengthy closed-door sessions. The agenda, known to only a few handpicked members of the government of the People's Republic of China, was addressing initiatives that could be considered for growing the economic, agricultural, military, and financial sphere of influence and internal prowess of China over the next ten years. Subjects on the table included nearly absolute control over the world's petroleum resources, the world's gold assets, diamond mining and trading activities, airline and maritime capabilities, as well as how and when Chinese military assets could be most efficiently deployed and used to deter other nations from using their military force to defend their resources after sensing the compromising of their government treasures.

The strategy that held the greatest appeal to the majority was a scenario that would cripple a nation or a region of great natural wealth by some catastrophic means. It would discredit and cast doubt on the viability of another nation's military force that might be brought to bear in order to defend perceived destructive events. It would embarrass and neuter the political and diplomatic infrastructure of the nation that appeared to be coming to the aid of the injured country. The plan, successfully executed, would mean The People's Republic of China, as the disinterested party in the Far East, would appear to be the logical choice by the injured nation to help defend and deter against further attack. They would also help rebuild immobilized elements of government infrastructure in the injured nation, and would be the one nation most able and willing to make funds immediately available to restore and rebuild the injured nation. A plan resulting from such a concept still needed additional study and resource development, but it was the basic strategy that enjoyed the most favor. But how to execute such a plan without risking governmental exposure still needed careful thought.

A small splinter group of planners was secreted in a secured room to brainstorm how activation of the plan could be orchestrated and carried out. The recommendation: use a small army of apparently civilian entrepreneurs to act as the government's surrogate. They would use the Chinese Mafia, the so-called Triad Society. These "entrepreneurs" would carry out the plan from beginning to near-end where the Chinese government would then step in to transition the injured nation and region back to health. The Mafia is rife with ties to international drug cartels, weapons smuggling sources, prostitution rings, and other resources that can make selected people and companies offers they can't refuse. They also have a plethora of economic and political ties that get things done.

Now what was needed was insight into whom, what, and when. The minister and all the meeting attendees quietly—and in staggered sequence—flew back to Beijing with the plans in their heads; no hard or soft copies of anything were to be carried back to Beijing by any of the attendees. Before departure all of the attendees were personally debriefed that they would incur instant death to themselves *and* their families if they revealed any morsel of information about these discussions.

In the first four months of the new administration, the North Koreans detonated a nuclear device and launched a barrage of six missiles into the sea of Japan; Somali pirates commandeered four merchant vessels, one of which was American; six American civilians were taken hostage by North Korea, China, and Syria; Iranian elections erupted into civil disagreement and protests; Venezuela and Libya were suspected of secretly conducting nuclear-weapons-assembly activities; Russia invaded Tajikistan; the Taliban in Afghanistan went on the offensive against UN peacekeeping forces; and the Chinese government forcefully quelled *peaceful demonstrations by Nepalese Buddhist monks on the border of the two countries.*

5

THE LOADING AND SAILING OF THE USS SALEM

Many tasks involve hours and hours of boredom and monotony interspersed with moments of sheer terror.

IT was February 23, 2017, at 1300 hours PST. Moored at US Navy Pier 6 at the dock in Bremerton near Seattle, Washington, the United States ship *Salem* (T-AK 41), a 564-foot-long, six-thousand-ton-capacity military cargo vessel housed a crew that was feverishly preparing to set sail for Hawaii. Designed and used exclusively for transoceanic shipment of ordinance and sensitive military cargo, she was a Kilauea-class naval cargo ship capable of cruising at twenty knots and configured for replenishment at sea. She was capable of carrying two CH-46 Sea Knight helicopters, munitions, a ship's complement of fifty-five crew members, additional fuel, water, and one thousand tons of dry supplies and refrigerated food. Since the *Salem* was destined for deployment to the Indian Ocean after dropping her cargo in Hawaii, she was going to be outfitted at Pearl for full Indian Ocean support operations and was not maximally outfitted for departure from Bremerton. For a minimal deployment, an outbound leg of her tasking from Bremerton by the Military Sea Lift Command, the MSC, the ship's crew was comprised of only four officers, a crew of twenty sailors, and twelve civilians. Two of the officers and some of the enlisted crew members were battle hardened from service in the Iraq-Afghanistan-Pakistan theater of operations in the Sea of Oman, but others were younger seamen who were on first or second enlistments. They were receiving their training and experience by serving aboard support ships of the fleet. The civilians were merchant seamen who only handled cargo operations.

As a rule, the US Navy would relegate most of its shipments of supplies, munitions, and essential military goods to MSC ships, commercial cargo ships, or an airlift. On occasion, however, certain military materiel requires special protection because of its advanced technology and its planned use. Such was the nature of the crates being loaded aboard the *Salem*, overseen by a squad of US Marine Security Guards. Once the crates were loaded and secured below decks, the Marines would be dismissed back to barracks and the *Salem* would sail relying on the isolation of the ocean to assure her security.

Six large containers below decks housed forty-eight environmentally sealed crates containing the latest versions of advanced AGM-86C air-launched cruise missiles and some auxiliary support materiel and spare parts. They were destined for the underground munitions test-and-checkout storage bunkers at Pearl Harbor Naval Base in Hawaii where they would be evaluated and prepared for transit to Hickam Air Force Base across the island. The missiles had been rendered temporarily inert for the voyage to Hawaii.

Lieutenant Commander Mark Wood, the captain of the USS *Salem*, was relatively new to the *Salem* after having served with distinction aboard three other ships in the Pacific Fleet a year earlier, in the process earning a promotion to his own captaincy. Lt. Commander Wood, a 2001 graduate of the US Naval Academy in Annapolis, graduated a tick above the midpoint of his class. His sixteen years of service had been honorable, impressing his superiors as an "up and comer" who should be given an opportunity to show his talents. Cargo operations aboard a ship like the *Salem* are not considered frontline, battle-ready duties, but nonetheless, the duty is a respectable proving ground for young officers and seamen who have intentions of making the navy a career.

The executive officer of the *Salem*, Lieutenant Senior Grade Rose Doolin, the officer of the deck, greeted Lt. Commander Wood at the top of the gangway when he came aboard at 1630 hours. Lt. Doolin had been overseeing the loading activities in preparation for the ship to sail at 1900 hours. Bleak and overcast with scattered rain and mist, the day was not unlike the past three days. The crew, accustomed to this type of northwestern Puget Sound weather, took it in stride. Lt. Commander Wood, returning from the MSC division headquarters across the base to obtain the *Salem's* sailing orders from the MSC staff, carried with him a pre-sailing weather report as well as intelligence and Pacific Fleet status briefings. The course the *Salem* was to take was across the mid-Pacific, avoiding any approach to land masses or other military ships of any other nation. The Salem was to be at sea in international waters for four to six days. The weather briefing identified a squall line of rain storms just south of the Aleutian chain of islands of Alaska for the first day at sea followed by overcast skies for the next three or four days of the trip. The captain of the *Salem* had been told by the MSC weather officer not to expect sunny and warm weather and calm sea conditions until the *Salem* was at least one day out of Pearl. The intelligence briefing didn't reveal any activity of a remarkable nature but did identify submarine transit activities by both the US Navy and the People's Liberation Army of China. Both activities were identified as having sailing courses that were in the Mid- to South Pacific, a significant distance from the *Salem's* course.

Lt. Commander Wood stopped at the top of the gangway, saluted the ensign at the stern of the ship, and requested permission to come aboard. Lt. Doolin granted the permission and the ship's loudspeaker system sounded the announcement that the captain of the *Salem* was aboard.

After boarding the Salem, Lt. Commander Wood and his executive officer went directly to the bridge to prepare to depart for what was expected to be a routine crossing. At 1745 hours a tender came alongside the *Salem* and the harbor pilot came aboard and proceeded to the bridge. Fifteen minutes later, two commercial tugs came alongside as well. Captain Wood directed the executive officer to prepare the ship for departure and complete the dockside pre-departure checklist. Twenty-five minutes later the Salem's deck crew had cast off the mooring lines and the tugs gently nudged the *Salem* out into the Puget Sound navigation channel. There were no lights, bells, sirens, or weeping wives or girlfriends as one would see in the movies. It was a routine departure with no fanfare. Little did anyone know or even guess that it would be the last voyage of the USS *Salem*.

6

An unprovoked surprise attack is heinous and deserving of retaliation.

TWELVE hours into the transit, the MSC staff weather officer's forecast was on target. On the bridge, Captain Wood was seated in the captain's chair drinking a cup of government-issue Navy coffee, which for a change wasn't bad. He smiled at Seaman First Class Bill Jones who had recently assumed the watch, manning the sound-powered phones on the bridge.

Jones has a big responsibility. He is a key link to being part of the central processing center of this entire ship in that everything goes through him and is then relayed to designated posts on the ship.

The captain interrupted his personal mental retreat, stating, "Seaman Jones, I'm counting on you to be alert and on your toes.

Before you came on watch the onboard navigation surveillance radar system went out due to a lightning strike. It appears that we will be going in and out of this wind and heavy rain. Call down to the wheel house and tell them to set the auto-helmsman on course 230 degrees."

Seaman Jones responded, "Aye, Captain. Wheelhouse set the auto-helmsman to a course of 230 degrees."

The Captain nodded his approval. "Seaman, contact the engine room and tell them to make fifteen knots."

"Aye, Captain. Engine room, we're operating on auto-helmsman. Set your speed at fifteen knots."

The Captain smiled as he stood and made his way towards the intercom. Upon reaching the intercom, he announced, "Boatswain mate Smith, report to the bridge."

I think that I'll get Smith to assign a couple of deck hands to a lookout position on the bow. Hmm, it wouldn't hurt to get the executive officer on the bridge as well.

"Seaman Smith, call down to officer country and tell whoever answers the call that I need the executive officer on deck ASAP."

"Aye, Captain."

While Smith relayed the order to officer country, the captain again retreated into his private thoughts.

I don't like the feeling I have in my gut. Visibility isn't bad now, but who knows what is going to happen in the next few minutes. We've passed through the worst of the storm, but.... At last report we were at least one thousand miles from any land mass, and thank God that we are receiving GPS navigation data and we're still able to uplink the data to the INMARSAT and SEASAT military satellite channel satellite systems every hour. The weather radar is still functioning and is showing another squall line dead ahead at fifty miles. Let me see. Just before the onboard navigation surveillance radar system went out, it was showing no other vessels within a range of thirty-five miles. That's good, but I don't want to be unprepared. Thank God the civilian electronics technicians are on board and working to repair the radar system, get it up and running and recalibrate it. It could take some time because the blown circuit boards have to be replaced. What was it that they said about how long it would take to complete the job? Oh yeah, they are figuring on about five hours. That is too long! It's a good thing that the short range harbor radar is working, but it only gives me five miles of visibility. I guess that will just have to do for now.

The ninety-five foot luxury cruise yacht, *Vancouver Escape*, was sixty miles ahead of the *Salem* on a parallel course, also headed for Honolulu. Destined for a vacation cruise to take its twelve passengers on to Japan, South Korea, and then on to Thailand, their experienced crew of seven consisted of the captain, the navigator, the first officer, the ship's steward, the engineer, and two other seaman. The navigator, knowing the course to Honolulu, had shut down the navigation surveillance radar and the satellite communications net to preserve power because one of the three massive onboard batteries for backup use had failed. Not considered a crisis, they had nevertheless reduced speed to ten knots to avoid the turbulence of the choppy waters in the rain storm. After all, they didn't want their distinguished guests to spill their martinis.

Ever the perfect host, the captain and first officer checked on their prestigious passengers in the dining room every fifteen to twenty minutes to assure there were no glitches in the bar service or the menu items for the twelve very affluent industry and Washington, DC, passengers who were enjoying a boisterous cocktail party in the dining room. It had been going on for more than an hour and everyone was thoroughly enjoying the food and drink. So preoccupied with the party, the passengers and crew of the *Escape* failed to see both the two military attack dinghies that quietly pulled up alongside their starboard bow and the ten black-wet-suit-clad intruders board the luxury vessel.

The captain had just left the bridge to check the partygoers, leaving the first officer on the bridge at the helm. In the next seven minutes, with perfect military precision, the captain, the first officer, the ship's steward, and the engineer of the *Vancouver Escape* were each shot with a single bullet to their brain. Six of the passengers suffered the same fate. The two remaining Philippine crewmen were positioned at the bow and at the stern respectively. They were given promises of safety if they followed instructions precisely. The remaining six passengers were given the same promises and instructions to appear mildly upset but able to assist with rescue once an appropriate vessel came alongside.

The engines of the *Escape* were then reduced to idle and the craft sat in the water as if awaiting rescue. The invaders, still covered with wet suits, had their faces sufficiently covered to avoid any possible recognition of their nationality. Each was equipped with an ear piece that provided communication with some source of control elsewhere.

Meanwhile, the USS *Salem* remained on course, but was unaware that it was on a near-collision course with the *Vancouver Escape*. The *Salem's* navigation radar was still out, but even if it had been working, the *Salem* was experiencing low-level radar and radio interference from an unknown source either on board or nearby. Unbeknownst to Captain Wood, his ship was now one mile from the *Vancouver Escape*, which lay dead in the water directly ahead.

Seaman Smith, acknowledging a message from the radio room, responded, "Aye, radio room. Captain, the radio room reports a low-frequency distress signal being transmitted from another vessel called the *Pride of BC*. Their location is dead ahead. Their crew reports a fire aboard with nine passengers." Unknown to anyone except the intruders, the *Pride of BC* was in fact in Nova Scotia, which would take anyone who checked a week to determine. The Vancouver Escape, however, was on a casual sailing plan that would allow it random, unscheduled changes in her course that would also go unquestioned for five to seven days.

"Very good, Smith. Relay a message to the engine room to reduce our speed to *All Ahead Slow*."

Seaman Smith relayed the message to the engine room, awaiting the next directive from the captain or a report from one of the other stations.

"Seaman Smith, try to get the range of the *Pride of BC* from the radio room or the navigation room and then contact the seamen on the bow and tell them to keep their eyes peeled for any sign of a navigational hazard in our path."

Dammit, the low-level EMI prevented me from seeing the ship on the harbor radar or from transmitting an acknowledgement to the Pride of BC *and to MSC headquarters. What the hell is low-level EMI doing all the way out here?*

"Seaman, tell the radioman to keep trying to answer the distress call from the *Pride of BC*." Striding over to the intercom, he barked, "Attention all hands. Rescue Boarding Party report to your duty station and prepare for a rescue. We have less than ten minutes."

"Captain, the radio room reports that the *Pride of BC* is one hundred yards off the starboard bow."

The Captain quickly grabbed the sound-powered phones from Seaman Smith and shouted, "Engine room, all engines *All Back Full*. Wheelhouse, steer hard left to course two–zero-zero."

In the next two minutes, the *Salem* approached the *Escape* to within twenty yards. The *Escape* had already begun to sink because the intruders had opened all shuttle cocks and had scuttled the ship. As its decks became awash, the intruders quickly made their way to the *Salem* via several black dinghies. Two RPGs suddenly ripped into the bridge of the *Salem*, killing the captain, the XO, and the two crewmen on watch there. Within the blink of an eye, the decks of the *Salem* were filled with twenty intruders who proceeded to shoot and kill anything and anyone who moved. Six minutes into the boarding of the *Salem*, she also lay dead in the water with all communications and navigation systems down. All USS *Salem* crewmen were dead.

No distress signals were sent, no position report was transmitted, and no officer or crewman was able to respond to the highjacking. In less than an hour the *Salem* suffered the same fate as the *Vancouver Escape*.

Stealthily the Chinese nuclear-cruise-missile submarine *Chairman Mao-Tse-Tung* pulled alongside the *Salem*, its deck plates open and prepared to take on the cruise-missile containers and any other valuable cargo that could quickly and easily be loaded. When the missiles had been transferred, the water-tight deck plates of the *Chairman Mao* had been sealed, and C-4 explosive charges planted aboard the *Salem* in sufficient quantity at strategic lower-deck locations to assure a rapid destruction of the ship with minimal explosive flash that might be seen by imaging satellites. The bodies of the dead Americans were sealed in a cargo compartment to avoid leaving any floating bodies or any other telltale signs that could reveal what had happened.

The *Chairman Mao* slipped quietly away to a distance of one-half mile and electronically detonated the charges aboard the *Salem*. In a muffled explosion, the hull of the *Salem* below the waterline was completely blown away. What remained of the USS *Salem* silently and slowly slipped beneath the surface of the ocean as the *Mao* submerged and disappeared on a course that would take her to 45 degrees 12.139 minutes north latitude, 124 degrees 5.074 minutes west longitude, eight miles off the coast of the state of Oregon, outside US national territorial waters.

7

THE RENDEZVOUS

*Talent and expertise performed in the
beginning can avoid catastrophe later.*

CAPTAIN Chen Wai Kee of the People's Liberation Navy and
captain of the honorable nuclear-powered cruise-missile-launching
submarine *Chairman Mao-Tse-Tung* stood at the navigation table in
the center of the control room of the vessel. Patiently, he instructed,
"Helmsman, call out the current heading and depth."

"Aye, Comrade Captain. Heading one-seven-zero degrees, depth
eight-zero, zero meters."

"Tell the engine room to reduce speed of engines to *All Ahead*
one-third and come to periscope depth".

"Aye, Comrade Captain. Reduce speed of engines to *All Ahead*
one-third and come to periscope depth."

The time was 1530 Greenwich Mean Time (0630 hours Pacific

Standard Time) and the *Chairman Mao* was slowly approaching a predetermined rendezvous point eight miles off the Oregon coast, directly abeam of the small coastal Oregon town of Pacific City. It was very dark and the ocean was relatively calm for this time of year. The waves were three feet high with occasional swells of five feet.

The engine room called out, "Comrade Captain, the *Chairman Mao* is at periscope depth."

Captain Chen, a serious tone ringing in his voice, commanded, "Sonar operator, call out all surface and subsurface contacts."

The operator replied, "No contacts in any direction, Comrade Captain."

"Helmsman, bring engines to *All Stop*. Periscope *Up* and activate air surveillance radar." Visually scanning the vicinity of the submarine through the entirety of 360 degrees for any navigation lights, deployed lights, or illumination devices, he nodded. "Good, there is no sign of any illumination."

The very crisp, direct words from the PLA minister of defense were emblazoned on his brain and were still clearly ringing in his ears during his one-on-one pre-mission briefing.

Comrade Captain, this mission is of the highest possible security clearance and utmost importance and secrecy. No one other than you, I, and two other party officials know of this task. A sealed envelope with your sailing orders will be delivered to the Honorable Chairman Mao-Tse-Tung *at dockside just before you sail. You may share it only with your first officer in the unlikely event that you become incapacitated for some reason. Your mission tasks, actions to be completed, circumstances to be met and overcome, and contingency operations to be implemented if the situation warrants, will all be in the envelope. Complete instructions are in the envelope for a four-phase mission profile. Phase A involves a confrontation. Phase B is a rendezvous. Task Phase C is another confrontation and Phase D is your return to the motherland. Failure in any of these phases is not an option. Your mission from beginning to end will*

*be conducted in strict radio silence. You will be operating nearly au-
tonomously. There is, however, a classified, very-low-frequency encrypted
channel set aside for you to report one of three messages: you can transmit MISSION SUCCESSFUL, ONBOARD CRISIS, or MISSION
INCOMPLETE. The frequency will be continuously monitored seeking
one of these transmissions to go directly to the party president. I will tell
you this much: you will be operating very close to the northwest coast of
the United States. At the appropriate time, you will be contacted from a
helicopter from the US mainland that will be dispatched to relieve you
of certain cargo. That cargo will then be returned to you in ten days' time
at the same rendezvous point. Once on board, you will secure that cargo
and proceed with Phase C of your sailing orders."*

"First Officer Quan Lee Duc, verify silent deployment activity.
All motors and power devices are to be muffled."

"Aye, Comrade Captain."

"Officer Quan, deploy the navigation rendezvous point beacon
to the surface."

The captain, in accordance with Phase B sailing instructions,
knew that it would only be a matter of time before two US-made
commercial version CH-47F Chinook helicopters would make contact. All was going according to plan. The crew members of the helicopters were loyal to a private civilian entity in the US. They were
being paid extremely well for their cooperation and secrecy.

"Officer Quan, stand by to surface. Make preparations to transfer one-half of the cargo to the deck for helicopter pickup once the
deck plates have been opened. You will oversee the cargo handling
and transfer operations. Ah yes, Number Two, be prepared to transfer the sensitive cargo in a rapid and secure fashion and avoid un-
necessary lights and unsafe activity."

Heading for operations bay, Number Two responded, "Aye,
Comrade Captain."

The *Chairman Mao-Tse-Tung* sat quietly submerged at periscope depth with surveillance equipment, radio receivers, and transmitters at heightened alert, awaiting contact.

At 1630 GMT (0730 PST) a short verbal, cryptic voice message in American English crackled over a discrete VHF channel. "Porpoise 1 this is Seagull 1, I have your beacon and am twenty minutes out. Seagull 2 is four-zero minutes behind me."

Captain Chen reached for the radio transmission microphone in the control panel above his head in the control room. In perfect English, without an accent, he responded, "Seagull 1 this is Porpoise 1. Message understood. We will be ready." All the radio exchanges were deliberately clipped and direct. If they were overheard or accidentally intercepted, they would be assumed to be routine traffic between deep-sea fishing vessels. Captain Chen then ordered the helmsman to surface and the cargo handlers to stand by to open the deck plates and be ready to transfer cargo.

Seagull 1 was a tandem rotor heavy lift CH-47F helicopter that was purchased from the US Army six years earlier. The Chinook was specially chosen by the purchasers because of its ability to handle loads of nearly twenty-four thousand pounds and its exceptional maneuverability in various climatic, altitude, and crosswind conditions that typically keep other helicopters from flying. It was purchased through a third party and was later sold to Mountain View Aviation at the McMinnville Airport in Oregon in 2011 under the guise of being needed for search, rescue, and fire-fighting operations. This aircraft and two others just like it were indeed used for the advertised missions but were kept in a hangar, maintained, and periodically flown on a regular basis by skilled and experienced aircraft and engine mechanics, all curiously of unknown Asian descent.

The pilot of Seagull 1 was simply known as Dan and was recruited by Trish Anatolia six months earlier along with three other CH-47 day-night-qualified pilots. None of them were given specific instructions on what the range of their tasks was to be for the duration of their contracts. They were, however, hired with the proviso that they weren't to ask too many questions, at times might be asked to fly nighttime and inclement weather sorties, and some flights might be required to deliver or pick up cargo from vessels at sea, with no questions asked. For these activities they were to be paid handsomely and were expected to keep their mouths shut and their eyes and ears open.

On this night, Dan's copilot was an Asian by the name of Kim. Dan neither knew what Kim's last name was nor where he had come from. Dan concluded it didn't make any difference as long as those very nice paychecks kept arriving in his bank account, and that Kim didn't do anything stupid in the air. He had known Kim about one month and the two had flown together on three previous missions. Dan was pleased to discover that Kim was as careful and meticulous as he. They were both expert pilots who supposedly had extensive background in the Chinook. They shared a degree of mutual respect for one another's abilities and demonstrated skill in handling the Chinook because of these earlier missions. They worked well together and that's all that mattered.

Just as Dan and Kim crossed over the Coast Range Mountains on a heading of 250 degrees, they began their descent from twenty-seven hundred feet to five hundred feet. They had left the McMinnville Airport 20.6 miles back just over twenty minutes ago and were headed to a rendezvous point in the dreary morning hours eight miles off the beach at Pacific City. As they crossed the beach, their altitude was eighteen hundred feet and descending. The low-light illuminators on the instrument panel gave off an eerie green glow. The Navigation Target Point sensor was locked onto a beacon eight miles off the coast and both pilots knew they had to be at an altitude of fifty feet once they arrived at the RP. They also knew they would be hovering for up to twenty minutes at a lower height for the pickup operation.

The *Chairman Mao-Tse-Tung* was fully surfaced, the deck plates were open, and the sensitive cargo containers were exposed. Minimal-illumination lighting outlined the cargo bay. Lifting cables had been attached to three of the six large containers. The cargo handlers stood quietly, searching the sky east of the submarine's position. They cocked their heads listening for the distinctive WUP, WUP, WUP of helicopter rotors in the dark sky. Gradually the Chinook approached from the east, slowly descending to twenty-five feet above the submarine's cargo opening. Kim lowered the two grappling cables that were to be attached to the containers. Dan held the Chinook in steady hover configuration at twenty feet above the sub's deck while the cables and slings were secured in place to assure that all crates could be brought up snug with the underbelly of the chopper. Once attached, Kim activated the onboard winches and pulled the cargo up to the Chinook. The submarine crew cargo handlers held lightweight nylon cables long enough to steady the containers as they were raised to the Chinook. This sequence was repeated three times until all containers were hoisted up.

The entire retrieval operation took just twenty-four minutes. The loadmaster aboard the *Chairman Mao* turned his signal flashlight upward toward the Chinook's cockpit and gave three green-colored flashes which meant *all clear and cargo secured*. Dan keyed his microphone button and transmitted the prearranged word *DEPARTING*.

There was a third transmission over the radio channel: "Porpoise 1, this is Seagull 2. I have your beacon and am ten minutes out."

Captain Chen keyed his microphone and simply said, "Roger, Seagull 2. We are ready."

Operations between the *Chairman Mao* and the two Chinooks were conducted with speed and precision. When Seagull 1 completed the loading operation, he returned to Mountain View Aviation and lowered his cargo to awaiting flatbed trailers, which quickly moved the containers to the elevators inside the hangers and then to the secure basement munitions bays and clean-rooms.

Seagull 2 completed his uploading without delay and headed back to McMinnville to follow the downloading actions that the earlier Chinook had completed. The *Chairman Mao* secured from transfer operations and quietly submerged on a heading of one-eight-zero degrees and began diving to a depth of eight hundred meters. In accordance with his sailing orders, Captain Chen was to avoid all sea lanes, all surface and sub-surface vessels, and any and all distress signals or requests for assistance. The *Chairman Mao* was to disappear for ten days, then reappear at the same rendezvous point where it met the Chinooks earlier. As per his sailing orders, it was easier and much safer to modify the cruise missiles close to where they were acquired and to then more expeditiously upload them into the *Chairman Mao's* firing tubes for later use.

8

ATTACK ON TEHRAN

General Quarters! General Quarters!
This is not a drill! General Quarters!

That announcement, enough to wake the dead or cause the living to
wonder if and when they will join the departed, always causes the
spine to tingle and the hair to rise. Not unlike any alarm announcing
eminent danger but perhaps in a more dramatic sense, it prompts rapid
movement directed towards a specific destination. Foreboding to most,
it initiates thoughts about loved ones and a life's work undone.

IT was hot in Tehran on a Friday morning in June, just as it always
is in late June to mid-July. Too hot to hurry anywhere, it did not
significantly slow one's rate of travel to a specific destination. In the
distance, the lyrical Muslim call to prayer could be heard. It was
being broadcast from the top of the Mauch Mude al Muhammad
Mosque, the central, largest, and most revered shrine in the center of
Iran's capital city. Time and technology had made a positive impact

on religious worship, as well as on the political and economic front of Iranian society. Not too many years prior that call to worship had to be sung from the parapets by the caller with the loudest voice— one who could project his call in all four directions through the use of a mouthpiece from a small but functional megaphone. Now, of course, the message was electronically broadcast from the external speakers positioned around the city center.

The Mauch Mude al Muhammad Mosque was considered as holy as—but somewhat less ostentatious than—the shrine at Mecca in Saudi Arabia. Each Friday hundreds of worshippers slowly but purposefully made their way to this mosque and others like it but somewhat smaller in size. Worshipers came with their prayer rugs carefully folded away in a variety of ways or encased in ornamental bags and purses to protect their sanctity.

In other parts of the city there was still significant unrest among the citizenry following the much contested presidential elections of 2016. Even a year later tens of thousands of supporters of opposition leader Mir Hussein Mousavi still gathered in front of Tehran University for Friday prayers while large numbers of security forces formed security cordons around the university. Foreign reporters and photographers continued to be banned from covering the events. In the flash of a moment, just as it occurred the year before—as if it were intentionally choreographed—the police unleashed tear gas, began beating the students and demonstrators with batons, and peppered the dissenters with rubber bullets. The crowds fell back, then regrouped with new signs and posters, pleading with police and civil authorities for an election recount, the opening of a dialogue with theocratic leaders, and the release of students and civilian demonstrators arrested in earlier, similar demonstrations. This same sequence of events had occurred two days earlier and continued for three days in a row thereafter.

The crowds were insistent that the 2010 and follow-on elections of 2015, which resulted in the reelection of President Ahmadinejad, were a fraud and that the ballots were fake. Clerics and parliamentarians were at odds with the current government leaders. On the fourth day after the 2010 election, former President Mohammed Khatmi called for a referendum on the election with regard to the legitimacy of the Ahmadinejad presidency. Following the elections of 2016, former Prime Minister Al Hambra Il Fousami sacrificed himself to make the same call for a recount of votes. Neither request for recount was successful.

Supreme Leader Ayatollah Ali Khamenei continued to call for all politicians to discourage further public demonstrations and disagreement by the people. These directions and mandates simply served to stoke the fires of dissent, not only among the people, but among and between parliamentarians and religious leaders. The country had been up and down in disarray and government control had reached a serious state of disorganization. In late 2016 the nation was grinding to a halt and became ripe for overthrow. No one seemed to be in charge; military forces were failing to follow orders of many of their generals. The fires of discontent had been stoked by the independence movements in Egypt, Yemen, Libya, Bahrain, Iran, Lebanon, Palestine, Israel, and Syria in the previous five years. The Iranian Republican Guard forces acted without authority in torturing and maiming civilian protestors. The Basij secret police mercilessly and deliberately injured defenseless old people, children, women, and even pets in the streets. A struggle to be heard by the leadership was obviously underway; equally obvious was that the leadership did not want to hear what the people were saying. The city and the region were vulnerable to upheaval from within and assault from outside. They were buoyed by the events throughout the Middle East. Nonetheless, some minor evidence of stabilization had been achieved. The government continued to blame the great Satan, the United States, Britain, France, and NATO for all the world's ailments. They even stated that the US government was behind the attack on September 11, 2001, on its own World Trade Center twin towers. The mood throughout Iran, Iraq, Afghanistan, Pakistan, and across the Middle East was one of suspicion, but with cautious optimism. Mistrust and fear still carried with it a willingness to cooperate and a desire to negotiate. Hope was still alive under the newly elected President Rashid Al Formadi.

Across town most of the worshippers were aware of the chaos in their country but were aware only of their own personal thoughts and challenges that faced them the rest of the day. They were not involved in the dissent but knew it would only be a matter of days before the people would have to take a positive stand. Still, others were intent only on basic survival issues such as the latest increase in the price of fresh fruits and vegetables that had come from the rich agrarian growing areas of southern Afghanistan or southern Iraq. Since the Americans had significantly decreased their presence in neighboring countries, oil production was closely monitored and controlled by internal Iranian and OPEC officials. Agricultural activities experienced a decline. And for its part, the government announced it did not need to defy the latest UN ruling to avoid producing weapons-grade plutonium since it was only building nuclear reactors for producing energy for commercial and public uses. But the diplomatic and military communities in the region believed that Iran was secretly launching plans to produce a nuclear warhead to mount on the Khomeni I intercontinental ballistic missile recently placed into full production. The Khomeni II extended range ICBM was rumored to not be far behind.

To add to the chaos, recently revived political competition among the rival sects in Iraq, Pakistan, India, and Afghanistan had caused a spike in the militaristic goals and visions of the more aggressive Imams of the strongest tribes. Only a loosely woven agreement between the former warring factions, geographical separation with provincial borders dedicated to each of the four major tribes, and the mediation of the more-moderate newly elected President Formadi kept another all-out confrontation from erupting. That agreement, too, appeared in jeopardy of dissolution. The government was in need of hard currency. Oil and food were necessary commodities that produced it. Opium products also produced hard currency, but thousands of acres of opium poppy fields had been destroyed by military operations. That was a possible explanation for the sharp increase in the price of oil. The lowliest of the social strata in Middle Eastern society continued to bear the brunt of taxation, little of which went toward creating comforts for the populace.

Of the crowd of Iranians making their way towards the mosque on this fateful Friday, a few were somewhat less than engaged, concentrating on both where their destination would lead them and the purpose for reaching that destination. They possessed neither the keenness of sight nor hearing to be distracted by sounds originating from the distant horizon. Over one thousand worshippers were already inside the massive mosque structure and grounds, diligently beginning to chant their prayers to the Almighty. Another six hundred to nine hundred were scant yards from the mosque, silently praying that there would be more space available than in previous days. After all, problems in Iran, the region, and the hemisphere were seemingly out of control. Prayer was a diplomatic tool that few politicians seemed to want to use anymore. Besides, worship was always more pleasant if there was ample space to lay their prayer rugs to offer their prayers to Allah.

In the distance to the south and to the west there was the beginning of a quiet but persistent, raspy, low guttural growl of small jet aircraft engines, not unlike a swarm of bees might sound. The growl became increasingly louder and louder until it could not be ignored any longer. Suddenly there was the high shrill resonance of many aircraft hurtling toward the earth at high speeds. Growing still louder and louder, the shrill penetration of the humid air by the high-speed aircraft caused the crowd of Iranians not yet inside the mosque to look upward to see where it was coming from and what it was. They weren't particularly concerned because they sensed it was another one of the increasingly common local air maneuvers that required overflights of the city. Besides, there were demonstrations still underway across town near the university that probably needed airborne surveillance.

For most of the over nine hundred worshipers not yet in the mosque, that awareness was the last thought they had. To all the worshippers already inside, their lives ended in a split second without a cry, no preceding alert or warning whatsoever. To observers, there were two more almost simultaneous explosions a mile away to the north, two more a mile to the south, and another two a half mile to the east. Destruction was sudden with fire everywhere. To the south and across town in the direction of the demonstrations there were three more detectable huge explosions. Then there were two more explosions one mile west of the city center, three more within a mile of the city center, and a final one two miles to the east. The sacred mosque crumbled and nearly vaporized from the intense, almost nuclear-like explosion, much the same way as the twin towers in New York in the now seemingly distant 9-11 attack. Unlike the 9-11 attack, the devastation was so much more rapid and comprehensive. Several miles to the south of Tehran at the Kharg Island petroleum distribution plant, three more explosions occurred, leveling buildings and facilities, detonating petroleum reserve tanks, and killing upwards of 250 facility workers. In all, twenty-four impacts at final count almost totally leveled the entire city.

Thick acrid smoke filled the air. Uncontrollable flames consumed nearly every building within a radius of five miles of the city center. Nearly everything and everyone was gone! Life as it had been only seconds before was gone, changed in the blink of an eye around the mosque and the other impact areas. There were no sounds of cries for help amid the searing flames. Stores, street vendors, and homes were gone. Government buildings, police stations, hotels, hospitals, schools, and medical facilities were gone. It was as if the Apocalypse had finally come, occurring with lightning speed. Devastation and death were instantaneous.

9

AMBASSADOR WOODARD MOVES IN

The transition of leadership, intended to be smooth, sometimes is fraught with unanticipated and unexpected disruptions. Ensuring that the transition is smooth under such circumstances requires a style of leadership that often times is not taught or learned from a textbook.

TWELVE hours prior to the attack on Tehran, in the lobby of the embassy, Ambassador Brad Williams had bid farewell to newly appointed Ambassador John W. Woodard, to his former aide, Station Chief Colin Morris, and to his personal secretary, Janice Strothers. Brad and Colin had presided over the acquisition, modification, and final activation of a central Tehran building that served as the new American Embassy in Tehran. Quiet diplomacy for over four tumultuous years between the governments of the United States and

Iran had resulted in a state of somewhat nonhostile wariness. Cautious relations between the two countries and a low-key agreement resulted in a ninety-nine-year lease of a former museum whose location, structure, and architecture made it the best place for the American Embassy.

Thirty-one years had passed since November 1979 when a group of Iranian students, emboldened by religious and political upheaval, stormed and seized the US Embassy, imprisoning all the Americans on the embassy staff for over four hundred days. They had vowed to try—and if necessary, execute—all the Americans as spies. The attack held the world's most powerful country hostage and paralyzed the presidency of Jimmy Carter for over a year. It wasn't until just before the inauguration of President-elect Ronald Reagan in January 1985 and the appointment of retired General Alexander Haig as secretary of state that circumstances changed. A back-channel message three hours before the formal administration of the oath of office from President-elect Reagan to the national leadership in Tehran informed the Iranian government that unless the hostages and all American property were returned immediately, a state of war would exist between the United States and the Republic of Iran, with all possible and practical force being brought to bear to free the Americans held in Iranian prison facilities. Within hours after the inauguration of President Reagan, the hostages were on their way back to the United States. Regrettably, Iranian resistance to international pressures to change after that was merely cosmetic, and Iran's international behavior became increasingly more covert in nature.

Prior to the mid-2013 signing of the lease—formalized between the two countries after two years of quiet wrangling—Brad Williams, a career foreign service officer, had led the US negotiating team. Considered a natural to be the next ambassador for the United States to Iran, he had managed to secure the old museum building that was located near the British Embassy and six blocks north of the Iranian parliament buildings. The four-story structure, built in the early 1920s, was considered to be an architectural marvel of its time. No expense had been spared to make it a quiet but striking example of reverence for the Persian empire. Perhaps the breakthrough in the negotiations came about indirectly because so many Iranian artifacts from both the former Persian empire and the Iranian people had accumulated, hence influencing the government to decide it was necessary to combine the relics contained therein into a newer, larger museum. As a result, the Iranian government commissioned the construction of a new, grander monument to Persia, Iran, and Muhammad, paving the way for the United States and Iran to reach a diplomatic agreement and establish an embassy despite continuing political differences in philosophies and international priorities. In fact, it was these differences that led both sides to decide there were more reasons to reestablish the American embassy than to continue to reject international pressures to reduce and avoid vitriolic rhetoric.

With the infusion of fifty million dollars worth of bulletproof, high-impact windows in the old museum building, modernized water purification and storage systems, synchronized electrical power, new security-sensing and reporting systems, and satellite communications equipment, the elegant old building was transformed into an American fortress without ever appearing to violate local architectural restraints. The only change to the outside of the structure was the standard addition above the doors of the large circular-shaped Great Seal of the United States of America with the imposing American eagle looking over the Tehran skyline. From this building, Brad Williams managed the affairs of state for the United States for two years.

After shaking hands and thanking Colin for his continued and exemplary loyalty and support, Brad dispatched Colin back upstairs where his replacement, John Woodard, was to assume his duties. Brad mused about the challenge that Dr. Woodard had accepted and the formidable tasks that lay ahead. He also took time to consider his aide. Smiling, he nodded, recalling that Colin was the consummate detail man. Often anticipating what his superiors wanted or expected, he always managed to surprise them with his efficient, timely, and accurate attention to detail. His physical appearance, slight of build and often thought of by many as a clone for the fictional comic book character Clark Kent, belied his capabilities. Always aware of the significance of the impending task, but unlike the fictional Daily Planet reporter, he didn't find it convenient to step into a phone booth to change identities. Performing his work without fanfare—often undercover without expecting anything more than to be included in the thick of the mission at hand—Colin had served the ambassador admirably.

Quickly but methodically, Brad stuffed the last of his belongings into a large handbag that soon would be picked up and carried down to a waiting car that would whisk him off to a hotel for overnight obscurity and then, the next morning, to the airport. Slowly he zipped up the bag and then reached up to remove his glasses.

My God, my nose itches, and on such a glorious day, too. Something interesting must be about to happen. Oh well, not to complain about a little irritation. At long last, tomorrow I will board a plane and head back stateside. I should be with my family in less than twenty-four hours. Sue sure will be glad. I'll finally have time to help her plan all those "honey do's" I've been neglecting.

After the momentary reflection, Brad got into the embassy limousine that would take him three quarters of a mile to the Tehran Hilton Ambassadors Suite where he would spend a short night before departing for the international airport early the next morning. As the limousine slowly drove away from the embassy, Brad turned to take a look out of the rear window to get one last look at the embassy building that was to be his legacy to both the United States and the Republic of Iran.

His stay at the Hilton was on his own accord, since Ambassador

Woodard had already assumed the office. Two ambassadors in residence was an awkward protocol circumstance, and since he already had his going away party with Iranian friends and embassy staff—and had given his farewell remarks—he only needed a few private hours to compose his end-of-assignment notes for his final report to the secretary of state.

In his third-floor office of the aesthetically designed and adorned American Embassy office, a mile from the city center, Ambassador Woodard was focusing on some of the correspondence he needed to scan to bring himself up to speed on some of the latest developments in Iran. Sitting at his desk, he was surrounded by approximately a dozen boxes of books—treasures that went wherever a new assignment took him. They were stacked in four neat piles near the floor-to-ceiling, elegantly finished mahogany book cases on the wall. Each was marked with broad, felt-tipped black pen that read "Amb Woodard – Books." Another four boxes were stacked across the room and were marked with the same broad, felt-tipped pen as "Amb Woodard – Personal Items."

So intent was his concentration to digest the information in front of him, he didn't take notice of a soft knock on the door. Without notice the door opened and closed. Colin Morris had quietly returned. "Sir, I just left Ambassador Williams. I saw him off to his hotel."

Slowly, Woodard looked up from the paper lying in front of him on his desk and nodded an acknowledgement of Colin's return. "Well, Mr. Morris, I assume that Ambassador Williams is ready to depart?"

"That he is, Dr. Woodard. Ambassador Williams asked me to convey his best wishes for a long and successful tenure, as he certainly is glad that you're here. He's ready to go home."

"Relieved might be a better term for his feelings, huh? Anyway it was most kind of Brad to wish me well."

"Please, Mr. Ambassador, as we spend more time working together, please feel free to call me Colin when you think it appropriate."

John Woodard nodded his assent, careful not to seem too eager to find accord with the suggestion. After many years in the medical field, the ambassador had become a man not prone to make snap judgments. Often operating within a margin of error that approximated mere millimeters or less, he had developed an ability to make decisions dispassionately but with carefully calculated haste. He was, like his aide, forced to wear glasses. Sitting behind his desk, he didn't give any indication of athleticism, but when he rose from his chair, he immediately gave the impression of a person who was in charge. He could be likened to an NFL quarterback. Given the time and protection to deliver, he could shred the opposition with accurate, delicate, surgical probes not unlike those he had delivered many times in the operating room. When he smiled, his teeth were slightly concealed by a cooperative upper lip. "Very good, Colin. I'm not much for protocol either except for formal occasions. So, when it's appropriate, you should advise me when I'm about to do or decide something that is ill-timed or inappropriate."

Woodard learned years ago when it was necessary to finesse offers of familiarity, and this was just such an occasion. Until he knew Colin Morris better and was better ensconced in the ambassadorial position, it was better to leave issues such as this to grow if they were intended to.

A resounding, piercing sound echoed throughout the office. BOOM! BOOM! BOOM! KABOOM! KABOOM!

"What the hell was that?"

Again the suddenly sickening sound resounded. BOOM! BOOM!

The ambassador quickly rose from his chair and made rapid, decisive strides towards the high-impact, bulletproof window. "Holy shit, the entire area is on fire. Colin, we're under siege. Fuck, the damned hotel where Brad was staying is gone. All that remains is totally engulfed in fire. What the hell is going on?"

Colin's face blanched as he neared the window. "Oh my God, I just left the ambassador not ten minutes ago."

"Lucky for you, that you didn't accompany him to the hotel. The whole building is gone! I'd say that we need to find out if Ambassador Williams has survived. Can you check your sources to see if there are any survivors? Meanwhile, I am going to call Washington and get in touch with Secretary of State Jane O'Donnell to inform her of what's just happened and see if they have any information on this. This is a major nightmare."

Wide-eyed and speechless, Colin nodded somberly. "A-a-a yes, yes, this place is going to be a real hotbed of activity. Yes sir, I'll check my local sources and see who survived. It could turn out to be one hell of a wild ride until we can determine what happened."

"Holy shit!" said Woodard. "This is a major nightmare. I'll call Jane, but first I better call Rosemary while I still can. I don't want her to go ballistic when this hits the press."

The ambassador's furrowed brow was evidence that he understood the gravity of the situation and that there was obvious peril for the personnel assigned to the embassy staff and their families. Nodding, he silently gave confirmation of his conclusion and the priority of his intentions.

This will probably be the last time for a while that I will put my wife ahead of my professional assignment.

"Before you leave could you tell me what the chances are that we have a secure phone that I can use?"

Colin, responding with the reaction of a man who knew the ins and outs of his assigned position, offered, "There is a satellite handset instrument in the third drawer down on the right-hand side of your desk. Do you have anything that you want me to do?"

The ambassador frowned as he reached for the satellite phone in the drawer. "I don't know, Colin. I think it best that you go check the status of Ambassador Williams. That's priority number one. Also, check the street rumors and survey the area to see if there is anyone out there, anything going on that will help us get a handle on what happened. Please don't overexpose yourself. I don't think that you'll be in any danger, but emotions could be running high. Be careful, and think first! I'm sorry. I don't mean to tell you your job. You know what to do so much better than I in these situations. I'm just trying to sort through the priorities of what needs to be done first. Your reputation preceded you and I don't want to lose you."

"I understand, Mr. Ambassador. I'll be careful. I'll try to be as observant and objective as possible without drawing attention towards me. First though, let me see if I can get any information on Ambassador Williams."

"Thanks, Colin. I think we're going to make a good team."

Noting Colin's retreat from his office, John turned to his encrypted satellite phone.

I hope to hell it works. The last thing I need is connecting to some unknown, possibly hysterical person in the Washington suburbs thinking that some American overseas needs emergency, top-level advice.

He dialed the three-digit number and pushed the ENCRYPT button on the front of the telephone cradle. Fortunately he'd been instructed on its use before he left Washington but hadn't thought he'd need it this soon. After a beep, it gave a distinctive series of two buzzes—not rings—meaning it was encrypted. Then two more buzzes and a voice on the other end intoned, "Yes, Mr. Ambassador, to whom do you wish to speak?"

Ah, I'm glad some things work like they're supposed to.

"I need to make two phone calls, please. The first is to my wife. Please stay on the line with me since this will be a short call. Then I'll need you to put me through to Madam Secretary. The number where you can reach my wife is…."

"Never mind, Mr. Ambassador, we have all the numbers each of our ambassadors call on a frequent basis. One moment please."

Christ, I had forgotten what government efficiency was like. I guess this is a good thing.

The familiar voice of Rosemary responded, "Hello?"

"Hello, baby, I just wanted to make a quick call to tell you I'm okay, but there's some confusion here that I need to sort through over the next week or so."

"I know, John. I've just seen a television report, but there are no details. Are you okay and is everyone there okay?"

"Yes, yes, but I don't have a lot of information right now and have somebody checking on things. I just wanted you to know that I'm okay and will get back to you soon. Please know that I love you and miss you."

"I love and miss you too, sweetheart. Be very careful and get back to me as soon as you can."

"I will. Goodbye for now. Operator, are you still on?"

"Yes, Mr. Ambassador."

"Okay, can you connect me with the secretary?"

"Right away, sir."

10

REFLECTIONS AND TAKING STOCK

A mirror gives off a reflection of the object or person standing in front of it. Searching for depth to see if there is something more that doesn't appear on the surface is often something a person does when looking at their image cast on glass. So too are the reflections found in the mind.

DR. Woodard sat at his desk waiting to be connected to Secretary of State Jane O'Donnell. It had been forty-five minutes since the last detonation had been heard in downtown Tehran. Deep in thought, he tried to make sense of what had just occurred by making a connection of recent events. It had been an eventful span of several years, with gas prices rising to unbelievable heights in the United States, the housing market still recovering from the collapse, the North Koreans still saber rattling, and the Al Qaeda in Iraq and Afghanistan continuing their offensive. As always, since the late eighties and the early nineties, the citizenries of the United States were angry with politicians in Washington over continued job losses, expenditures, and a sluggish economy. How would they react to this catastrophe?

I wonder what it all means. There has to be some sort of connection. The damned Russians said that they would bury us economically, but we turned the tables on them. But this.... If some terrorist group is trying to bring us down, what would be the easiest way for them to accomplish that feat? Did we play into their hands when we invaded Iraq? What about Iraq or Afghanistan? We haven't finished the job there and now it's looking like that battle will go on for who knows how long? It was Colin Powell who said we should take on a Pottery Barn philosophy with regard to those countries—if we break them, we buy them. Hmm, I suppose if I were going to try to topple a superpower that I couldn't defeat in hand-to-hand combat, I would try to spread its power so thin that.... Yeah, and then if you take an economic necessity that they rely heavily upon and jack the prices up.... Damn, we've handed our new president one hell of a mess. This is something that we certainly do not need.

The ambassador cleared his throat and slowly rose from his chair. Walking heavily towards the heavy glass window to again survey the damage, he held the phone receiver to his ear, sighed, and slowly shook his head.

Damn, this is all I need to face my first day on the job.

A familiar voice on the other end of the line suddenly disrupted his thoughts. "John, this is Jane. I'm sorry to keep you waiting, but I was just watching the breaking story on Fox News from downtown Tehran—well, what's left of it—and got a three-sentence update from my CIA representative on events there. Needless to say, no one in Washington knows anything, except that it happened. What can you tell me? What's the state of the embassy? Are our embassy people okay? Are you in one piece? How is Brad holding up? Shit, I have a thousand questions and I guess I should just shut up and let you talk.

I have several of my core people here in my office. Try to be specific where you can because you're on speaker and they're taking notes."

"Thanks for the heads up, Jane. I'll do my best to avoid circumstances where information is unknown or sketchy, at best. Yes, I fully understand your anxiety about this. The truth is that I'm a bit rattled too. I can't begin to describe in detail what I see from my office windows. I'm damned glad the embassy is reinforced steel and concrete and the windows are bulletproof-shatterproof glass. Otherwise, we would have an outdoor exposure here on the third floor. I have no information about the embassy staff yet or their families. My station chief is out trying to gather quick-look information. He'll be back shortly and I'll give you an updated, detailed report. I can hear the embassy backup diesel generators running, so we have power, and water filtration is working. We may find ourselves acting as a field hospital, but it's too soon to know that now."

After a brief pause, Woodard continued, "Right now, I can't begin to describe the breadth of destruction I see here. The city is almost leveled with fire and smoke present no matter which direction I look. This much damage and destruction tells me there is undoubtedly massive loss of life, and my air force service in Vietnam tells me this appears like a deliberate attack from the air. There is no reason to believe that there were nukes involved—just extremely high explosive munitions. As you might expect, the Iranian government is probably in shock and at a standstill. I can't say with certainty, but the Iranian government might have even been decapitated. I have no judgment about the cause, origin of the attack, or even if there was a specific tactical or strategic target. The damage is so widespread that it seems as though the attackers just wanted to inflict as much destruction, confusion, and death as possible."

Woodard deliberately avoided responding to the earlier question about Ambassador Brad Williams. Since Williams's hotel was leveled, there was little chance anyone survived in that structure. His intuition, which had never failed him, was that Williams was dead. But he wanted Colin's report before he said anything about casualties.

Janice Strothers, the ambassador's personal secretary, came into the office and handed Ambassador Woodard a handwritten note showing a list of known damages, casualties in and outside the embassy compound, an unsolicited comment from an Iranian security guard stating that "only a superpower could have done this," and the urgent cries for medical assistance from people on the street who made their way to the front door of the embassy. At the bottom of the note, Janice had written that she had instructed the US Marine platoon sergeant to allow wounded civilians into the compound for first aid, but to be alert to the possibility of suicide bombers among them. John Woodard gave Janice an approving nod and thumbs up gesture. He then gave Jane a quick rundown of all the items on the list. "Jane, I had best be seeing to my duties here. I have to gather as much information as I can in the next hour. I'll call you back then with an update as soon as I can." Woodard paused, and then continued cautiously, "I'm a little nervous about the security guard's comment. If that's what he thinks then that's what a lot of others in this town will think. As you know, the US and the Israeli's are still the biggest boogie men in the region. I'd like to know ASAP if you learn that Israel had complicity in this attack."

Jane O'Donnell responded tersely, "Good, I understand. So far I have no word from Tel Aviv that they had any involvement. I know they probably wish they had. I'll await your call back to me and give you an update at that time. Meanwhile, based on your initial response, the official US position on this will be that we are as overwhelmed by this catastrophe as everyone else in the world and will stand ready to assist the Iranian people where requested. I'll recommend to the president we leave it at that for the next few hours till we hear back from you."

11

PRESUMPTION OF GUILT
TEHRAN

*Many things emerge from a disaster. confusion, disorientation,
fears closely followed by panic, despair, and general chaos.
Usually someone steps to the front to quell the disorganization
and lead the way back to a relative state of calm.*

AMIDST the havoc and destruction created by multiple explosions that had sounded from all directions in Tehran, an Iranian Army officer with the rank of captain on his shoulder straps and the insignia of Records Administrator on the collars of his open-neck uniform shirt was forced to bring his all-terrain vehicle to an immediate stop on his way from his quarters to the American Embassy across town. On more routine days his military task was to monitor intercepted, unclassified correspondence and message traffic from the embassy and then report internal embassy emergency or crisis data to the Iranian Army chief of staff's office for their assessment. If all his communications were severed, his Plan B instructions were to get on his ATV and physically go to the embassy, present his special credentials, and offer any assistance to the American Ambassadors office. Now, confronted with a more catastrophic Plan B than he ever imagined, with death and destruction at every turn, he looked with horror at debris, acrid smoke, and fire blocking every avenue. Captain Aref moved cautiously forward to the most centralized point in Tehran. Dismounting the ATV, he immediately realized that his most important duty was to serve in a rescue and recovery capacity. Dazed by the unimaginable commotion and destruction lying in front of him, he was overcome with the empty feeling that nothing in his years of training had prepared him for this tragedy. He started to leave his vehicle to help the surviving victims, only to, as an afterthought, return to retrieve a large bundle with a red crescent emblazoned on it.

It is a good thing that I never go anywhere without my government first-aid kit.

Satisfied that he had what was needed, he quickly resumed his movement towards the scene in front of him. In the block ahead, he saw an elderly man and his wife sitting in the street, both with cuts and abrasions caused by the debris fallout from the explosions. Nearby was a mother with three small children. Crying uncontrollably, she held in her arms a child exhibiting no movement. Her other two children were crying too, but their cries were more out of fear than from injury. All the people he encountered had blood seeping from various cuts, abrasions, and contusions. Thankfully, none seemed to show evidence of chest wounds or gushing open gashes.

Thank God I see no critical injuries. None of my training would have prepared me to act as a paramedic or an emergency services re-

sponder. I know some basic first aid that is useful, but, no, I don't have the ability to do any major triage.

All of the afflicted tried to muffle their moans of distress as he started to administer to their wounds. First, he stopped to see the mother with the children. The woman was covered with scratches and abrasions, as were two of her three children. The third child still showed no signs of movement. Checking for a pulse, he found none. He could only wrap the child more tightly in the blanket that was hanging loosely about her lifeless body. After gently setting the lifeless form on the ground beside the mother, he began cleaning the wounds of the mother and her other two children. Satisfied that he had cleaned the wounds as well as he could, he began to apply bandages and look them over for other more serious injuries. Next he moved through the smoke and small piles of burning debris toward the elderly couple huddled in the street.

Nearing the couple, the captain stepped over large concrete blocks, adroitly sidestepping debris in his attempt to reach them, to offer what aid and assistance he could. Before moving closely to them, he quickly looked around in all directions to see if there were others moving to his location. Smoke permeated the landscape as cries of pain and agony arose amidst the piles of rubble and debris. Captain Aref frowned as he rubbed his eyes in an attempt to relieve the tear-producing caustic air that seemed to be everywhere. Looking about again, he was shocked to note that chaos seemed to be everywhere. Suddenly, out of the corner of his eye, he caught sight of a bright piece of shiny metal. Clearly and blatantly out of place, it shouted for his attention. Stopping quickly, he knelt down to see what it was. With great care he began dislodging it from the soil that cradled it, only to discover that it was a small plaque roughly the size of a mailing envelope. Scanning it carefully, he noted an inscription on it written in a language he had studied only eight years earlier in the university.

The inscription is in English! Hmm, what do you know, the inscription indicates that this came from an AGM-86C air-launched cruise missile. It appears that this was manufactured by the Brandon Aviation Corporation.

It said:

Components and sensors are provided by Lambert Aerospace Company, Richardson Corporation, and Hairston Airplane Company. Systems engineering and integration supplied by Anatolia Enterprises, McMinnville, Oregon. All parts made in the USA.

I don't understand. My God! Could the Americans have really done this? Why would they have done such a terrible thing? I cannot imagine what kind of a country the United States is that it would kill hundreds of people without provocation. Surely they must have gone mad!

Quickly the captain arose, placed the metal label in his kit bag, and moved toward the stricken couple, his mind racing. Reaching them, he laid down his bag with his discovery inside and quickly but gently attended to their wounds.

I need to get hold of my general at the headquarters and then my friend Colin Morris, if he still is my friend. If anyone will tell me the truth, I hope Colin will.

Looking up, his face blanched in horror.

Oh God! The hotel nearest the new American Embassy is in ruin.

Scanning the landscape in a ninety-degree arc in front of him, he spotted someone approaching.

Who's that coming from the direction of the embassy? Ah, it looks like Colin. No, it couldn't be. But it is. Yes, it is. Allah must be smiling on me to bring us together at this crucial moment. It was meant to be.

Quickly the captain rose to his feet, careful to assure the older couple that he would send help to care for them and transport them to the nearest shelter. He paused for a moment, recalling the shiny plaque that he had placed inside the first-aid-kit bag. He called to Colin and waved his arms wildly.

At a distance of less than fifty meters, Colin recognized the captain rapidly closing the smoky and smoldering distance between them. Appearing to be on a mission, as the distance closed to twenty meters, he noted Captain Aref was trying to speak to him.

The captain cupped his hands in preparation to hail the approaching aide, trying vainly to speak over the din that surrounded them. "Colin, over here, over here! I need to talk with you!" When they met, they shook hands in an overly enthusiastic manner, showing they were indeed glad to see one another and that they did in fact share some sense of rapport.

"Thank God you weren't injured in the blast, Captain!"

"Thank you for your concern, my friend, but when I show you what I have found, our friendship and spirit of cooperation may be at an end." The captain quickly reached into his kit bag, withdrawing the plaque.

"I've made a surprising discovery that perhaps you can shed light on. He handed the plaque to Colin who took it to examine."

Colin looked at it for a moment, then said, "Holy shit."

The captain said with an accusatory tone in his voice, "This is bad news, is it not, Colin? This is not just bad news; it is catastrophic news on top of that dastardly attack. I request, no, I demand we take this to Ambassador Williams immediately!"

Colin said, "Aref, my friend, I have no evidence at this time, but this is not the work of the United States. As for Ambassador Williams…." Colin turned slightly to his right and with a waving motion, replied, "I think the ambassador is somewhere in that rubble, which once was a hotel before it was leveled."

"Oh my God, may Allah have mercy on the ambassador and his family!" The captain then paused to reflect on the circumstances in which he now found himself. "But is there not a replacement ambassador who has just arrived? Someone from the embassy must explain what, if any role, the United States had in this devastation."

Colin responded, a distant ring to his voice, "Yes, the new ambassador is near, but he is in an emergency-security location to assure that he's safe from any unexpected harm."

"That is good, Colin. I hope it's not in any of the many safe houses the government has made available to you. Those who would do him harm will soon find him. I am still not sure what I think of this situation based on the metal label I found. I hope to Allah I can trust your word that the people of America would not do what we see here today."

"Trust me, Captain. The US knows nothing of this. Only the new ambassador can explain this to your president and the Imam. Additionally, Ambassador Woodard is safe. No one would think to look where he's now located in a very secure environment. Now, can I quickly help you with this elderly couple? They need to be taken to a shelter, if one even exists. If we can't find one, let's take them to the embassy grounds." They looked at each other, then looked around at the total devastation, and intuitively reached the same conclusion. They helped the couple to their feet and headed to the embassy.

I doubt that telling Captain Aref that Ambassador Woodard is in his third floor office in the American Embassy would be appropriate at this moment. That would be almost like telling him that the embassy is surrounded by a platoon of US Marines who would rather die than either have the US Ambassador assassinated or have the American flag flying over the embassy burned in public in this time of crisis.

12

KEEP A LID ON IT
TEHRAN

*Things aren't always as they seem. Sometimes life
seems to be nothing more than an illusion.*

LESS than two hours after the series of explosions, one of which
was a mere eight blocks north of the American Embassy around the
Shirudi Sports Complex, the ambassador was back on the phone
with a third contact to Jane O'Donnell. In his second call back to
the State Department, he was connected to a deputy undersecretary
who confirmed that the United States was as surprised about this as
the rest of the world. John angrily responded, "The rest of the world?
Are you telling me you think this came from *within* Iran?"

"No, Mr. Ambassador, I'm telling you we don't know yet where
it came from or why! When I know more I'll call you back." The line

connection then terminated.

Why, he hung up on me! I guess it's to be expected when there's so much chaos on both sides of the world.

Ten minutes later, on the third phone-update call, he reached Secretary of State O'Donnell. "Yes, Jane, I called Rosemary. She's handling it very well. Thank you for dispatching the Secret Service to soften the news, but right now I'd like to know what all the secrecy is about."

"Secrecy, what do you mean, John?"

"Well, the CIA station chief here said his contact people at the White House told me to keep a lid on things. I was told that the word of the day is that we don't know anything, but we are looking into it. Anything that comes my way that even remotely indicates that we have any involvement is to be handled with the highest degree of secrecy and diplomacy. In other words, Jane, I sense that I am to be like a nesting bird waiting for the eggs to hatch."

"That's really strange, John. The president just found out about it. She hasn't even had time to convene the National Security Council together for a meeting. Between you and me, this attack on Iran is a catastrophe—a holocaust. Let me say also that the political timing is terrible. The president is having one hell of a battle with Congress on a myriad of other activities. Now we're faced with giving immediate and substantive aid to Iran using resources that are already stretched to the breaking point, and at the same time denying our involvement and proving to the world that we are not to blame. We have precious little left to give, but we're going to dig down deeply to give what we can."

"What's really going on, Jane? If I can trust anyone right now, it's you. I need to know some things and I need to give you some initial impressions."

"Okay, John. Go ahead and ask what you want, and tell me what you need me to know."

"Okay, Jane. The hotel down the street from my office was leveled. Brad Williams was staying there awaiting transport to the airport. I'm afraid Brad may have been killed in the blast. I'm waiting for confirmation and may have it in thirty to forty minutes."

"Oh my God, he had waited so long.... Would you like for me to take care of notifying his wife and family?

"Yes, it would be best coming from you. I will follow up with a call to Sue after you speak with her."

"It is doubly difficult to talk with her since I had to be as persuasive with him as I was with you to get him to take the job. If he's dead, it's my fault. But I'll make the call as soon as you get a confirmation. I don't want CNN or Fox News to break this before I do. They already strongly suspect there's more to this holocaust than anyone in the administration is willing to admit."

"I understand, and I must admit that I was hoping that you would suggest that. I've heard that Christian Amanpour from the news media is already in the streets here. She is reporting that the destruction is widespread and random. So far she has said there is destruction at the Shemisipour College of Technology, the Atomic Energy Organization headquarters, the Tehran West Airport, the Islamic Culture and Communication Organization, the Mehr Abad Military Air Base, the Doshan Tappeh Air Base, the Iranian Parliament House just six blocks south of us, many mosques, metro rail stations, hospitals, schools, and local aid stations. Even the embassies of Russia, the UK, Turkey, and Germany are reporting damage. Rumor has it that the Khargh Island petroleum refinery export terminal and even Qum have been hit. There is too much destruction to enumerate any further so I'll have someone here compile a list of other institutions and sites that are affected. One thing that strikes me in a cursory look at the list of buildings and facilities that have been destroyed or disabled is that there is no pattern to this attack. It's random and indiscriminate, so we need to turn up the heat on getting answers and making decisions."

"I sent my station chief out to get a feel for what is going on and get an initial assessment of the damage, and if possible, some insight into who and why. I also asked him to see if he could find out if there are any foreign visiting dignitaries in the city. Things here are so disjointed I'm wondering if this was an assassination plot. If it was, a random, indiscriminate series of explosions would be a good way to cover it up."

"Good plan! I can see that you're on top of things, as usual. My staff CIA liaison is here and is shaking his head and shrugging his shoulders about the assassination theory but will check his sources further. Meanwhile, my staff is convened here and is prepared to give you a short update on what we know, or don't know, so far."

One by one, the staff went through brief statements about internal Iranian government problems, external intergovernmental disagreements between them and their neighboring countries, deployment of military forces in the region, and social unrest in the country.

Consciously listening as the secretary's staff brought him up to speed with what information they had gathered at that point, his mind and his subconscious were riveted on the pillar of thick black smoke rising from what appeared to be a large, intense fire in the direction of the hotel that he could see from the window in his office. As the moments went on, he concluded the one single thing they knew was that they didn't know anything.

Not being "in the know" was foreign to his nature. In the past years both in medicine and politics, John Woodard was a man always well informed before he began work. Today's events were an anomaly for him.

Jane O'Donnell's staff finished their fifteen-minute initial update, which failed to reveal anything either of them didn't already know. It did, however, as is said frequently in Washington, put them both on the same page of the script. "So, Madam Secretary, when you hear something more, I know you'll get back to me and I will do the same for you."

"You never cease to amaze me, John. Since we have known one another we have always kept each other apprised of important information. It has been a welcome relief to me to have you there and reporting what is happening. You have been wonderfully responsive. I just wish your assumption of the ambassadorship would have been less chaotic."

"Thanks, Jane. As soon as any new news breaks here, you'll be the first to know. I'm expecting a call from President Rashid Al Formadi's office any minute now and he'll be looking for answers, explanations, offers of assistance, and anything else that can bring clarity to this disaster. As you know, I am acquainted with him and his family personally because of a medical problem they had a few short years ago. I was the treating physician. So, he may be a little more patient with me than anyone else. But he is being pressed by the Ayatollah for counteractions. Since you are the only person who I can really trust right now, I need your advice and counsel."

"Sadly, outside of you, the president, and the vice president, that's exactly how I feel. The formal US position is that we'll help where it is requested and we will assist in finding out who did this and why. Please express President Chenoa's deepest sympathies for the loss of life."

After terminating the connection, the ambassador remained at the window, surveying the damage before him. His mind retreated into private thoughts as he sadly shook his head, stuffing the cell phone into his coat pocket.

What a colossal mess! This is going to take years to clean up. That might be the easy part. The political fallout will be huge and, unfortunately, enduring.

While still reflecting on previous conversations with Jane, he pondered what he should do.

When Jane came to me to check to see if I might have an interest in becoming the ambassador to Iran, she cleverly appealed to my ego by mentioning that my calling to public service had become more important to our nation as an international figure and a person who knows how to diagnose and prescribe for those who can't do it themselves. It is amazing that she knew about my having treated the nine-year-old daughter of Al Formadi, one of the few quasi pro-American diplomats of Iran, to re-store her impaired vision. She actually thinks that because of that act—a kindness that any physician would have willingly done had they been in my place—a diplomatic bridge between Iran and the United States was helped to be built. I wonder why President Chenoa didn't come to me instead of sending Jane.

He continued momentarily to reflect upon his only trusted con-tact in Washington. Nodding, he reflected upon the persona of a woman completely consumed with her job. Her attire, certainly not from Vogue, nevertheless was stylish and very professional. Her hair style was short and chic, her makeup was applied sparingly, and her overall appearance was that of a strong, sensible, and capable pow-erhouse. Jane was always someone he could count on and trust with his life.

13

ASSESSMENT AND
DAMAGE CONTROL I
TEHRAN

Sometimes you have to wait for the smoke to clear before
you can actually see the fire. The same is true when it
comes to solving an apparently unsolvable mystery.

FOR years the Iranian government pursued many policies that
gave the country perceived strength, a promising economy, and technical prowess. These attributes gave Iran legitimate standing among
the community of nations; other inter-Iranian initiatives were more
self-serving and of less value to the world at large. There had been
international opinion that the United States had done too much
grousing over the preceding ten years about the lack of Iranian contributions to the world community and too little to support medi-

cal, drug, terrorist, weapons sales, and international hunger issues that the United States and a few other nations had shouldered. One did not have to look far or deep into Iran to find strong governmental opinion on the need to showcase their nuclear power, missile technology, and cyber development accomplishments on which they based their national power. They also blustered about the will to use their influence and power against the satanic initiatives of western nations. In point of fact, their diplomatic and military rhetoric was just that: bluster. In the minds of many Arab and Islamic nations, the evidence of who launched the attack on Tehran, and why, was irrefutable. They sadly and conveniently had poor memories about the good and noble things the United States had done in the last six decades for Europe, Africa, South America, and Asian-Pacific countries. And now the crown-jewel capital of the Islamic world lay in shambles with a governmental structure that had apparently been decapitated in a matter of twenty minutes.

Ambassador Woodard was mesmerized with the damage. It was more widespread than he had ever seen. He went again to the third-story windows of his corner office to survey the damage. The sky was still filled with black smoke. Intense flames could be seen in the direction of the Bu Entrada refinery, four miles away to the northwest and in the downtown government-center buildings to the southeast. He stood in silence for almost two minutes listening to the verbal report from his station chief, Colin Morris. The report was mostly about the structural damage done to the nearby hotel and three sacred mosques. Slowly, but with apparent purpose, he began to ask the more humanitarian questions that were so vital to be identified.

"About how many Iranians have you seen or received reports about having been killed? Any reports on the number of fatalities?

"It is hard to say, Mr. Ambassador. Perhaps as many as twelve thousand or more, but I will have to get in touch with some of my Iranian contacts to confirm that number. A huge number of casualties have been reported at the mosques, but other than that the government is unable to release any information. I suspect government capabilities are paralyzed."

"Those poor bastards, can you imagine what their last thoughts might have been? My God, how awful!"

Colin nodded, "Nothing—no information—can be regarded as credible at this juncture except for what we see. We do, however, have in the courtyard of the embassy 257 wounded who require first aid. Some are resident American citizens and some are more seriously injured than others. Our Marine staff corpsman is attending to them and we have a state department nurse assisting as well."

"Okay, I'll go down there in a minute to see if I can help. Colin, tell me, what Iranian government actions do you see or know about that are set for aid and medical assistance?"

Colin shook his head ruefully. "None to speak of; things are very chaotic."

"You mean there is no leadership and no apparent plan, right?"

"That would be a correct initial assessment."

"What about emergency service vehicles and hospitals?"

"It is pretty grim, I'm afraid."

"That's not surprising! There are never enough to begin with, even without a disaster."

"Mr. Ambassador, I have some sensitive information that I need to share with you."

"More sensitive than what I've already heard? Jesus, man, I'm almost ready to roll up my sleeves and head out there to see what I can do to offer medical assistance."

"That would be ill-advised right now."

"Really! Why? I know, damn it, the situation is dire and the dangers may not be over yet! But I'm just so frustrated that everyone seems to be so helpless."

"That's to be expected, Mr. Ambassador, but listen to me first.

As I started to say, I ran into a trusted Iranian Army officer, Captain Aref. He is the embassy liaison between us and their Foreign Ministry. I met him a few years ago when he was on exchange duty in the Iranian Embassy in London. He's the sort of person who is very well connected in not only his government, but in the military intelligence of governments of at least four other Middle Eastern nations. I suspect he is secretly a higher-ranking military officer or national government department official than he is allowed to admit. He also knows that I suspect that he is more than he masquerades. Nevertheless, I treat him as he requests, and we many times shrug off pieces of incredibly sensitive information that could only be garnered from a highly placed, inside source. I never press him to identify sources or methods. And I suspect he knows I am more than a station administrator. It's an unspoken subject between us. We simply regard each other as a credible source of information and we protect our relationship. Anyway, it seems that he discovered something both interesting and incriminating in the rubble near the mosque."

"And just what would that be?"

"He found what purports to be a nameplate with an interesting inscription on it."

"So, are you going to beat around the bush or are you going to come to the point?"

"What would you say if the nameplate had some English inscription with American aerospace corporations' names on it?"

"Are you serious?"

"Deadly! The inscription referenced several well-known American aerospace firms with which I know you are familiar. Since I know you reside in the Pacific Northwest, there is one firm you may be more familiar with; it's the Anatolia Enterprises of McMinnville, Oregon."

The ambassador turned away from the window, glaring at his aide. "Yes, I know that company, but moreover, are you telling me that this is not the result of a prepositioned explosive, car bombs, or the act of some terrorist force or some tribal group run amuck?"

"At the outset, so it appears. Sir, I think that we have a very bad situation here."

"No shit! It is unfathomable to me that it could be anything other than an airstrike or a missile attack. The damage is widespread and somewhat random from both what I have seen and what you and the secretary have reported. The detonations were large explosives and the targets seemed nonexclusive and dispersed, almost as if the damage was intended to decapitate the Iranian government and to do as much damage and destruction as possible. No, Colin, it is completely insane to think this was a US-inspired and -initiated attack, and yet, who in this area has such weapons besides us?"

Woodard shook his head while staring at the floor, trying to digest the unhappy news. "You say that this Captain Aref actually thinks that this was an act perpetrated by us?"

"So it seems. I did everything to convince him that he needs to keep his discovery to himself until we can shed some light on who the perpetrators are. But his ability and even his willingness to suppress this information are very, very short."

"Colin, you know damned well that it wasn't us. I can't prove it yet, but we didn't do this. Our military couldn't pitch a pup tent in the desert without this government knowing it. I assume that you assured him of that fact."

Colin nodded an unconvincing *yes*. "Anyway, Mr. Ambassador, my role is to serve as a relay, pass information that I gather on to you for relay to Washington. So I need to get back out on the streets to see if there's any other data to pick up."

The ambassador nodded, somewhat detached, as if concurring but thinking of other, more important and higher priority actions. "Listen, Colin, you are right and you need to get back out there and continue to find out what is going on, but I need you to do two specific things while you're there. First, please check on the rescue operations in place—if there are any—and get a feel for casualties, and second, see if you and I can get together with Captain Aref and continue to emphasize to him to, if possible, keep this under his hat until we find out what is going on. I'm suspecting that he can't or won't. After all, this is his country, his city is in ruins, and he has seen elderly and innocents dead or dying, and to top it off, he thinks the US did it. No, I agree, he won't keep this to himself for very long, so time is not on our side. I suspect I will be hearing soon from someone in the Iranian Foreign Ministry and I can't and won't stall them at the front door. I want to be an open book to their president, or whoever is in charge. We need as much credible information as we can gather, as quickly as we can. We sure as hell don't want this to blow up on us. Right now, diplomacy is our most important weapon—both in the streets and at the top of all governments represented in this town and across Europe and the Middle East. We have to let the people know that the United States is going to have a disaster team of personnel with medical supplies and shelters in here ASAP."

"Yes, sir! I think that is a very wise decision. Anything we can do to defuse any mistrust is essential. I will get back in touch with Aref immediately."

"Good! Thanks, Colin. I'll begin making some additional diplomatic and international phone calls to attempt to limit political damage."

14

TIME TO GO TO WORK
OREGON CITY

*Being reunited with an old friend after a long separation can bring
about a variety of responses. How has the separation, because of
different career paths and geographical location, affected the friendship?
Is there still a common thread that can serve as a connection?*

SOMEWHERE in the subconscious of Lee Grady, he heard
the soft but persistent, annoying ringing of a bell. He felt as though
he were lying in a small boat on a serene lake, gently rocking and
feeling the dreamy effects of being a bit inebriated. This was somewhat of a pedestrian thought for someone of Dr. Grady's stature in
academia and government circles, and a bit of a departure from the
unconventional theories and innovative thought he had brought to
the field of criminology and investigative information discovery. The

annoying ringing continued unabated somewhere in the distance. At the same time in his dreamy state, it was almost as if his brow were being gently caressed by a soft, feminine hand belonging to someone he couldn't quite focus on. This subconscious thought must have come from recent flirtatious encounters he had experienced at a civic government reception, as well as from the overall feeling that he would like to have a steady female companion in his life again. He had met a woman named Kathy Moen, who seemed more acquainted with civic, local, and national governmental issues than seemed customary for a real estate agent. But there was also Trish and others whom he had come to know more or less intimately. After all, it had been seven years since the love of his life had passed away from cancer, and he was still a relatively agile, healthy male with normal male desires and impulses.

The ringing grew louder. Though distracted by it, he was still not quite able to place its origin. It continued to get louder and louder. Suddenly, Lee shot upward until his upper torso made a perfect right angle with his soft perch on the sunroom sofa. He shook his head to dislodge the cobwebs. Lee hadn't changed much from his college years, other than to experience the thinning of what used to be a thick growth of closely cropped, dark brown hair. He still wore glasses, but they no longer defined him—they had become a mere accessory. Lee's vigor carried over to his seemingly endless quest for answers to the problems of the day. His mind was keen and always in motion.

Damn, what a time for the phone to ring, just when I really conked out. I guess the eighteen holes and the early tee-off time were more demanding than I thought they would be. Getting older is not for sissies. I'm not old, but right now I feel older than usual. Indeed, his sixty-eight-year-old body was still wiry and athletic. The years had been physically kind to him, and regular workouts, eating right, and carefully striving for moderation seemed to have worked. His chiseled jaw line, masculine good looks, and steely blue eyes presented a man of determination and consistency, with a degree of unpredictability that made him a person to be reckoned with by either an intellectual or physical adversary.

The phone continued its persistent ringing as he stumbled to his feet from the sofa. "All right already, I'm coming. Isn't it enough that you woke me from a completely wonderful dream?

Lee picked up the phone, looking at it as though it were the enemy.

"Hello!"

"Hello? Is this Dr. Lee Grady?"

"I answer to Lee. Yeah, speaking, but you can drop the 'doctor.' I'm pretty informal. Ah, sorry it took me so long to get to the phone. In case you don't know it, you interrupted a much-needed nap."

What a bozo! Why in the hell would he have to ask if this is Lee Grady? If he needs confirmation, he must be selling something!

"This is Phil. I hear there is no rain predicted for the Pacific Northwest for at least sixty days!"

"Say again! Would you please repeat that?"

"This is Phil. I hear there is no rain predicted in the Pacific Northwest for at least sixty days!"

Lee was briefly speechless. This was code, a summons, something he hadn't heard in nearly a year. He knew the voice on the other end was an anonymous dispatcher who probably had his dossier in front of him and was simply relaying directions from a high-ranking government official. Only three or four seconds passed, but Lee's mind was racing. First, he knew that Phil was really FIL. It was governmentese shorthand for Federal Investigative Liaison. The statement about rain was a personal code only used by some federal investigative branch of the US government to alert Lee Grady, and only Lee Grady, that they had a job for him to do.

Since Lee had signed on as a freelance investigator several years earlier, receiving encouragement from his wife, Sandy, an attorney for the Federal Prosecutor's Office, to do so, he had responded to the summons maybe two or three times a year, but it had been some time since he had been called this way.

Lee now needed to give the countersign to this phone call, to acknowledge the caller and agree to meet and talk.

"That's what I thought you said. Ah, uh, yeah. Yes, where I live, we either experience a drought or a flood."

"We are dispatching a person to meet and talk with you at this time. He is familiar with your area and is someone you know and with whom you are familiar. I am to give him instructions and directions where the two of you can talk. The location is your choice. It should preferably be some public place. Do you know of such a place that is, let's say, within twenty minutes from your residence?"

"Ah, let me see, there's the...how about Little Cooperstown in Willamette?"

"Willamette?"

"Willamette is a small community off I-205 that is an extension of West Linn."

"Fine, can you meet at four o'clock this afternoon?"

"Yeah, I suppose so. Yes, I'll be there. Do you know where the Ram Pub is?"

"Our man will find it. Four p.m. today. Don't be late. This is a matter of the utmost urgency and is time-sensitive."

Lee returned the receiver to its cradle. Scratching his head, he slowly eased his body onto the bar chair and stared out the window.

I wonder what the hell this is all about.

15

DAMAGE CONTROL II
TEHRAN

Taking steps to avoid a confrontation, opening up the lines of communication is time-consuming and frustrating because both parties in the dialogue come to the table with different perspectives.

AT the same time Lee Grady was hanging up his phone in Oregon, following this surprising phone call, Ambassador Woodard was sitting at his desk in Iran trying to assimilate all that had taken place, planning for this important first meeting of his diplomatic tenure in Iran. Now, only a day into the job, he felt somewhat overwhelmed by the events that had taken place.

Somehow I am going to have to present a convincing argument to the president and government of Iran. I need to take any and every opportunity to buy us as much time as possible to find out what the hell happened. I only hope I can keep a lid on this and keep these theocrats from making any precipitous decisions. Otherwise, my instinct and Jane O'Donnell's warning that this entire region is going to blow up with the fallout consuming the entire hemisphere may come to fruition. Who's to say that it won't have even more of a far-reaching effect? This could be the prelude to WWIII.

A knock on his office door brought the ambassador back to reality. "Come in."

The ambassador rose from the chair behind his desk and made assured, confident strides towards the door.

"Colin, I see you have been able to make contact with Captain Aref."

Smiling at the Iranian captain, Woodard extended his hand in a gesture to make the captain feel welcome.

"Yes, sir, Captain Aref is a busy man amidst all of the turmoil and confusion, but he felt that meeting with you was a priority."

The ambassador nodded, making sure to meet the captain's steady glare head on. "I understand. At a time like this, there isn't a moment to waste. Captain, won't you please take a seat. Rather than be seated at a conference table so that they could face one another across the table in a formal us-and-them format, the chairs were arranged in the office away from the table, in a living room setting, so as to create an illusion of an informal atmosphere.

The ambassador extended his arm, palm up, to direct them each to a chair so that all three men were seated in angular fashion to one another, all well able to see each other's facial expressions and bodily gestures.

Woodard carefully studied the Iranian captain sitting across from him. He had a typically dark complexion with coal black hair, and he was slight of stature. Aref's military bearing was strikingly similar to military officers of nations like Russia, Germany, and China, but there was also the American influence, which avoided the usual stiffness of posture. He reflected momentarily on the goose-stepping demeanor of Russian officers he had occasion to deal with in the past. There was also something nagging at him. This seemingly low-ranking military officer was worldly and informed, had a confident bearing, and, according to Colin, reportedly had a somewhat direct line to many seniors in the Iranian government. It was an age-old ploy in diplomacy to take a fairly senior military or Foreign Service Officer and pass him off as a low-ranking, relatively unimportant local or city official who would be accountable for little that happened in his domain. This would cause most people to be more candid with him and less intimidated by his perceived station in life. John's intuition told him to be candid with Captain Aref, not too effusive with facts, show sympathy for the situation, and radiate honesty and candor. It seemed to John that Captain Aref was probably a colonel or even special inspector. Whoever Aref was, John and Colin were direct, honest, and genuine in their heartfelt sorrow.

"Yes, time is crucial. I am expected back at my headquarters and am almost overdue in informing them of my whereabouts and in updating them on the status of needs of the American embassy, so I do appreciate you agreeing to meet with me on such short notice in this chaotic environment. Now, to the point: even though I have spent much time in the US and believed I knew and understood American attitudes, values, and beliefs, I find myself troubled in accepting the evidence that I have uncovered."

The ambassador nodded knowingly. "But what you have found is very difficult to discount, correct?"

"That is correct, Mr. Ambassador."

He reached into his pocket and slowly unveiled the plaque and handed it to the ambassador. "When I found this at the site of the bombing near the mosque, well, it was difficult for me."

Woodard nodded as he carefully examined the inscription on the plaque, which the captain had handed him. He turned it over to examine the back, the edges, the printing, and especially the words. Since he was certain the captain was not going to let him retain the plaque, he wanted to be assured he could provide a detailed description of what he held in his hands. "This is certainly incriminating, isn't it? But I assure you I have been in contact with the highest levels of government in the United States and have been told with certainty that this holocaust was not of our doing." As John spoke those words, he looked Captain Aref in the eyes, with a steady gaze. He wanted to leave the impression that he spoke the absolute truth and that it was based on fact and authority. John and Aref locked their gaze in what seemed an interminable moment. When Aref broke the silence, John felt assured he had conveyed truth and honesty and that Aref had accepted it.

"Yes, but I'm sure there is an explanation?"

"I agree, there is an explanation to be found. But at the moment, Captain, you have caught me with insufficient information to give your country's leadership an unequivocal explanation. All I can promise you is that I will get to the bottom of this as quickly as is humanly possible. Further, I promise you that I will keep you apprised of what is going on at every turn."

The captain nodded. "That is reasonable, Mr. Ambassador. So what do you expect of me?"

Woodard smiled as he slowly hunched forward to look directly into the captain's eyes. "I know you must report what you have discovered in the rubble, as soon as you can, but I would only request you be as fair as you can and express my heartfelt sadness at what has happened to the good people of this city and the nation. I continue to believe this is not the work of my government and know that an investigation has already begun in the United States. As the United States ambassador to your country, I intend to report this same message to your president and foreign minister as soon as I can be granted time. I expect that it will be sooner than I am prepared to give a full and complete report, but I am determined to present as many follow-up status reports as it takes to identify the source of this horrendous attack."

The captain nodded his head in silent agreement. "I would hope that you will learn something definitive within the next twenty-four to forty-eight hours. My superiors' lines of communications are in disarray right now, but it won't be long before they will be comparing what they know with each other and will be asking for efforts to collect evidence. As you might know, I am compelled to forward this plaque as a piece of information that is key to what has happened. I am required to make an interim report as soon as I return to my headquarters. So I appreciate your efforts. Your diligence in this matter, Mr. Ambassador, is sincerely requested. I also have it on good authority that my foreign minister will be here anytime now to solicit your aid and support."

That latter alert about the foreign minister's impending visit lent credence to Colin's observation that Aref was, indeed, higher placed than his rank indicated.

"You can count on my cooperation, Captain. And I do appreciate your tip off to the visit of your foreign minister. I respect that your line of communication within your government is much better than mine, so I will be prepared for his visit. In the meantime, I will let you know anything that comes my way. I am very serious about discovering who is behind this dastardly attack, and why."

Rising from their chairs, all three men slowly began walking toward the door.

"Thank you for coming to see me, Captain Aref. I know you are a busy man, and quite frankly, I have a lot of stones to unearth so that we all can get to the bottom of this."

16

REUNION
LAKE OSWEGO

Clandestine meetings always carry an air of anticipation and even suspicion. The challenge of solving the mystery, however, is often so powerful that it evokes more than cautious expectation.

THE time was 3:45 p.m. when Lee got into his Corvette for the fifteen minute drive to the Ram in Little Cooperstown. He pondered what he had heard during the brief conversation with "Phil."

These spooks are always so melodramatic and mysterious. Do you suppose that every phase of their lives operates that way? I suppose it's not hard to figure out why they would choose to operate that way with me, particularly if they have a new assignment for me. Maybe I should be grateful. All they're trying to do is keep all the good guys protected so that no one is ever compromised or runs the risk of being inadvertently or deliberately killed. What the hell, it's been slow here and I was starting to get bored with my golf game. I need a challenge and a change of scenery, so maybe the timing is good. Still, I need to be cautious.

Nonetheless, Lee was irritated. Probably more so because he had not been called for some time and was growing accustomed to relaxing. It was nice not having to always be preoccupied with looking over his shoulder. Since the Anatolia affair, he had been forced to remain vigilant. After the Anatolias and their accomplices were securely incarcerated, the attorney general of the United States called him to Washington to personally and privately congratulate him for an investigative job done exceptionally well on that case. Lee's actions led directly to the arrest and conviction of no less than six "most wanted" fugitives and the exposure of two highly placed moles in the Department of Justice who were collaborating with the crime families and the Anatolias. The attorney general's accolades under these circumstances were presented quietly and privately to avoid the potential for reprisals. In the meeting, the attorney general told Lee to remain alert to any unusual events, phone calls, or new people in his life. Lee knew all too well that crime families have a long memory and can be extremely vindictive when they think someone has been responsible for their exposure.

All of that is a past issue that requires continual vigilance and an awareness of today's surroundings. I hope the case is closed! Come to think of it, I've been a bit careless lately. As soon as the air was cleared I knew I was skating on thin ice by renewing my connection with Trish. That's not like me. I'm usually more standoffish than that. I must be getting old, but she was a fine and loving woman even though she was somehow distantly connected to her father's underworld activities. It was funny: the FBI could never tie her directly to the syndicate. Damn! I need to wake up. The Anatolia family affiliations are very clever. If they ever wanted to get me, they would wait until I least expected it. I could easily let my guard down, and then, ZAP! Yep, they would do me in. I suppose it's possible

*they might have even broken the code. They might be the ones who sent
the coded message I received and already have the wheels in motion to
send "someone" to meet me....*

At 4:00 p.m. Lee stepped out of his Corvette after having scanned
the parking lot looking for anything out of place, including people
sitting in parked vehicles who appeared poised for an unobstructed
getaway. He slowly approached the pub steps, his head turning un-
obtrusively, looking for one or two men moving in his direction. But
nothing was out of order; no one seemed interested in him. That was
a good thing. Slowly he walked into the bar and paused.

He fleetingly thought that this would be a good time to catch
him off guard. Veering to the left inside the lounge, he quickly
checked to see that nobody present appeared to care or take special
notice that he had walked in. A scan of the tables and booths in a
rapid but careful, semicircular sweep of the premises ensured that all
appeared to be okay.

*There's hardly anyone in here. Oh yeah, that makes sense. The late-
lunchtime crowd is gone.*

Noting no presence of another patron, Lee began to walk slowly
and nonchalantly towards the booths to the rear across from the bar.
If this guy was a "spook," he would probably choose a spot in the
room where he could see in all directions—a somewhat inconspicuous location. Lee was about to turn the corner to scan the booths in
front of the bar when a man stood and offered his hand, a gesture of
welcome.

"Lee, remember me from a few months back at Dave's Famous
Ribs?"

"Holy shit, Eag! I should have known you were probably behind
the call. I'm glad to see you again. I know we agreed to stay in touch
and planned to meet again before too much time went by, but I guess
I wasn't expecting to meet again so soon...and why all the formality?
You could have just called me."

"I know, I know. But I wanted you on this case and the only way to do it was to get you tasked through FIL. That activates your security clearance, certain protection measures, and, by the way, starts your paycheck. So let me be direct since time is of the essence. I need to know some detail about recent contacts you've had with Trish Anatolia. You can skip specific details."

Lee smiled, knowing exactly what his friend meant. Pillow talk in the afterglow was acceptable, but what happened between the sheets was off limits.

"As you now know, the call to you earlier today wasn't a fluke. I'd like a little more information about her. She has somehow been able to fly under our radar to this point. You mentioned when we last talked in October that you were acquainted with her. I didn't think much about your comment back then, but recent events have caused her name to surface in connection with some possibly illicit activity. You seem to be our only connection. Also, if you've seen the news on television or heard it on the radio in the last six hours, you know there's been a catastrophe in the Middle East that is yet unexplained. No nation or group has taken credit for it. If it was done for political purposes, certain groups or countries wouldn't be able to contain themselves from rushing to news outlets to let the world know of their plans to overthrow legitimate, national political or religious authorities. So we're running down all the leads we have on past activities that were dead ends or unresolved in the recent past. There were some details about Ms. Anatolia that never quite came together. I knew you were involved several years ago and the agency is familiar with your…ah let me say various credentials, abilities, and, of course, social connections, so my job is to enlist your assistance. Your mission, should you choose to accept it, is to follow this string as far as it leads in the hope that there is a tidy knot at the end."

Lee grinned, nodding knowingly. He didn't want to be obvious, but the "Aha, so that's what this is all about!" light went on. He decided to face it head on.

"Well, well, well! Now I know. I am important to the CIA because I have an *in* with Trish, right?"

Jerry matter-of-factly looked into Lee's eyes without a trace of emotion. "That's about it, Lee—an *in* with her and superior investigative talents that might come in handy in solving the current Middle Eastern crisis, if we get that far. To be very frank, our timeline to get some answers to some very difficult questions is extremely, *extremely* short. You noticed that was two 'extremelies.' In my business, everything is on a short fuse and many times is black or white and pretty cut and dried. We pretty much learn to keep personal issues out of it and stick to facts, schedules, times, dates, places, and people."

Lee snorted. "You mean bloodthirsty, win at all costs? You call a spade a spade, right?"

"Let's not be so cynical. When national security is at risk and it involves saving lives, we let few things get in the way. You have an opportunity to become a huge part of that and there are people in high places who believe you can be essential in getting at the truth."

Lee nodded, knowing that this was the right thing to do. "You've probably read all the accounts in the papers and heard all the news reports, so you know the initial details about the cruise missiles. There are a few people who think Trish may have a connection. Notice I said *a few*. I'm one of them. The others in my community are focused on foreign governments, organized terrorist factions, or splinter groups. If any of my colleagues who are investigating those sectors run out of airspeed and altitude, their resources will be redirected to the most promising of leads. I happen to think there is more to Trish Anatolia than even you know about. So, anything you can share with me will be helpful."

Lee nodded again. But as the two men continued to talk, Lee noticed that every time Trish's name was mentioned in the last ten minutes, it was associated with the Middle East attack. So he took seriously what he was about to say, and was intrigued to see where this was going, but more importantly, to find out what he didn't know about Trish Anatolia. "Well, I knew Trish while I was at Naval OCS. I met her as Trish Knight but was told that her original family name was Anatolia. Her dad, Trush Anatolia, a.k.a. Knight, still retained the family name for his import-export business interests. I think it was called—"

"Yeah, yeah, Anatolia Enterprises, yes, we know all about that."

"Well, after her supposed death, just at the time I had completed boot camp, she moved to the West Coast as the wife of Vinnie Trabogo. Anyway, as time would have it, I became involved in an undercover sting operation run by the FBI and came to know Trish and the rest of the Anatolia family better than I should have. I mentally wrestled with pretending I cared for Trish while at the same time reporting events and observations to the FBI. When Trish agreed to turn state's evidence, she was convinced to change her name to Pat Brown and enter the witness protection program."

Mayhew nodded. "Did you know that Anatolia Enterprises is alive and well?"

"No, I thought they…I thought she…."

"If Trish told you she made some changes, she may not have told you explicitly what those changes were. The home base isn't located in Seattle anymore, Lee. T-Line Enterprises, flying above the Anatolia name, is now being run by her son up there and it's totally on the up and up. There's another, more transparent, somewhat secretive subsidiary of Anatolia Enterprises operating elsewhere."

"So where is this ugly beast located now?"

Jerry glanced around to see if anyone might have moved into one of the adjacent booths. Seeing no one, he then leaned forward closer to Lee as if he were going to reveal a piece of sensitive information. "How would McMinnville grab you? At least that is what we suspect. We think that it is embedded in Mountain View Aviation,

Inc. That is where you come in."

"McMinnville is a pretty small burg. It's a strange place for an operation like that to be located, isn't it?"

"Not really. Small places sometimes don't attract much attention, especially if the affiliation appears to be legitimate. Are you familiar with the new location of the Spruce Goose, the eight-engine, wooden-transport seaplane aircraft built by Howard Hughes in 1947?"

"Yes, in fact, I went through the hangar to see it not long ago."

"Well, across the highway at Mountain View Aviation, Inc., we suspect that there are all sorts of interesting things going on. At least we have more than a passing interest in what's going on, but it's difficult to be both inquisitive and anonymous."

"So, that's where you think I could be helpful?"

"Well, yes and no. Let's just say we're pretty damned sure that's where Trish and her slime-bucket mob are doing their dirty work."

"And it's still called Anatolia Enterprises?"

"Not officially."

Jerry nodded, slowly rising from his seat.

"Come on, I'm going to take you where I'm staying. I have something I want to show you. I think that will convince you that you can play a key role in helping us put this operation out of business."

17

BEGINNING WITH AN INTRODUCTION

WEST LINN

It has been said a picture is worth a thousand words. Nothing can stir your emotions so completely as seeing the bold, unbiased, nonjudgmental depiction of an event displayed through the eye of a camera. Likewise, contact with an old friend, or even a lover, can be the same sort of bold depiction that gives unexpected clarity to a situation. It can indeed sometimes be a welcome or a painful revelation.

RETURNING to his motel in Oregon City, after the meeting with Jerry Mayhew, Lee went to the reclining chair and slowly sank into the soft leather. Once seated, he gazed out the window at nothing in particular, his expression troubled.

I think Jerry felt he had to retrieve the sensitive satellite imagery and recordings of the intercepted cell phone calls from his room security safe to convince me. I didn't really believe that Trish would play a part in the missile strike in Iran. Well, at least not at first, but the nondescript, state-of-the-art electronics activities referred to in one of the cell phone calls seemed very suspicious and nefarious.

He frowned as he continued to stare out the window, reflecting on the day's events. Now, he had to go to Washington late tonight on the redeye flight.

Those damned photos and cell phone recordings were very convincing. I wonder how I could have misjudged Trish. Usually I'm a pretty good judge of character. In my business, a person doesn't get second chances. I think I have let my guard down. I have let my emotions overrule my training and good judgment. This was a well-timed wakeup call. Now I have to figure out how I can pretend that I know nothing about her presumed activities and nothing about her new Anatolia Enterprises operation in McMinnville. She is one damned good looking woman, and from now on, my time spent with her will be like flirting with a black widow. What's the name of the front organization? Yes, it was Mountain View Aviation.

A shrill report from Lee's telephone disrupted long-forgotten memories, brought back to life from this afternoon's meeting with Jerry. Annoyed at the interruption, Lee made his way to the kitchen and picked up the receiver from its cradle.

"Hello, this is Lee speaking."

"Hello, you. Is this a bad time for an Oregonian to call her friend?

"Trish! What a nice surprise. What time is it?"

"My watch says that it's nearly 6:00 p.m. That would be 1800 hours in some people's vocabulary. But in mine, it's cocktail time."

Resting his elbows on the kitchen counter, Lee returned the volley. "No matter, in any person's vocabulary, five or a little after is a perfect time to greet another Oregonian…rather, an Oregonian to be."

"Ah yes. Well, I'm calling to invite you to join me for dinner."

"That sounds nice. When did you get back from Seattle?"

"Two days ago, but we can talk about that at dinner."

"Where and when? I'll need time to take a shower."

"How does Little Cooperstown in Willamette sound? It's not fancy, but I'm not in the mood for fancy. I suppose ninety minutes would give you enough time to spruce up and drive from Oregon City to meet me, right?"

"Sure! So, what's the occasion?"

"So that you can welcome me back to Oregon. Does there have to be an occasion?"

"Absolutely not! Anytime you are near is a celebration. In fact, I've been thinking about you a lot lately. You said that you've been here for the past couple of days?"

"I did. Yes, I got in a couple days ago. I had some business to attend to in McMinnville, plus, I want to show you the property I'm thinking of making an offer on in Lake Oswego."

It's going to be tough, knowing what I know now, to play super sleuth and make her think it is so wonderful that we have found each other again and that she is an important, "new" addition to my life. I will need to decline an all-night affair tonigh, though. I'll just tell her I have an important consulting appointment out of town for the next day or so. She won't like it, but that's going to have to be the way it is. If I play my cards right, this could turn out to be easier than I thought. All I have to do is find out about her McMinnville business, Mountain View Aviation, without sounding too curious. Maybe I should suggest a visit to see the Spruce Goose and casually mention that I could be persuaded to see her business property in McMinnville. Hell, that wouldn't be much of a leap. Planes are planes and a lover of planes wants to see them all. On the other hand, a voice inside me warns that I shouldn't be too optimistic about any of this.

"Is it a house lakeside?"

"Good guess. You remembered my love for water and nice views."

"Yeah, right. I also recall that the view from a motel room was sufficient."

"Come on, Lee. Be nice. We shared much more than a few casual rolls in the hay, don't you think?"

"I'm sorry. You're right. The time we spent together in Newport was very special. I suppose you know that you're looking at high-priced real estate, don't you?"

"Well, it's not like I can't afford it."

"I apologize. I have no right to suggest parameters for your purchase." Lee glanced at a picture of Sandy and his two daughters, Nicole and Chiron. "So, you've really decided to take up residence in the Portland area?"

"Lake Oswego, dear, and yes, I was pretty clear on that issue the last time we were together."

"I wasn't sure that you were serious. As I recall—"

"That's not fair, Lee. At the time I really had no choice. Besides, I'm very serious when it comes to finding a way to be near you. We've already wasted far too much time."

"Do you plan to do your design work from your home?"

After a long pause, Trish said what he was hoping to hear. "Lee, my business plans have changed a bit. I'm not really in the design business anymore. I turned all of that over to Truman. Oh, I'll probably have to fly to Seattle once in a while to ride herd on Truman or give him some pointers, but yeah, I think I need a little separation from the company. Besides, I might have found something that is very intriguing as well as profitable here in this area."

Yeah, right. Uh huh, you mean like being in business of supplying missiles to rogue nations.

"Let's talk about that over dinner, Trish. I'm always interested in what you do; you know that. I must tell you, though, that I have an overnight redeye flight out of town to keep a consulting appointment tomorrow that I made some time back and can't get out of. So we need to make the most of our time. My work shouldn't take too long over the next day or so, which gives us time later this week for some quality moments together."

"I'm sorry to hear you don't have much time tonight. Are you sure I can't persuade you to change your appointment plans? I'll make it worth your while."

"I wish I could change my plans, but this client has made me an offer I can't refuse. Well, I'm not getting any closer to the shower standing here talking to you. So, I'll see you in an hour. Love you." He hung up the phone.

Trish hasn't changed her stripes one iota—still the aggressor.

Frowning, he slowly made his way towards the shower.

She's the complete package, but I'm not going to rush into anything serious, like I did the last time. Besides, I now have confirmation there's a mysterious side of her that I always suspected, but couldn't quite identify. This time I have an important mission to complete, and I don't need any more mystery in my life. Yeah, Trish, this time it's my turn to play the cloak-and-dagger game.

Thinking of Trish's many attributes and the good times they'd shared, a smile spread across his face.

Is it possible this could work out in our favor?

His subconscious yelled a resounding *NO!* But he pushed it aside, for now.

Trish really hasn't changed much since the time we spent together while I was attending OCS in Rhode Island. Those were good days. I wonder if she's still as fiery as she was when we first hooked up. My God, she could swear with the best of them, and when she got mad, well, she was really something. The aging process has been kind to her. Her body hasn't lost much of its shape either. Yeah, this could be one hell of an assignment.

*One thing is certainly different now. She seems so much more busi-
ness-like. I guess that goes with being in charge of a big company. Yeah,
I suppose. And, there's still something that doesn't seem quite right to me
about Trish's new business in McMinnville. How in the hell does she
conceal something as pronounced as missiles? Is it all true? It doesn't take
a rocket scientist to figure out the logistic pieces of the puzzle, but how
does she transport and store them so that she doesn't attract unwanted
attention? She sure as hell doesn't use UPS or FedEx. Truman's role, like
she said, is totally separate from Anatolia Enterprises, or at least that is
what Jerry says. Truman's supposed to be the accountant and the CEO of
T-Line Enterprises, and yet, is it a subsidiary of Anatolia Enterprises? I
wonder.... Hmm! I wonder.*

18

LITTLE COOPERSTOWN
WEST LINN

Little Cooperstown displays an abundance of reminders from MLB,
NBA, and NFL stars, as well local collegiate stars from the past.
Displayed openly, there isn't even a hint of deception.

AT 6:50 p.m., Lee greeted Trish in the waiting area at Little Cooperstown. He was a bit early and so was she. It may have been because they were anxious to see each other. Or maybe he was anxious and she was already nearby, wanting to see who else was present.

"My God, Lee, this place is hopping! Is it always this busy? If it is they must be rolling in the green stuff."

"Well if it's too busy for you here we could go somewhere else." Casually he glanced at his watch. "Trish, the dinner rush is just about to subside. I doubt that this crowd is going to last much longer."

"That's good to hear. I also hear that the food's good and the service, well, I've heard that it's top notch. I've had a hankering to…. If you don't find eating in a…."

"No, I'm fine with this place. It isn't like I haven't been here before, Trish. Besides, I think the décor is outstanding."

"Yeah, I suppose if you like sports, it's memorable. Also, my realtor is meeting us here for dinner."

"What? Who is it?"

She slowly and subtlety rubbed her hand across the front of his pants, smiling slyly. "You don't mind, do you?"

Lee grinned devilishly. "Let me see. Do I mind the fact that your realtor is meeting us or do I mind that you seem to have taken a liking to a certain part of my anatomy?"

Trish winked. "What do you think?"

Lee blushed. "Ah, no, I don't mind. I've always enjoyed meeting new real estate agents. We'll have to watch the clock though. I hope he or she's not longwinded. So, where is your realtor's office?"

"She is a she, and she has an office in Lake Oswego, just off the lake."

"I met a realtor not long ago who has an office in Lake Oswego. I'll have to ask if they are acquainted."

Trish frowned, eyeing him suspiciously. She stared at the pictures on the wall, appearing to be somewhat disinterested in his comment.

Trish abruptly halted the playful exchange. Rising, she stepped forward to greet a woman approaching. Following a brief exchange, she turned toward the table where he sat and introduced her guest. "Lee, this is Kathy. Kathy Moen."

Lee smiled, immediately recognizing her from the Civic Center reception a few weeks earlier. Kathy was a fiftyish, diminutive blonde with subtle strands of silver in her hair. She had an air of self-confidence about her that comes from education, experience, success, and training that few women have in one curvaceous, athletically toned body. Compact, with all the curves in the right places, she exuded a contagious, outgoing personality that seemed likely to attract people to her like bears to honey. Her smile, displaying even, white teeth, was natural, not forced, as can sometimes be expected from a professional salesperson. But unknown to both Trish and Lee, Kathy was not a professional salesperson. She was born and raised in Seattle, Washington. She graduated from Seattle public schools and, like most natives of the Pacific Northwest, attended college there as well. In her case, she graduated from the University of Washington in 1975 with a degree in political science, was a natural athlete, and starred on the women's swim team, ski team, and lacrosse team. In the fall of 1975 she entered graduate school at Reed College in Portland where she completed her master's degree with honors with a thesis in European diplomacy negotiation strategies. Before her graduation in 1977, a small team of federal government recruiters were on the Portland campus seeking candidates for openings for several nondescript positions in government offices in Washington, DC, and positions overseas that promised adventure, solid pay and benefits, and a chance for upward mobility. Kathy was intrigued and brought a copy of her resume—brief as it was—and interviewed. The recruiters politely discussed her academic record, her plans for the future, her natural athletic abilities, and what she planned to do after graduation. She told them she thought she might want to teach political science or stay in school to obtain her doctorate. She was nonspecific but seemed eager to get on with her life. She interviewed extremely well.

Later, Kathy interviewed with three other representatives from industry, with a small exclusive junior college in California, and with a congressional staffer from the office of a local congresswoman who represented the Seattle district in Washington, DC. She heard nothing from any of the recruiters or interviewers until late June, three weeks after graduation. One day there was a knock at the door of her parents' home in Seattle by a man and a woman who introduced themselves as recruiters from a government organization simply described as a consolidated federal employment pool. They showed identity cards and credentials. She recognized the man as the recruiter she spoke with earlier in the spring. She invited them in and after thirty minutes of polite conversation and random talk of what her plans were for the near future, they became very specific. They were from the CIA. They wanted her to join the agency and be available for training and security processing in two weeks. They were prepared to offer her a check for six thousand dollars right there and then as a signing bonus. With successful completion of appropriate indoctrination and training, they said she was a candidate for special diplomatic and liaison activities in Europe. Trying not to show her wild excitement, she had to bite her lip to calmly say she believed she would accept their offer.

Over the years, Kathy became a highly effective diplomatic operative for "the company." She completed small arms weapons training, martial arts defenses, and annual refresher updates to all physical and intellectual skills needed for her profession. It was not overtly obvious, but she most assuredly could defend herself. She obtained sensitive and sometimes critical political, military, and financial data that allowed the United States and special international friends from European and Middle Eastern nations to avoid catastrophic confrontations. More than half a dozen times she helped selected US, British, German, and Saudi diplomats or wives avoid extremely embarrassing personal disgraces when they were caught with attractive acquaintances who were not their spouses. She married a colleague from the Directorate of Operations at the agency and enjoyed a fifteen-year marriage before he was killed in an unfortunate, clandestine undercover operation in Iran. She read the after-action report, but those responsible for exposing her husband's operation were never specifically identified. There were, however, possible ties to a Chinese mafia operation that appeared as though they were directly related to an ambush and the use of a Chinese double agent who sabotaged the mission. The trail back to China or any Chinese criminal element was cold and very obscure.

After three more years of secret undercover support operations, Kathy felt emotionally exhausted and burned out. She asked for and received a sabbatical leave of absence to go back to the Pacific Northwest to rest and do something else for a while. But it was with the proviso she could be recalled to limited duty if circumstances warranted. She settled in Portland, Oregon—a town she had often enjoyed in her college years and which held a degree of charm, sophistication, and friendliness she had often longed for. She obtained her realtors license and became intimately acquainted with the region, developing many new friendships, both female and male. Once a month, someone from the company called to simply tell her that her skills and talents were missed, but that the terms of her sabbatical were being honored. More importantly to her, the lucrative salary for nearly thirty years of service was continuing. Occasionally they would also give her an update report on persons or activities in the Northwest in which the agency had interest. Thirty days ago they informed her of certain unspecified activities of Trish Anatolia, and she was asked to observe and track Trish's actions. How fortuitous it was that Trish had expressed interest in certain real estate properties, which afforded Kathy the opportunity to not only get better acquainted, but also get to know who Trish knew and what her plans were. Now, a new side of Trish's life had apparently emerged. She hadn't expected to see the more romantic side of Trish, but it had suddenly appeared.

Lee nodded his approval, his smile revealing something more than a mere appreciation of the introduction. "I'm pleased to meet you, Kathy," Lee said.

Failing to conceal her surprise and apparent elation with the introduction, Kathy's cheeks immediately turned a reddish hue. "I think that Lee and I have been briefly introduced before," Kathy said.

"Hmm, when was that?" asked Trish.

"I believe it was a brief encounter at the Civic Center. There was a Symphony Society reception there and Kathy was with a fellow from Salem."

Kathy smiled, nodding her head in agreement.

"Will he be joining us tonight?" asked Lee.

Trish bristled, noticeable irritation starting to surface. "Okay, okay, I get the picture. You are acquaintances?"

Lee noticed the irritation and got a small amount of satisfaction from Trish's reaction, but knew he needed to tone down his approval of Kathy as Trish's newfound friend and realtor. He also wondered—since he knew nothing of Kathy's background—if it were possible that she and Trish were actually co-conspirators. Deciding discretion was the better part of valor—and feeling a distinct disadvantage in this situation—he decided that a low-key role would be a better path for him to follow. "Trish, we haven't seen you in some time and it was unfair of us to take advantage of you, even though it was unrehearsed. I apologize. We're just glad to see you and want you to know this area is a fairly small community. Everybody eventually runs into everybody else sooner or later, right, Kathy?"

"Yes, there's nothing more to our previous encounter. I'm glad to see Lee again, but this meeting is all about you, Trish. I am so pleased to meet with you professionally and hope that our business relationship works out to our mutual benefit."

Lee slowly observed the change in atmosphere between all of them and sensed it was less antagonistic.

She looks a lot like Trish, blond and easy to look at with a trim figure that is hard to overlook. Maybe Trish's hair is a bit longer with just a hint of grey. On the attractive meter, both would probably rate a nine or ten.

Neither is overly endowed, but that's for show anyway. Kind of like golf, you drive for show and putt for dough.

Lee said, "So, I guess we are having dinner and then you are going to take us to see the place that Trish is thinking of buying, right?"

"Yes, and I trust that you must be with Trish to make sure that I don't sell her a lemon."

"Lake Oswego isn't exactly the citrus capitol of Oregon, now is it?

She grinned, nodding her head, appreciating the compliment on the quality of real estate in the upscale, Portland suburban neighborhood. "No, no it isn't. In fact, I think that we need to think in terms of gems when it comes to describing property in this lake community. Well, are we going to order dinner and drinks, or shall we be off? The sellers would like to reclaim their home by eight this evening if that will work for you."

"Maybe we had better see the property first if that's the case," said Trish. "Lee and I have some unfinished business to take care of and he has a flight out at midnight tonight to see a client. So, the sooner we get to it the better. Besides, he and I can eat later. Then again, when we're done seeing the property, if you'd like—"

"Thanks, but no thanks. Sometimes it's best to go with the old adage that two's company and three's a crowd. Besides, I too have an appointment later." They left the foyer of the restaurant and walked to Kathy's car for the drive to the property. Only short comments about the weather and the traffic ensued during the short drive across town. While driving, Kathy returned to business and said, "So, are you prepared to make an offer today?"

Trish chuckled, obviously enjoying the opening. "It's possible, but I would like to hear Lee's opinion first."

Kathy's smile immediately evaporated, a look of surprise on her face. "I see. So his opinion is important in making a decision?"

"You might say so. I think that I already know what I want to do, but he is so much more analytic and aware of values than I am. Another pair of eyes and ears is useful in making a big decision."

Kathy nodded. "Why yes, a second opinion is always valuable."

At the property a few moments later, Kathy and Trish were interested in showing the whole house to Lee for his approval. He followed Kathy as she led them through a quick tour of the premises of the Lake Oswego house on the lake.

"I think you would be very happy here, Trish."

Appreciative of the opportunity, Trish noted, "It isn't just for me. I sort of figured that you might have an interest too, Lee."

Kathy smiled. "Have I missed something here? Are you two thinking of getting married?"

"No, we're just old and very good friends. This is going to be a purchase that has to please Trish." Grinning, he continued, "I'm just along to serve as an impartial and unbiased judge."

Later, while headed back to his house in his car, Lee broke the silence. "I think you made a wise decision. The house is beautiful. If nothing else, it will give you a fantastic retreat from the hectic life of the business world in Seattle."

"I thought I told you that I have turned all of that over to Truman."

"I know, but I didn't think that you would be completely divorced from all the business aspects of the company. Was Kathy correct when she said that you could have possession in two to three weeks?"

Trish nodded. "Yeah, and it will put me closer to a group of people I have been working with."

"Oh, you mean since you turned your operation in Seattle over to Truman?"

"Yes. We can talk about my new operation in McMinnville at another time, okay? I'm thinking about giving you the grand tour, but first I have to get moved in and tie up some loose ends."

"Sure, sure, I understand, but could you tell me what this group is all about that you mentioned?"

"Oh, they're just a group of people that, ah, well, let's just say that they have diverse interests."

Lee frowned, nodding as though offering encouragement for her to continue. "So, you are interested in…."

"I'm interested in what our government is doing. Some of my business interests and profits are tied to what they're doing now in the Middle East and Far East. Some of those initiatives are downright political in nature, some are disingenuous, and others are outright bullshit, and you know it, Lee. For instance, the events in Southwest Asia and now the crisis in Iran today…doesn't that bother you just a little bit? We profess to have a democracy, but the United States Congress can tie up needed legislation for an eternity on just a whim. The president needs to be able to act without restraint when it's necessary."

"And just when is it necessary?"

"How about after 9-11? How about the USS *Cole*? How about the aids epidemic in Africa? How about North Korea and Iran building nuclear bombs? Lee, how about the environment, the banking crisis, or the bailout of big business? The list goes on and on."

"You mean give him the power to launch an unprovoked, preemptive strike or go to war without having to go to Congress?"

Trish glared at him momentarily. "There are other international issues that are troublesome, like our attempts to bully other nations into doing our bidding; like Britain, Australia, and the Baltic states that want entry into NATO so badly; like the control exercised by certain countries over the petroleum reserves around the world; like the valuable mineral deposits and food stores that are closely controlled by certain nations. Those are the things that are managed by the so-called world order that need to be better managed and led, and I have legitimate concerns about these issues."

"I'm noting a contradiction here. The US administration and selected consortiums of nations do some things we like but some we also don't like. So what's the solution, Trish? I don't think you would like all the answers, but maybe would like to have a say-so in some of the solutions."

"I'm just saying that we need to…." Trish then exhaled in exasperation. "Come on, honey. Let's talk about this later when we have more time and less urgent things to attend to."

Lee shook his head, trying desperately to disguise the disgust written all over his face.

Shit-o'dear. Trish is starting to sound more and more like the father that she apparently worked so hard to bring down. Who is this woman? Has she changed this much or is this who she has always been? Is money her new God or does she now covet power?

Lee's cell phone interrupted further inquiry and discussion. "Hello?"

"Can you talk?"

"Not at length right now. Who is this?"

"Kathy. Don't ask how I got your number. Just be grateful that I have it."

Lee's face immediately reddened. "Ah yes, ah, sorry, I didn't recognize your voice and there's a lot of background noise here right now. Are you on your cell phone, Charon? The background noise makes it—"

"I get it. I just wanted to say that we should meet and talk sometime soon and that I hope you don't feel an urgency to make any permanent decisions in the present situation."

"Well, that's a possibility, but I have to leave town tonight to meet with a client. Can we discuss it on the phone tomorrow?"

"Yes, absolutely. When do you anticipate you'll be free?"

"My work will keep me tied up for a day or so, but we can talk about the kids tomorrow. Will that be okay?"

"Yes, that will be fine. Please call me early. All you have to do is push the send button and my name will pop up."

"Okay, bye for now."

After terminating the call, Lee turned towards Trish, motioning to his phone. "My youngest daughter...I guess I may have some tentative plans for a few hours later this week. I'm sorry. Time with kids is precious, and sometimes, their problems can't wait to have a dad's perspective. I promise I'll make it up to you. That's okay, isn't it?"

"Well, what if I wanted to do something, just the two of us?"

"Well, then I'd have a real conflict, wouldn't I? It's you or my daughter. I thought during that SOS call from my youngest that you'd probably have business stuff to attend to. Besides, a little father-daughter bonding from time to time is a good thing."

Trish ducked her head, her cheeks filling with color. "You're right. I just...."

"Trish, you have to give me a little maneuver room. Balancing my work, my daughters, and this dating thing is still a little bit new to me—especially with you. You're a longtime special person to me and you've been away. I need to relearn how to balance our time together. Besides, you've been here a couple of days without telling me. If I had known you were here, I could have readjusted appointments a bit."

"So, now I'm thinking about taking you to my hotel."

"That sounds nice." Lee chuckled, winking at her wickedly.

19

GETTING ON BOARD
WASHINGTON, DC

*Sometimes an old haunt is the best place to ponder
serious issues and arrive at logical conclusions.*

THE next morning, following the meeting with Lee Grady in
Oregon, and after taking the late-evening flight from Portland, Mayhew sat in the old, massive dining room of the Army-Navy Club
in downtown Washington, DC, having breakfast. Tired and very
groggy after having deplaned at Dulles International Airport a scant
three hours earlier, he gulped down his coffee. He shook his head
recalling the hectic nature of the past couple of days. A quick flight
to Portland to meet with Lee in Lake Oswego was followed by a late
flight to respond to the call from DC from the director of central
intelligence—the DCI himself. The purpose of the meeting was to

both get and provide updates on the investigative findings related to the missing and unaccounted-for cruise missiles that had been fired on Tehran less than three days earlier. Mayhew was not reacting well, physically, to the new and stressful day. Still, all things considered, his mind was sharp and still calculating as he weighed the pros, cons, data, assertions, conclusions, and conversations he had been exposed to in this time of extreme turmoil.

He liked staying in the A-N Club, as it was called, since it was right across the street from Farragut Square, which was on 17th and K Streets. But the club itself was on what some thought a more prestigious address: a street next to the square on Connecticut and I Streets in Washington. A statue of Admiral David G. Farragut, first Admiral of the Navy, stood in the center of the square, looking with a stony, disapproving glare to the east towards the White House. The statue was surrounded by small, bronze naval cannons as if they were placed there to thwart any assault on the admiral's lofty perch. Mayhew had often thought Washington prided itself on being a navy town, so this was a fitting tribute to the sailor who saved the union.

At the outbreak of the Civil War, David Farragut consented to receive a commission in the Union Navy and was named flag officer-in-command of the West Gulf Blockading Squadron, with instructions to enter the Mississippi and capture New Orleans. He was placed in command of eighteen wooden vessels—including his flagship, *Hartford*—a fleet of mortar boats, and seven hundred men. He was successful, but not without costs in ships and men.

Two years later, in 1864, Rear Admiral Farragut was again summoned into combat. This time he was ordered to lead an attack on Mobile Bay, the last Confederate stronghold in the Gulf of Mexico. Mobile Bay was not only protected by Fort Morgan and a fleet of wooden vessels but also by the formidable Confederate ram *Tennessee* and a field of explosive mines called torpedoes. Farragut's fleet of wooden ships, along with four small, ironclad monitors, entered into battle against more strategically positioned confederate emplacements. The smoke of battle became so thick, blocking his vision. He climbed the rigging of the *Hartford* and lashed himself near the top of the mainsail so he could see the scope of the battle unfold. It wasn't long before one of his vessels struck a torpedo and sank. His fleet, confused, stopped in place in the crosshairs of confederate gun emplacements. That's when Rear Admiral Farragut rallied his men to victory, shouting, "DAMN THE TORPEDOES, FULL SPEED AHEAD!"—a rallying cry still used by military men and women in and out of battle, by politicians locked in mortal combat in Congress, and by liberal publishers, newspaper editors, and the world's most disliked band of mercenaries, the Paparazzi, all out to scoop one another in breaking whatever story could bring them the most fame.

Jerry had read this story in the Army-Navy Club many times, and even he had quietly thought how the famous "Torpedoes" phrase went when he was out of options in some godforsaken corner of the world. But now, here he was again in Washington—a nice place to visit but a hell of a place to work—in hopes of being successful and making a friend or two whom he wouldn't have to reward with a quid pro quo. It was former Speaker of the House of Representatives Tip O'Neil who once said, "And if you want a friend in Washington, you'd better buy a dog."

The club was only three short blocks from the Old Executive Office Building, also called the "Old EOB." During the period between World War I and World War II, the EOB building had served as what was known then as "The War Department." It now housed the staff of the National Security Council, the executive office of the vice president, and various high-level advisors, directors, former ambassadors, historians, and economists, as well as a bevy of experts in foreign, domestic, medical, military, and academic policy.

It was quiet every day in the Army-Navy Club. The paintings

of General Pershing, General MacArthur, Admiral Nimitz, Admiral King, General Eisenhower, and even General "Stormin' Norman" Schwarzkopf hung on the walls with looks on their faces that said, "Be proud!" and "Do your best!" and "Never give up!" and "Always take care of the troops!" The place was a throwback to great years gone by, an admonishment to today's generations to "do the right thing," and encouragement to all to take care of one's comrades and one's country…no matter what!

It was only 7:30 a.m., and in this historic place with all its old military ghosts, it was always quiet, even though there were moments when some old soldiers and sailors were known to kick up their heels at happy hour. In the bar at 4:00 p.m., having a few too many Scotches or bourbons, they often were known to break into a chorus of "Anchors Aweigh" or "Over Hills, Over Dales"…and heaven forbid, some young upstart would start singing "Off We Go into the Wild Blue Yonder." Yes, this was that kind of a place, where tradition prevailed. Officers and gentlemen wore coats and ties. Ladies wore conservative dresses that never showed cleavage or too much leg. There was even a sign outside the men's room, conspicuously mounted on the wall at eye level so each officer and gentleman could see it when he returned to the bar or dining room after taking a leak. It said, "Gentlemen, please adjust yourselves." That was polite English, military-ese for saying, "Make sure your fly is zipped." Mayhew liked this place. He always found a way to stay here every time he came to Washington. The agency always seemed to find a way to get him a room here on short notice. He especially liked the library room with the mahogany paneling from the Far East, row upon row of book shelves along the walls, and the tall, red leather wingback chairs where retired generals and admirals refought old, and sometimes recent, campaigns. It reminded him of a cartoon in the Sunday papers of long ago, where there was a character called General Bullmoose who sat in the same kind of high, leather wingback chair, sometimes pontificating and sometimes merely clearing his throat by saying, "Harrumph!" Other times he would just fall asleep in the chair, with the daily paper in his lap and a brandy on the table next to him. Yes, this was that kind of place.

Right then, that day, that week, was a time to take stock and recommend to the president a course of action. To do any less could mean a retaliatory attack on the United States or its worldwide assets and resources, and absolutely, the loss of innocent American lives, inside and outside the country. Within twenty minutes after the attack, the news networks were full of breaking news alerts showing the horrific damage in Tehran. The pundits and the speculators had not yet had time to second-guess the government investigators and had not collared an eyewitness who could claim he saw an American lighting a fuse on a cruise missile. So far the only thing the media got right as of noontime in Tehran was that the damage was apparently caused by at least twenty-four cruise missiles with extremely high explosive munitions on board, launched from the land, sea, or air somewhere within an eight-hundred-mile radius of Tehran. The news network Al Jazeera claimed it must have been the result of an American and Israeli plot to annihilate the Muslim population. NBC and CBS claimed there were high-placed, unnamed sources in the Pentagon, the State Department, and the White House who inferred there were cruise missile assets missing and their theft had been covered up by admirals, generals, sergeants, petty officers, and anybody and everybody in the US government. Fox News had film crews fanned out across Washington, including Capitol Hill, and the members of Congress were elbowing their colleagues out of the way to get to a microphone and a TV camera to express that those who did this would be brought to justice. The BBC, Sky News, Pravda, France Today, and every other network in Europe had on their payrolls every single source they had ever used to gather inside information, with the intent to dig up anything they could. Almost every news organization, while claiming impartiality and no bias, reported stories that were just the opposite. They all concluded from what little circumstantial evidence existed on this disaster that somehow only the United States was in a position to launch this attack. Now they were digging further to determine if the United States acted alone and why the president gave the execution order.

Russia and Germany were requesting—no, demanding—the UN Security Council be convened to seek answers and mete out sanctions and punishment. Things were going to get much worse before any nation would call for calm, cooperative, and deliberative thought. In fact, the longer this went on, the more obvious it was that the world was racing toward a kangaroo court to accuse, convict, and execute the country behind this—the United States.

In Mayhew's mind it was obvious that someone else did this to make the US look culpable. But then again, he had a little more inside information than the networks and the general public—not much more, but enough to stay focused on legitimate leads. He knew that, even though foreign retaliation against the United States or any other country would be unjustified and unwarranted, countries would be looking for the guilty party. In spite of statements from the White House and personal calls from the president to world leaders, the frenzy of the situation was not abating. Even the Brits, the Canadians, and the Japanese were starting to keep US diplomatic overtures at arm's length. The Saudis were even now saying they were looking at ceasing all shipments of petroleum to North America. The diplomatic, political, and military clock was ticking. There was a limited amount of time to get the facts. In international relations, most nations would expect decisive results in seven to ten days, but this problem was more complex and answers were not readily apparent. Mayhew had been told that the current ambassador to Iran had been given piecemeal reports to placate the Iranian government. The answer to who and why was still elusive. However, if all the parties could be encouraged to be patient for up to three weeks, even in two-to three-day increments at a time, all involved in trying to resolve the problem could be staring at an answer and a solution sooner rather than later. Delaying tactics for governments was a task for ambassadors and statesmen; keeping the victims, who were already demanding retribution, at arm's length would be a problem.

Inside the administration, everyone was quietly, quickly, and feverishly searching for answers. A lot of pressing domestic issues had been shunted aside. This was the most serious, potentially catastrophic action to confront the administration since moving against Iraq. Unfortunately—or fortunately, depending on one's vantage point—most of those who were searching for answers were politicians. They were trying frantically to find out what had happened and who was responsible, before CNN found out first. NBC even released an unsubstantiated report that a US Navy admiral had turned rogue and ordered naval cruise-missile forces to launch the strike. The White House and the DOD were in a frenzy to discredit that report before it took on a life of its own. Nonetheless, this was an incident of apocalyptic proportions that definitely didn't need a media spin on it. The administration and selected members of Congress were calling for an investigation and wanted this Iranian incident to just go away. Most politicians were quietly speculating that the United States didn't do it, but they didn't have a clue as to how to find out who did. They were probably thinking that somebody in Iran, or even Europe, should just nab the bastards that did it—any bastards—and move on. Some were even willing to throw the Israelis under the bus to get this behind the United States. Politicians in Washington would always think, "It's not my job," or "It didn't happen on my watch," so, "Convene a tiger team at the State Department and let them recommend a fix to it." This time it wasn't going to be that easy.

To complicate matters, there were ultra-conservatives in both houses of Congress who were starting to say the United States should gird its loins and prepare for a global fight. They saw this incident as an opportunity to finally make the world over and eliminate all the populace and political regimes that have never liked the United States and would scream to the world that the United States was advocating genocide, keeping them in poverty and debilitating them with a worldwide scourge of the AIDS virus when it delayed or threatened to terminate that year's financial support.

On the other side were the ultra-liberals who had already started planning national budget contributions to reimburse the poor victims of this catastrophe and who were pressing hard to turn the other cheek and try to cure the ills of the world. They believed there was a presidential and military conspiracy to neutralize the Iranian regime, and that we should just own up to it and try to make reparations and recompense. They wanted to see someone prominent in the administration's political spectrum—along with all respective supporters—be hunted down, exposed, and publically prosecuted. Then they would get the media and the Department of Justice to sift through all the offices in the Departments of State and Defense, as well as the aerospace industry, to find the conspiracy and execute the guilty parties.

There definitely seemed to be a rising tide to significantly alter the source and thrust of national power in the United States. Trying to get either the right or the left sides to do what was right and not wrong, be rational, and try to think things through, was like trying to keep the sun from rising or trying to hold back the ocean's high tide.

It was also a particularly bad time financially for the United States and the rest of the world. The reality was that if the real culprits who caused the Iranian debacle could not be found, the United States of America, as it was known, could cease to exist.

Jerry took this quiet time at breakfast to think about some of the things that had happened and how they were related or seemingly unrelated.

Hopefully the US and Canadian military analysts in NORAD can retrace the trajectories of the cruise missiles and determine where they came from. This will be no easy task for the infrared systems in space, since cruise missile heat and light emissions are small and hard to discern. This would be a work in progress and would take some time, of which the US has little. The only international loyalty that seems to exist is from the Province of Bermuda, who we provided supplies, life support systems, and reconstruction supplies for when they suffered a devastating blow from a hurricane. This was good for Bermuda, but did little in this global crisis for the US.

His years as a "spook" taught him to jump over that old adage of trees and forests, and think not only outside the box, but beyond reality. He set the McMinnville photos, Lee's relationships with people of influence in the Willamette Valley, the Anatolias, and the Al-Qaida and Afghani problems aside.

What if it's somebody else? What if it's some group or country that would think they are too far away, working different agendas, are apparently unrelated, and think no one would ever suspect them? What if there is someone on the inside of the Iranian government who is manipulating things? Are there any incidents of surreptitious terrorism against any of the other components of US critical infrastructure? Are there any unexplained incidents in US petroleum, transportation, banking, state and local government, medical care, water systems, or electrical-grid-networks management? Or could there be a crazed US general or admiral who lost his cool and took a hundred fine NCOs and young officers with him to activate this launch? What if it was an assassination and the raid was a cover for it? No, no, no, those concepts are possible but not plausible and are a bit too far out of the box.

Is it possible it's not a government at all? Could it be a private entity like the mafia, or a group of Muslim extremists, a Middle Eastern terror-

ist sect, a group of theocrats, or some quiet but powerful group of indus-
trialists? Let's see.... What is going on in the world? China is apparently
focused on Taiwan. Moscow is focused on the G-14 economics meetings
where they are discussing distribution of oil resources. Caracas is hosting
the OAS meetings on drugs, Tokyo is hosting global warming meetings,
and Toronto is working the worldwide conference on AIDS. The US is
still grappling with strong, opposing political points of view from the No-
vember 2016 presidential elections. US financial and housing markets
are in disarray and no one has a quick fix. Who stands to gain and who
stands to lose? What's the prize? Prestige? Power? New alliances? Technol-
ogy? The end of US domination and both the demise and loss of influence
of the US, oil, and money? Hmm, OIL AND MONEY—could that be
it? Hmm, I wonder.

Suddenly something from an event that had occurred the day before popped into his mind, displacing his train of thought. He had been checking the reports from some intelligence MI-5 colleagues in London, from the General Directorate for External Security and the Sûreté in Paris, the Masaud in Israel, the Bundeswher in Germany, the national Public Security Intelligence Agency in Tokyo, and the Nationalist Chinese CIA Office in Taiwan. The only item that even mildly piqued his interest was an article in the Sûreté report that noted a man resembling the likeness of the Chinese terrorist and assassin Wah Hu was seen boarding a plane to some destination the observer didn't have time to follow up on. Mayhew recalled that two years ago, Wah Hu and his partners in crime, Yee Hah and Chung Mai, had mysteriously been seen one or two days before several events, each having horrible outcomes. One was the saran gas inci-dent in the Tokyo subway system; one was the freak and mysterious launch of a Russian ICBM from Plesetsk into a retrograde trajectory toward Oslo; one was the munitions impact on the USS *Cole* in the gulf; and another was the mass annihilation of more than three thousand innocent civilians in a dirty bomb detonation in Nairobi,

Kenya. Mayhew's mind raced as he took one last swallow of coffee.

I should check this out and call Lee while he's still airborne to tell him of my thoughts. Everybody is certainly thankful that Ambassador John Woodard engineered the Herculean effort to keep the lid on the uproar over this event. I'm sure that the lid is very porous by now and the Iranians are getting restless; I would be, if I were in their shoes. I sure wish I had the means to talk directly with the ambassador. I know that John is a reasonable guy and one in whom I can confide without ridicule over unorthodox rationales. It is time to go to the EOB for the appointment.

20

BRIEFING
AND SHARING
WASHINGTON, DC

*In each person's life there is a time for revering the history
of the past, a time for pondering the significance of important
events, a time for problem solving, and a time for humor.
All work and no play will make Johnny a dull boy.*

THE Old EOB was just as stuffy as it had always been. Mayhew remembered when he had been assigned here on the fourth floor during the first Bush Administration and worked for the National Security Advisors who had rotated through the office: Bud Miller, John Dexter, Colin Patterson, and Frank Carlton. None of them wanted to be there, but like all appointments to the White House, when the president calls, you answer.

Jerry had an appointment in Room 435 with Thelma J. Massadoti, director of Middle Eastern policy and economic support. She was second-generation Italian. Thelma's father had served in the Italian government in the late fifties and early sixties as a mid- to high-level official, negotiating the future of Italy, which was still in economic turmoil after the Second World War. The Italian government was striving for political relevance and sustained economic growth, and lusted after a military presence in NATO with the Allies that included the US, Great Britain, France, and Canada. Her father was successful in finding "a place in the sun" for Italy in spite of its somewhat dubious policies enacted and perpetuated by Il Duce, Benito Mussolini. Through all of this, Thelma's life was sheltered, tutored and educated by her multilingual father who managed to persuade her to stay away from the Russians, be skeptical about the Germans, and go find an education and a life with the Americans. Later, she immigrated to the United States on a university scholarship, parlayed that into a master's and a doctorate in international relations, and married a Harvard University classmate who died after fifteen years of marriage, leaving her a respectable inheritance. In the intervening time, her father became the deputy foreign minister of Italy and continued to coach his little girl in the finer points of diplomacy. In spite of her knowledge, and ability, she never chose to ascend to the higher levels of the Foreign Service, but instead became very comfortable as an in-country operations specialist. She became the go-to person when the US ambassadors to Italy, Syria, and Iraq wanted to know what to do about various political and economic confrontations. Thelma even handled a few diplomatic and personal indiscretions when high-ranking members of the American, Italian, and various Middle Eastern countries' officers of Foreign Service got caught in their skivvies or with their flies open.

Thelma Julianne Massadoti, now affectionately known as TJ by her friends and colleagues, was a trusted, well-informed, well-connected member of the National Security Council staff. The National Security Advisor, Lieutenant General John Laughlin, USAF, Retired, sought her counsel on many matters, both foreign and domestic. Her advice was always sound and on target.

With the overnight assistance of a member of his staff in the Directorate of Operations at the agency, Mayhew had done his homework on this appointment. The complete assessment of Massadoti's profile and the functions of her directorate in the NSC staff were on his BlackBerry by 0430 that morning. He had a summary of all the data on TJ Massadoti's background, political philosophies, political connections, friends, and enemies, and knew who she was seeing. He guessed she had information to trade and assumed she had tasking for him. He also assumed this since the Director of Central Intelligence had called him personally and asked him to see her posthaste—an indication that it was important. She must have something the National Security Advisor and the president wanted accomplished.

Now a woman in her early sixties, TJ Massadoti had spent years working her way through the chain of organizational hurdles until she became an assignee from the Department of State. After years of service in Washington and the Middle East, she was finally recognized for all her attributes. Jerry's resume had preceded him, and she anxiously awaited the meeting so that he and she could exchange evidence.

TJ had been in the office since 6:15 a.m. that morning, collecting a variety of intelligence reports from the White House Situation Room, which she had set aside to share with Mayhew. After TJ finished synthesizing the data and drafting reports, she sensed that it was time for her to ease back and allow a couple of pros to take charge, switching gears herself to complete some mundane activities while keeping the issue to be discussed with Jerry and Lee everpresent in the forefront of her mind.

Mayhew entered her outer office and introduced himself to the administrative assistant. She flattered him by repeatedly saying, "Yes, sir. Yes, sir. Ms. Massadoti instructed me to advise her the moment you arrived. Would you please walk this way?" She walked with a very pronounced limp, all the more surprising when Mayhew noted that at the junction of her skinny legs and small foot, she was wearing high-heeled shoes. A closer look revealed that she had evidently broken a heel from one of them, choosing to continue to wear the shoes anyway. Since she walked with a bobbing-up-and-down gate, and had asked him to "walk this way," he did, managing to imitate her bobbing gate into Thelma's office. It was one of a few fleeting moments of humor that didn't escape TJ's attention.

Seated at her desk in front of a window that overlooked the West Wing of the White House, Thelma grinned incredulously at the Abbot and Costello—or was is it The Three Stooges?—routine parading into her office. Rising from her desk, chuckling mildly, she thanked her assistant for her prompt efforts to usher the guest into her office. Professionally, she extended her hand, smiled warmly, and intoned, "Hi, I'm TJ. No need for you to introduce yourself; I know who you are. Somehow, Jerry, your reputation precedes you."

"I'm flattered that you've done your homework. But I've done mine as well and know who you are too. I'm just not sure right now how we're going to become connected."

Following a few additional introductory pleasantries, she indicated that she had given up an invitation to a late-afternoon party in Georgetown to continue working, so as to ensure that Mayhew received all the data needed to find out what happened in Iran. She indicated that she fully expected to be brought up to speed, to learn anything and everything that he knew, as well as be fully advised on how he proposed to proceed. TJ's demeanor suddenly changed, assuming a very businesslike manner. "The Director of Central Intelligence called me directly and said you and I needed to talk ASAP, to compare notes. He said also that all activities related to this catastrophe are code-named BLACKTHORN. He sent me an encrypted copy of your latest contact report from discussions you had in Oregon with a Dr. Lee Grady. He also sent me some intelligence sighting reports from state and CIA operatives overseas, regarding certain Chinese, Greek-American, and Iranian Shia, Sunni, and Kurdish terrorist movements."

"Thanks, TJ. That information helps a lot. Now we can get right to the point. The Chinese data points have come from credible sources in the French Sûreté overseas but are somewhat disjointed and lack time sequencing. The Greek-American associations are directly related to some recent contacts Dr. Grady has had on the West Coast. The religious-sect contacts have come from the staff of Dr. John Woodard, the new ambassador to Iran. You and I have seen the same reports from him."

"I haven't made the connections between these sightings and their activities, but my intuition says they are somehow related."

"Good, we're on the same frequency. I believe the same thing, but I can't make the connections either. We're missing some data points and I'm not sure where to start."

"So, here's what I know, Jerry."

TJ commenced a rapid-fire dissertation of facts, figures, report summaries, and State Department assessments of activities. She proceeded to cover the world, talking about activities in China, North Korea, Iraq, Syria, Canada, Saudi Arabia, Pakistan, India, and even Australia.

After hearing her report and quickly but carefully examining the printed data before him, Jerry sighed in resignation. Frowning, he shook his head in disappointment. "Thanks for the reports, TJ, but unfortunately they don't help me much. In fact, all they do is emphasize how inflamed the emotions of the Iranians were, not to mention the Iraqis, the Syrians, the Saudis, the Pakistanis, and yes, even the Chinese and North Koreans."

"The Chinese and North Koreans? What the hell is it of their business?"

"Let's not dismiss them too quickly. We must wait until we can at least conclude they are just being sympathetic to their Middle Eastern, radical brethren."

"I guess I agree that I shouldn't be so hasty at this early date."

She smiled reflectively.

Mayhew sure knows his stuff. It's good that he's joined the team. I'd be fairly lost without his experience and corporate memory.

Slowly she turned and started to leave the room so that he could continue studying the documents.

Damn, I know he's right, but it pisses me off that I couldn't figure it out without being told. Yep, there certainly could be a Far Eastern connection that is too obscure to identify.

After thirty minutes, TJ returned to the room to see what Jerry had discovered from the documents.

Noting her entry, Jerry looked up and smiled as he set the mound of papers he had finished studying aside. "The DCI told me we have an operative on the West Coast who wanted to go into semi-retirement and felt a little burnt out. So, she was given a leave of absence but with a caveat to render monthly status reports on her whereabouts and activities. She recently indicated she was selling real estate and had shown some property in a small western Oregon town and it had warehouses and an airport on the land. She indicated she had shown the property to a Greek-American by the name of Trish Anatolia. To make the circle of intrigue even more interesting, my old friend and college classmate, Dr. Lee Grady, is seeing Ms. Anatolia and has somewhat of a love-hate relationship with the Anatolia family."

"I heard about that in some extraneous report. It seems that there was some tie between Grady and the Anatolias, but I wasn't clear what it was. I do know he does periodic, classified work for both the FBI and CIA and is regarded as very effective and meticulous. So what's the tie between his innocence and her guilt?"

"You do have a way of getting right to the point. My answer would be just as succinct as your question. The answer is NONE, I think. Lee and she have a romantic connection and our semiretired operative has unsuspectingly shown the Oregon property to Trish Anatolia, met Lee, become interested, and has now created a relationship with Lee and Ms. Anatolia that might give us some answers to the Middle Eastern cruise missile attack."

"To make matters even more intriguing, there were sightings in this small western Oregon town of some Asian gentlemen, Mr. Hu, Mr. Mai, and Mr. Hah, who were overly friendly and offered large sums of money for female companionship about two weeks before the Iranian attack and three days afterward. If I think the unthinkable, what does Anatolia have to do with Wah Hu, Chung Mai, and Yee Hah? Furthermore, what are those arms dealers and assassins doing in a small town like McMinnville, Oregon? I think the answer can be found between Grady, our operative there, and Trish Anatolia. It worries me that we may find the answers there but may risk the lives of our operative and Lee Grady."

"The thing that has had me stymied from the beginning is why the name of Anatolia Enterprises and all the American aerospace companies who build cruise missile parts ever appeared on a nameplate curiously discovered in the rubble of buildings in downtown Tehran. Was it deliberate? What the hell is Anatolia now doing in the exotic technology of avionics? Did someone want the US to be culpable? Is there an ulterior motive where some other nation could gain from a US misfortune? Damn it, TJ! You know we've got more questions than answers and the question list is getting longer. We've got to get back out in front of this and get back in control."

"Okay. I don't think we have enough to go on to recommend to the president what the US should do. The DCI and the director of national intelligence are in agreement on this. The DNI has scheduled an interagency information briefing for 10:30 this morning at Bolling Air Force Base. You and I need to be there before the briefing start time to check on who's in and who's out. It's an old Washington game to determine where there is support and who they think is going to be thrown under the bus."

"Okay, but I need Lee Grady here to synthesize all the various points of view. He's great at that."

"Good, tell him to be on the next available flight to Washington."

Mayhew nodded. "I've already taken care of it. I asked Lee to catch a flight last night before I left Portland. He should be in a cab on his way to the Old EOB now. I'm sorry if it seems presumptuous of me, but since he's a cleared asset on the DCI's payroll already, his perceptive powers seemed useful. I'm presuming he will be going with us to the meeting. Who's going to be at this meeting, and what constituency do they represent?"

TJ paused, smiling reflectively. "Thanks for having the foresight on Grady, and yes, I'll have my assistant send his clearances to the DNI's office." She rose from her desk, went to the window of her office, and stood there for a moment with her back to Mayhew, her arms folded across her chest. She was looking down at the West Wing of the White House as if trying to be objective while considering how to measure her words. Finally she turned and walked around to the front of her desk and, half seated and half leaning against the front edge it, she pursed her lips and nodded with conviction. "The DNI, of course, will be there. Vice Admiral Ellison Manley, Retired USN, is the sailor's sailor. He makes a point of over-preparing and being scrupulously fair and impartial. He has no axes to grind and carefully avoids goring anyone's ox. He's not only a fine military leader, but he is also an honest, unbiased, and loyal politician. He knows he serves at the pleasure of the president and was appointed and confirmed by the Senate because he's liked by both sides of the aisle. His judgment is implicitly trusted."

TJ continued, "The others present are the directors of the three key intelligence information processing centers that have insight into all the factors that influence today's world and have the evidence and assessments to support their observations. They too try to be objective but will have a course of action to recommend if necessary. The director of the National Counter Intelligence Center, the NCIC, is Dr. Gerald Marbry. He was a professor of international affairs at Northwestern University in Illinois. He's a career academician and has held various positions of responsibility in the State Department and the Department of Defense. He's also been a member of the president's National Foreign Intelligence Board, the NFIB. He is very thorough in his analyses and becomes very brusque when he thinks someone doubts the veracity of his work."

Smiling as though apologizing for being too longwinded, TJ continued, "The director of the National Counter Terrorism Center, the NCTC, is Retired US Army General John Dotch. He is an attorney and was the former judge advocate general of the Army. He's well connected to the legal community, to all the judges in the Supreme Court, and to various captains of industry as well as selected members of Congress. His loyalty is unimpeachable, but if his intuition is that an issue seems to be poorly justified and has too much speed, he'll start checking sources along with people in other communities."

Mayhew cleared this throat. He always squirmed a bit when it was announced that there would be those who had political agendas present for a meeting . He found over the years that those kinds of people had slower timelines and liked to seek approval rather than to act and then ask for forgiveness.

TJ frowned, inquiring, "Do you need a break?"

"No, please continue; I was just getting rid of a little irritation in the back of my throat."

Nodding, TJ resumed her briefing. "The director of the National Counter Proliferation Center, the NCPC, is Dr. Adam Wooten. He is a former Republican member of Congress, the former director of the Defense Advanced Research Projects Agency, DARPA, a former director of the Air Force Research Laboratories, and a lead systems engineer from deep black projects at Area 51 in Nevada. He is fair, inquisitive, thorough, and unbiased. To his credit, he is also suspicious of any R&D effort that is not sponsored by an American industry or academic institution. He has been known on many occasions to send authors of National Intelligence Estimates back to their drawing boards to revalidate facts about foreign capabilities."

Mayhew interrupted, "You know, TJ, you are a wealth of information."

Appearing to ignore the compliment, TJ continued, "There should be no others of significance there, and each will have an exec there with a nonspeaking part. Normally, meetings of this magnitude would have a White House observer there; someone from the House Permanent Select Committee on Intelligence, the HPSCI, from the House side; someone from the Senate Select Committee on Intelligence, the SSCI, from the Senate side; and the usual drones from the CIA, the NRO, the NGA, the NSA, and the DIA. In this instance, however, the president gave Admiral Manley specific and explicit direction to find out what happened—who did this—and to waste no time or effort in identifying the culprits and recommending a course of action. She said keep the group small, high-level, proactive, goal oriented, and pointed toward a solution and a course of action. The DNI has already asked each of the directors for global summaries on activities in their respective areas of responsibility and has specifically asked them not to collaborate on their findings. This might cause them to temper their findings and associate their facts with what is probable or possible. He told each of them he would vet their findings himself with their real-time input."

TJ chuckled as she waved her arms to signify a conclusion to her dissertation. "That's about it. At this point, that's all I know. I'll spend whatever time it takes the remainder of today, after the DNI's meeting, to finalize the logistics and work the details of your and Grady's involvement in the decision-making process for the meeting. What's needed now are clear minds to synthesize facts, determine effects, assess impacts, and focus on possible solutions. Based on our conversation, your views, the global exposure you have, and the sources that seek you out and give you information, I think you, Jerry, should give thought to what solutions and actions we recommend to the president."

"You were very thorough, TJ. This should help me a lot." At that moment, TJ's personal administrative assistant opened the door to announce that Dr. Lee Grady was downstairs.

TJ said, "Thanks, would you please go down and escort him up? And Brenda, would you please assure that Dr. Grady is cleared to go with us to the DNI's meeting this morning? Thank you."

Mayhew stood and said, "This is a good time for me to talk to Lee and bring him up to speed on what you and I have discussed, and get his preliminary assessment. If there's somewhere he and I can have a few minutes alone before the DNI's meeting, it will be extremely important and helpful."

"Yes, of course. Brenda will give you an office next to mine to confer. Please plan to give me an update in the car on our way to Bolling."

"Yes. Absolutely. I think Lee and I already have most of our thoughts synchronized. We just need to compare some of the details you and I have discussed in the last forty-five minutes."

21

DAMAGE CONTROL III
TEHRAN

*Containing a virus is an ongoing process, as trying
to keep it from spreading is of paramount concern.*

DR. Woodard extended his hand to warmly greet Captain Aref,
escorted by Colin, as he entered the ambassador's office. The meeting
was hastily arranged at the request of Captain Aref, but Aref stated to
Colin that there was some new information that had arisen, which
needed to be shared to allow the ambassador to assess its relevance.

"So good of you to come to see me; I know your time is precious."

"As is yours, Ambassador. We're all operating under the gun."

Woodard smiled. "Well put, Captain. Well, I have very little to
report. There has been insufficient time since we last met to validate

several leads that seem relevant. All of our agencies are hard at work trying to determine what happened. We continue to profess our innocence and ignorance about why and how this has all occurred."

"I didn't expect Rome to be built in a day, but the leaders of my country are feeling a lot of pressure. It would be an understatement to say that they are searching for answers."

"What pressure are they experiencing?"

"As you probably know, there is a significant power struggle underfoot for control of the oil in our region. The players are the Chinese, the Russians, and the North Koreans. Of course, your country is right in the thick of it. The winner—or winners—of this prize is going to have a huge international advantage, both militarily and economically."

"I would agree with that." John began to calculate who stood to gain the most and who would stand to lose. He was quickly thinking of how diabolical a plot would be that involved the Russians or the Chinese, or both, if they first decided they wanted exclusive rights to the black gold of the Middle East, and then decided how they could make the United States a "third world" country, while at the same time making their involvements transparent. He thought of all this in split-second calculation while not wanting to share his views with anyone but Jane O'Donnell. John knew this concept, and the sources that were beginning to surface since the attack would prove to be valuable leads for the political, military, and intelligence operatives who were feverishly pursuing them across the globe. It was becoming more and more crucial that the survival of the United States as a superior nation and viable power broker was hanging in the balance. It had occurred to John that the United States could easily slip into a nation isolated from the rest of the world as a pariah, more concerned with its internal survival and the livelihood of its people than having any role at all in the world's community of nations. He did not want to share these survival instincts and vulnerabilities with Captain Aref, whoever he was, or with anyone outside the US diplomatic corps.

Captain Aref searched for meaning in the ambassador's incomplete utterance. He had been thoroughly briefed on this American medical-doctor-turned-politician. Aref was aware John was a close personal friend of the Iranian president and was well connected in Iran, the Middle East, and across the United States. Ambassador Woodard was not a man to be interrogated like a common political dissident. "Are you thinking that perhaps the attack could have been perpetrated by one of the nations I mentioned?"

"The thought certainly has merit, doesn't it? It needs further examination and evaluation. To coin a phrase by a past American president, 'Trust but verify.' I would like to take this under advisement and would hope you and I could compare notes later. Look, not to put you off, Captain, but perhaps we could meet later today or tomorrow morning. By then we both may have more information. Who knows? One of us may have an answer to at least one or two of the many questions still unanswered."

"I will plan on contacting Colin later this afternoon, Mr. Ambassador. I want to thank you for being so forthright and cooperative. Working together is so much nicer than being on opposite sides, don't you agree?"

Dr. Woodard smiled, confirming, "Yes, there is no substitute for cooperation. I will look forward to seeing you later today."

22

ON THE ROAD AGAIN
WASHINGTON, DC

*High-level, secret meetings, sometimes boring but always steeped
in information that may or may not be pertinent, are necessary
to assess the level of danger posed by an unknown enemy.*

JERRY had indications before he boarded the flight from Portland to Washington the evening before that there was to be a high-level strategy meeting to examine facts and suggest a course of action. No one knew much, but it was a good time to meld together what they did know. He thought it prudent to not indicate to TJ in their meeting that he was pre-briefed on the impending DNI's conference, lest TJ think he was checking the validity of what she knew. The DCI's office directed him to be in Washington and be prepared to attend. Invitations were still pending at that time, but it was projected to be held by the president herself. So, the invitees would definitely be there. Jerry intuitively knew it was a key data exchange, so he took the liberty of directing Lee to do whatever was necessary to be in Washington the next morning. *No matter what it took* seemed to be the message conveyed. This was to be the meeting to end all meetings—the mother of all meetings. Everyone who knew anything at all in the US government would be there, and, against all Washington rules, all attending were directed to reveal anything and everything, regardless of how insignificant they thought the information might be or what it might reveal about their respective agencies. There was a sense that revealing certain facts might even mean the demise of sister agencies. The old adage of "knowledge is power" was set aside. This matter could mean the difference between World War III and international peace.

Lee arrived on the ground at Dulles at 9:00 a.m. The Secret Service escort met him with a car to get him to the Old EOB before 10:00 a.m.

"Shit, there goes my social agenda for the next few days. Oh well, duty calls.

He did, however, have a few hours with Trish that turned out to be more passionate than before. There was urgency to their lovemaking that hadn't existed before. By the time he had left for the airport later that night, he felt exhausted and yet unfulfilled. He owed those contradictory emotions to his new mission to get close to Trish, while simultaneously having to be prepared to find out possible treasonous activity. Once aboard the United Airlines aircraft, he seated himself in business class and prepared to catch a thirty-minute power nap before beginning to assimilate all the information he had been given the day before. That information included what Jerry had revealed to him, what Trish had said, and most interestingly, what Kathy Moen had up her sleeves. Who was she? His intuition told him there was more to her than she had let on.

Oh well, hopefully I can connect with her when I return, if it can be worked out.

It was 9:52 when Lee was brought to the fourth floor of the Old EOB. He knew Jerry had already arrived there ahead of him and would have some new information. Lee was anxious to share with Jerry what he concluded and was looking forward to getting updated data to either reinforce what he thought or discount what he had deduced.

Jerry brought Lee up to date on the discussion with TJ. For his part, Lee shared his thoughts over the last sleepless hours on the red eye from Portland. Both Jerry and Lee spoke in clipped, rapid, unfinished sentences, which are commonplace in Washington in intelligence data exchanges. Each knew time was of the essence. Lee shared with Jerry how he had some random concepts about this whole affair and needed more data to sift through so he could discount those that lacked substance and merit. One of the things the CIA and FBI liked about having Lee consult on events like these was his way of thinking. In this case his approach was to think about this crisis in terms of what didn't make sense, rather than what did. For example, the US didn't need to obliterate Iran to get whatever it was that was wanted there; the purported US attack on religious and government sites such as the mosques and parliament were antithetical to American strategic warfare; there were two or three major nations who had been uncharacteristically quiet about their impressions of the events in Iran; and this whole affair almost seemed like a magnification of an international Mafioso revenge attack. Lee leveraged his Anatolia conspiracy to draw those comparisons. Jerry said, "Good, let's share that with TJ on the way across town to the DNI's meeting."

At 10:06, Jerry and Lee Grady walked into TJ's outer office. The administrative assistant was more somber and businesslike than she had been yesterday. Somehow, she and others in the Old EOB seemed to know something extremely serious was unfolding. Upon their entry into the office, she arose from her desk and briskly ushered them into TJ's office.

As they entered, TJ arose to greet them, extending her hand to Lee who courteously shook it while turning to Jerry and then looking back at TJ.

"TJ, this is Dr. Lee Grady, who is well aware of everything. He will have some valuable input to our course of action and is completely up to speed with events, including this morning's Dow Jones nose dive."

Lee smiled, nodding an acknowledging greeting to TJ. "You can just call me Lee, TJ. I am very happy to be here and share, but quite frankly, I'm curious to hear what you have learned.

"I'm afraid that my information is somewhat speculative at this point. I'll get my coat and we can continue this conversation in the car on the way to our meeting." After retrieving her coat from the closet in the corner of her office, she brusquely started toward the door. Lee and Jerry exchanged mute glances with one another that seemed to say, *Okay, let's mount up*, as they quickly fell into place behind TJ.

23

INVOLVING MORE PLAYERS
WASHINGTON, DC

Necessity is the mother of invention. The process, though urgent, should not be rushed. Be quick, but do not hurry.

TJ, Jerry, and Lee quickly descended in the elevator to the basement where a car and driver was waiting for them. Their driver was a US Army Delta Force Ranger who had two tours in Iraq and one in Afghanistan. No ordinary driver, he was typical of the elite White House motor-pool drivers. He was the ultimate professional, taking both his job and the tasks he was asked to perform very seriously. In these times of uncertainty in overseas locations and in the Washington area too, special people were needed to do special jobs. Sergeant First Class Byron "Bing" Jackson, US Army, was skilled in hand-to-hand combat, was an expert driver in escape and evasion maneuvers in heavy traffic situations, could rapid fire his 9mm Beretta with expert marksmanship, and if need be, could unemotionally kill an adversary who was intent on doing serious damage to those he was entrusted to protect. As a rule, TJ, Jerry, and Lee would have been just ordinary passengers in the exclusive White House taxi service, but today, Bing was told they had the extremely confidential White House "four five alpha" priority, normally reserved only for the president. Bing knew the gravity of his task: doing his best even if that meant having to "become involved."

Bing stopped the black, nondescript 2016 Lincoln Mark VI at the south gate to Bolling Air Force Base and showed his ID to the gate guard. Jerry and TJ followed suit by holding up their blue CIA badges. Lee held up his as well and felt a little uncomfortable since he hadn't used it in some time. Conforming to the security procedure, TJ also held up her White House badge. The guard nodded with satisfaction.

"Thank you, Colonel Mayhew, Dr. Grady, and Ms. Massadoti. The DNI has asked that I inform him the moment you pass the gate."

Mayhew nodded, returning the salute. "Thank you, Sergeant. We appreciate your service."

"Thank you, sir." Ever present was the unspoken word between military officers and enlisted personnel, regardless of service affiliation, that says with a look, eye contact, a nod, or a salute, that they are in this together, they will take care of one another, and their military brotherhood and sisterhood is the tie that binds their service and their nation together.

With the identification process concluded at the south gate, Bing drove on, two blocks down Nellis Boulevard, then taking a right onto Chappie James Drive until he navigated the Lincoln into the shared main reception entrance of both the Defense Intelligence Agency and the National Intelligence Agency. Almost as if by plan, they were met by Air Force Colonel Elroy "Peso" Moyer, a much-decorated air force officer from conflicts he would rather forget. Colonel Moyer led them through the security turnstiles, through the massive foyer where artifacts of war were displayed—including a captured SCUD missile the Soviets sold to any and every nation that would buy the 1500-kilometer-range rocket—and finally up the long ramp to the second level where the aroma of the Starbucks coffee from the only commercial booth in the complex permeated the air. After taking an immediate right to the elevators that took them to the third floor and to the offices of the DNI, Vice Admiral Manley, they were greeted warmly by the admiral. "I'm glad you're here. I have some interesting things to tell you, but I must admit that I haven't tied all the events together. Hopefully you can do that Mayhew, so we can get the dirty bastards that did this."

"That's why we're here."

Moments later they entered the DNI's briefing room. Awaiting them were three persons, rising as TJ, Lee, and Mayhew entered. They all shook hands and exchanged routine pleasantries. One of the three, Dr. Marbry, offered, "I knew your father, TJ. I met him at a previous international political discussion that he chaired when he was the deputy PM. Needless to say, the meeting went very well."

Blushing, TJ displayed some discomfort with the small familial tidbit. "Thank you. I'll have to remember to ask my father how things finally sorted out."

After the formal introductions, they were seated at a round table in the DCI's office. The three gentlemen seated across from TJ, Mayhew, and Grady were the director of the National Counter Proliferation Center, the director of the National Counter Intelligence Center, and the director of the National Counter Terrorism Center. They were the key intelligence agency contacts TJ mentioned earlier who knew, unequivocally, what was happening in each of their respective areas of responsibilities with regard to foreign and domestic anti-US activities. They did not, however, do information integration and interpretation. That formidable task would fall on the shoulders of TJ, Mayhew, and Grady—if the outcome of the meeting made that possible.

Admiral Manley, the first to speak, offered, "Ladies and gentlemen, we are here to discuss what we know about events that have occurred this past week—before the crisis in Iran, less than two days ago, that was the result of the cruise missile attack on Tehran, now code named BLACKTHORN. Let me be brief. The US is not responsible for the attack. US-manufactured weapons were used. The world thinks we are guilty and most foreign parliaments and political regimes are organizing plans of reprisal that will make the US suffer in excruciating ways. You each have information that may seem unrelated but could be directly related to who did this, how they made it appear as though the US is guilty, and more importantly, why? Dr. Marbry, would you please go first and tell us what your analysts and sources have found in the NCIC."

"Thank you, Mr. Director. I personally welcome the involvement of Ms. Massadoti, Dr. Grady, and Colonel Mayhew. We need knowledgeable and fresh eyes to view this mass of extraneous facts. In the interest of time, I'll be succinct. There have been several worldwide events that have been funneled to the NCIC in the last month, and especially in the last two weeks. Our event analysts have reviewed the circumstances surrounding each event and have looked for such things as relevance to other domestic and foreign activities, the outcomes of meetings and forums, and the possible impact of decisions and actions that appear to have come as a result of those meetings. Some of those events have suspicious or inconclusive outcomes. I will focus only on those that seem important to current events. If other data is requested, I will make my center completely available to any of you."

Marbry continued, "Six weeks ago there was a five-day meeting in Beijing in the Ministry of Defense involving ten to twelve of that country's top missile and space launch physicists. Without boring you with information on the credibility of our sources and methods for obtaining information on the meeting, let it suffice to say that six of the attendees were specialists in the design and manufacture of missile guidance and targeting capabilities. Three attendees were top aeronautical design engineers for cruise missile technology. One scientist was an intercontinental ballistic missile designer, and the remaining two were high-explosive munitions designers. There were a number of high-ranking military personnel representing that nation's rocket forces and an equal number of representatives from the defense manufacturing industry. The exact number and identity of persons attending are vague right now since there were many people coming and going, in and out of the meeting. The results and actions coming from the meeting are still undergoing analysis. We don't know much more right now about the meeting, but the details are still trickling in."

Marbry added, "Coincidentally with this meeting, there was also a meeting of the foremost computer software designers in China, held in Shanghai. They met for six days and we know the agenda discussed a review of the major, critical international infrastructure dependencies. Also, curiously, there was a significant spike—increase, if you will—in the data and voice message traffic between Shanghai and Beijing."

Marbry paused, looking about the room to see if there were questions or comments. Hearing none, he went on to say, "Since we detect, track, and analyze traffic about meetings between high-ranking foreign officials, there was one other meeting picked up on, but it occurred nearly six months ago in the Santsung Mountains of Western China. It was held in a compound known as Shangri-La. The identities of the attendees and the results of the meeting, even after these few months, are uncharacteristically elusive. So, we are tabling any actions about that meeting as probably unrelated to anything discussed here."

Amidst Dr. Marbry's presentation, Colonel Moyer quietly slipped into the briefing room and placed a sheet of paper in front of Admiral Manley. He held up one finger to Dr. Marbry, gesturing to wait momentarily before proceeding. When the admiral finished reading the memo, he nodded to Colonel Moyer, who then departed.

"Dr. Marbry, please continue. I think this can wait until you are done."

TJ and Jerry looked briefly at one another, knowingly acknowledging that a new piece of information had just entered the room but was not to be shared yet. Jerry turned to glance at Lee and was assured that Lee knew what was going on by the nod he received from him.

Continuing, Marbry intoned, "I only have a little more to pass along. It seems there were two topics that we are certain were addressed in all the meetings I have cited. They were: abilities to interrogate the software control capabilities on the world's economic management systems and the manner in which electrical grid and air transportation networks are controlled. We have human intelligence reports that the way the US manages its economic and transportation systems via central computer networks was a topic of a closed-door session. I might add that there was a third event, or series of events, that we have been made aware of: movements of up to fifteen of that nations' citizens who Interpol and other western nation security departments have tracked in transit to such places as the Pacific Northwest, Baghdad, Tehran, Moscow, and Washington, DC. Their specific goals, objectives, and missions are, as yet, undetermined. The makeup of this group of persons, some who have been identified and some who have not, are professional arms dealers, mafia-type terrorists, strong-arm assassins, known weapons technicians, and a few well-trained, undercover information gatherers and mole-handlers. Over the last two weeks, seven of these in the latter two groups have surfaced and disappeared twice. We last tracked them going into Saudi Arabia before they vanished."

Admiral Manley nodded as Marbry reclaimed his seat at the table. "Thank you, Dr. Marbry. Well, General Dotch, would you now tell us what you know of findings in the NCTC?"

Lt. General John Dotch, widely known for his no-nonsense brevity, began in typically clipped, wartime-command-post, lawyer-ly-style one-liners. "Thank you, Mr. Director. I'll try to be even more succinct than Dr. Marbry's report. I have had my data sources and analysts focused on this event in Tehran. I instructed them to track weapons specialists and military equipment that have moved into the Middle East in the last four weeks. I can corroborate Dr. Marbry's identification of the fifteen or more suspicious individuals and know three of them as Wah Hu, Yee Ha, and Chung Mai. They are known technical assassins. They have been associated with several events worldwide having to do with the mysterious disappearances of highly technical drawings, designs, and authors and designers of advanced aeronautical penetration systems, electronic listening devices, countermeasures employment, and the use of strong-arm tactics. We have tracked them for two years. We have found them to be careful and meticulous in covering their tracks, and they have been suspiciously present when catastrophic events occur. Their travels, movements, and activities have been very diverse and have occurred in extremely short timeline turnarounds. It has been hard to keep track of their movements. They have been very well informed about the abilities of the local police and national law enforcement capabilities in the countries in which they've traveled. They have continued to be two steps ahead of our agents and local authorities. If I could confirm it, I would tell you they seem to have moles planted in key US government computer centers or have hacked into computerized information facilities. We have found them getting careless of late, however. When they seem to be overcome with satisfying their carnal desires, they have tended to be a little less cautious about covering their tracks."

As General Dotch concluded his report, TJ, Jerry, and Lee looked at one another as if to say, "Did you get all that? Is it imperative to ask questions now?" All three nodded to one another as Lee started to enter additional notes on the pad in front of him.

"Dr. Wooten, would you finish by telling us what you know of reports reviewed by the NCPC?"

"Thank you, Mr. Director." Dr. Adam Wooten, PhD, possessing a distinguished career in academia and government, the perfect man to serve as the director of the NCPC, continued, "As you all know, the National Counter Proliferation Center is more interested in the movements of highly sophisticated technology, the transfer of these capabilities between the US and foreign nations, and vice versa. We give special surveillance to military equipment that could be deleterious to the interests of the US if it were to fall into the wrong hands. We are good, but we are not perfect. Many times we know what happened but don't know why. You may recall the shipment of nuclear missile fuses to Taiwan that was supposed to be helicopter parts. You also may recall the flight of nuclear weapons aboard US Air Force B-52s across the continental US. Some of the unexplained transport activities that occurred in both those incidents were how the computer-generated transfer orders and aircraft flight plan data seemed to direct them to do exactly what they did. Afterwards, when we tried to locate those transfer orders and their derivation, they had mysteriously disappeared from computer records."

Colonel Moyer reentered the room, handing the admiral another memo. As before, he held up one finger to Dr. Wooten. Admiral Manley read the note and then nodded to Colonel Moyer. Colonel Moyer apparently recognized the admiral's glance as a nonverbal gesture that there would be no response forthcoming. The admiral then nodded to Dr. Wooten to continue.

Lee watched the drama that played out before him, pondering silently as his mind began to wander, straying from what he had heard up to that point.

Holy Shit, what's happening now? I assume the admiral will lift the mask of secrecy shortly.

Dr. Wooten continued, "A similar event was the shipment of forty-eight advanced US-manufactured, air-launched cruise missiles from the US naval secure shipment docks in Bremerton, Washington, aboard a US-registered vessel, the USS *Salem*, bound for Pearl Harbor. After twelve hours at sea and after a routine navigation position check, something happened, and we don't know what. She missed her next two automated, fifteen-minute routine position checks, so an interrogation scan was sent via the civil government's space-based National Maritime Surveillance System. The *Salem* didn't show up anywhere. A US navy destroyer was transiting the area and was diverted to search the area. A Canadian oil tanker en route to Hawaii was also diverted to take a look-see as well. To make a long story short, they found debris in the vicinity where the *Salem* was to have been, and it appears that she went down at sea, for some unknown reason, with all hands and her cargo of forty-eight advanced cruise missiles. That's the most dramatic of all the pieces of evidence that could be even remotely related to this week's events in Iran."

"One additional series of data points has to do with the cruise missiles. I had my analysts look at the cruise missile manifest and classified shipping order. The missiles were the newest versions of the Air Force's AGM-86C conventional warhead, air-launched cruise missiles, or CALCM as they are called. Earlier versions of the missiles were used operationally in the first Gulf War. The CALCM has an all-weather, day-night, air-to-surface capability with a range of five-hundred-plus miles. They are manufactured and integrated with components from various other aerospace company features and have improved accuracy, increased resistance to jamming, and are regarded as excellent penetrator munitions. The air-launched configuration of these missiles makes it unlikely they could have been used in the attack on Tehran, simply because they would have required extensive modification in both guidance avionics and in launch platform refitting to allow launch from a ground or submarine system. They could be modified, but it would take a very sophisticated laboratory and production facility to alter the guidance and the launch mechanisms. We are continuing to look for such a clandestine facility but have not yet found one in the Pacific Rim nations."

Admiral Manley cleared his throat as he rose to face the gathering. "Thank you for your input, Dr. Wooten, General Dotch, and Dr. Marbry. I hope Ms. Massadoti, Dr. Grady, and Colonel Mayhew have heard enough and have acquired enough data to have relevancy to help them with their task. I have three other data points for us all to consider, forwarded to me from the National Maritime System, the government's underwater acoustic detection system, and the Canadian government. The memos I received during this meeting confirmed this information."

Smiling, he noted all in attendance focused upon him with a level of interest not noted previously. "First of all, a review of the maritime surveillance system's satellite number 4—which is in a slightly different orbit than satellite 2—which recorded the Salem's last navigation fix, has shown receipt of a low-frequency distress call from a private vessel located within a few nautical miles of the *Salem*. They claimed to have nineteen persons aboard and were taking on water after an onboard explosion. They identified themselves as a Canadian-registered, privately owned vessel, the *Pride of BC*."

After scanning the room, he continued, "Secondly, the Royal Canadian Mounted Police reported to the FBI and then to me just an hour ago that the *Pride of BC* is safely in port and moored in

Halifax, Nova Scotia—the other side of the continent—and it's been on the east coast since late August of last year."

Smiling, he added, "The third data point from NOAA's National Underwater Acoustic Sensing System is really interesting. The report came in to me at 0430 this morning, and I had it verified just an hour ago, and I wanted to share it with you. Fourteen minutes before the *Salem's* last navigation fix and within three minutes of the *BC's* distress call, the system picked up soft-screw noises from a Chinese *Mao-Tse-Tung*-class cruise-missile-launcher submarine within eight nautical miles of the *Salem*. The sub was evidently trying to run silently but didn't know NOAA recently and quietly upgraded the acoustic sensing system to be three times as sensitive."

The admiral braced himself on the table, surveyed the room again, and concluded, "Ladies and gentlemen, unless anyone has any additional data to add for Ms. Massadoti, Dr. Grady, and Colonel Mayhew to chew on, I suggest we adjourn and be available to reconvene in three hours, if necessary. I have your complete written reports on your presentations for use by Ms. Massadoti and her team and summaries of the assessment reports I just covered for all of you to review. Ms. Massadoti, if you and your team will come with me, I have a special conference room available for you, and anyone else you would like to invite, to deliberate on what you've heard. I just hope to hell you reach some plausible and realistic conclusions and courses of action. As we speak here and now, there are some very ugly anti-American demonstrations going on in Tehran, Baghdad, Riyadh, Athens, Rome, Paris, Moscow, Mexico City, Berlin, and everywhere else. Our 'friends' the Russians have requested an emergency meeting of the UN Security Council to review the events of the last two days and to recommend follow-on actions. They all agree we are the bad guy and they are moving for a unilateral retaliatory response against overseas US assets and even some actions inside the US to make us feel worse than shitty."

The admiral turned towards the door leading from the conference room, and in precise military presence, commanded, "Come with me and I'll show you to the conference room where you can debrief and plan what I hope will be a plan of attack to bring this issue to a satisfactory conclusion." Before he could reach the door, as if by prearranged scripting, the encrypted pagers, BlackBerrys, and instant-notification devices of all the principals began buzzing and vibrating or became illuminated. Also, as if by prearranged signal, they all reached for their devices. They each looked at the devices, then looked to Admiral Manley, who said, "Well, I guess the heat has been turned up on the urgency burner. The JCS have recommended and the president has authorized all US military forces to go to Defense Readiness Condition Three in consideration of the escalating level of violent anti-American activity around the globe. To the degree that our government has increased our military readiness, it is imperative that we gather the maximum amount of intelligence as rapidly as possible.

24

THE DNI'S CONFERENCE ROOM MEETING
WASHINGTON, DC

*A large group meeting, not dissimilar from a lecture, makes
large amounts of information available to the multitudes in
a very efficient manner sans the provision for discussion.
The small group meeting encourages discussion and a
sharing of ideas. From the sharing comes ownership.*

ADMIRAL Manley escorted TJ, Jerry, and Lee to his personal
conference room. Excusing himself, he explained, "I have to provide
an update on all current changes in the global hostilities status to the
president as a result of BLACKTHORN. I suspect you would operate better without my presence anyway."

After thanking the admiral, the threesome sat down around the big circular table, each with their respective notebooks filled with more than twenty pages of notes, observations, and opinions. Lee opened the discussion in his usual analytical manner. "I understand that DEFCON 3 action was necessary, but it could complicate our data-gathering activities. I guess we need to work faster. We need to put all we've just heard into perspective by starting at the beginning. The attack on Tehran is riddled with both items of consistency and incongruities. If time allowed, I would like to dissect each and every factoid and trace their relevancies and relationships to one another, but unfortunately, time is not on our side here. Suffice it to say, there is a decided lack of information on motive, intent, and communications-connectivity contact trails. All those dangling actions tell me there is a deliberate underlying pattern that says the finger of guilt for this activity is clumsily pointing to the US. That, coupled with the random nature of target destruction in the city tells me, therefore, not all possible conclusions that a skilled analyst might reach have been completely thought through. In summary, if the US had done this, command and control records, to include presidential decision sequences down to and including launch control directions, would be well documented. They are not."

Mayhew nodded. "I agree. I didn't mean to interrupt. Please continue."

"There are remarkable similarities in the agenda items for the three meetings held in China on missile and space capabilities, software integration considerations, and infrastructure systems management. It looks as though, as I scan the detailed human intelligence reports in the written synopses of the meetings, someone or some group was data mining in search of a central command and management capability to monitor air and space targeting and guidance, methodologies to usurp and disguise software command and control, and have the ability to disperse relevant facts from worldwide computer assets. They denied salient facts to US systems managers and confused US decision makers who rely on rapidly displayed and presented data. All that tells me *how* this happened; not *why*, or *who* did it.

Pausing to collect his thoughts, he continued, "There is not a lot of data on the movements of terrorists of note around the globe. Again, if time allowed, I'd want to see convergence reports done on Interpol, FBI, CIA, and individual nations' reports on the activities and whereabouts of known perpetrators of sabotage. I'd also want to see the most prominent reports on international crime objectives, specific vulnerabilities, and the major paranoias of the US, Iranian, Russian, and Chinese governments. Obviously, I have discounted other nations because the ones I just mentioned have the greatest potential to have had either government sanction or collaboration, or lack an organized crime element with sufficient sophistication to launch a spree of this magnitude. I am familiar with some of the activities of Wah Hue, Yee Ha, and Chung Mai, and I know that they have access to the resources necessary to carry out this type of attack. I just don't have enough information to implicate a government yet."

TJ nodded her head, her thoughts racing ahead.

Grady really knows his shit. I'm starting to feel better, if that is possible, considering what we're faced with.

Lee continued, "Finally, there is information here received from Tehran that includes bomb damage assessment reports stating that all the cruise missiles that impacted in Tehran may have been the same kind as those loaded aboard the USS *Salem*. Yes, I heard Dr. Wooten's observation that the CALCMs would have to undergo extensive modification if they were to be used in this attack. But missile modification could very well be part of the conspiracy. Were they in fact the same missiles? Let's assume for the moment that they were. If so, how did they get from the cargo hold of the *Salem* to the Middle East? If we connect the dots in the Pacific, it would seem that the Canadian vessel in distress was no Canadian vessel at all. It would also seem that the best way to transship stolen cruise missiles without being exposed to overhead surveillance would be to move them under the ocean's surface. If indeed these cruise missiles were our cruise missiles, is the Chinese government behind this or could they have simply been a go-between for some mafia-like terrorist organization? Another possibility could be a third country with whom the Chinese would take a risk, knowing they would stand to gain some major, significant economic or political advantage. What they may have done, after all, could be regarded in this asymmetric-threat world as an act of war."

Lee shook his head, frowned, and then continued, "If we review the actions at Chinese, North Korean, or Sumatran naval submarine bases, we may be able to show what happened to our missiles. Jerry has shared the overhead imagery of what appears to be cruise missiles in Oregon. Given a little more data, we may even be able to reconstruct the scenario of how the missiles got shipped for modification and then again transshipped to the Middle East. Earlier this week I thought it was a stretch to try to tie the Tehran attack to Mafioso-style actions. Proving parts of this might now be doable knowing what we know about the Anatolia family holdings in the Northwest and around the world, their surreptitious ties to the technical assassins, and the data uncovered by the CIA agents working this case near the Anatolia underground facilities in Oregon. I am still processing the reports of meetings between individuals with cyber skills and the group of ranking executives in Moscow, as well as their talks about the use of oil resources. The hairs on the back of my neck, which are seldom wrong, tell me there is a tie between them. Jerry, you look like the cat that swallowed the canary. Do you have something to add?"

Jerry had been sitting at the table, reflecting and listening to what Lee had to say, trying to leapfrog ahead to a hypothesis.

There must be a common thread that weaves through this maze of seemingly unrelated information and ties it together into an answer, a story, a plot, a conspiracy.

Jolted to attention by Lee's query, he responded, "As a matter of fact I do. I think you're on to something here. If I were a betting man, I would guess someone recruited the Anatolia Enterprises because of their illicit weapons merchandising activities—which we've suspected for some time—and made the profit too enticing for the family to turn down. Probably, unbeknownst to the Anatolias—specifically Trish Anatolia—the perpetrators also needed a scapegoat in case this whole deal went south and they wanted to distance themselves from the entire affair. The added cushioning layer could be the technical assassins who may have civil ties to China but not official government associations. As you implied earlier, Lee, for the Chinese government to risk this, the ultimate prize must be really valuable over the short and long term. Now, I suggest that we take the time to work our way back through this maze. The evidence appears to support the contention that someone needed US munitions of some sort, preferably missiles, to orchestrate a demonstration. To pirate a US vessel carrying such missiles and to go to great lengths to conceal the theft of these munitions tells me the risks were not only great, but the ultimate prize was exceptional. There had to be a grand plan or scheme that was going to neuter the lone remaining superpower, the US, and create an opportunity for the emergence of a new, more benevolent-appearing friend of the people. To conclude, I feel that the meeting of the cyber specialists and the oil technologists needs more examination. I continue to strongly think that there is a tie."

Lee interjected, "I agree. There have been low-level reports in the media and quiet concern among the corporate and investment industry leaders that the recent downturn, late in the trading day, in the Wall Street market prices is both curious and unexpected. Every trading day for the last two weeks, the market has suffered a dramatic sell-off of assets resulting in a sell-off panic by investors. No one could determine where these sell orders had come from or how they wound their way through the worm-protected network, but the market is taking a definite nose dive. My suspicious mind believes there was a Newtonian principle behind these actions, and they were designed to elicit a specific cause-and-effect relationship."

Lee paused and then continued, "Let us not fail to look at any and all activities that were occurring simultaneously. What was happening with the oil executives two thousand miles away in the West in Moscow? Were they convened to discuss how better to use 3-In-One oil for Russian and Chinese bicycles, or did they have more grandiose political and economic visions in mind? Again, my suspicious mind says all these events were inextricably intertwined, and there was a master scheme at work here.

Anxious to contribute to the dialogue, TJ waded into the discussion. "All this could be true with a few added twists and turns. If we assume the worst, and all the events are related, it looks like it could be an international scheme involving the collusion of political powers with the involvement of civilian criminal elements. If this is the case, it represents an act of war. So, I think that we need to focus on each of the influencing powers separately. Let's deal with data that we know. Interpol has fed data to the FBI that seems to suggest that we should focus on some loose ends. If an Asian mafia-type group was behind part of this, how do we expose them and put them out of business? If the Chinese government had a proactive role in this, how do we prove it and broadcast to the world that the dirty bastards behind this were not Americans, as it has appeared? If the Russian government were colluding with the Chinese government and the Asian Mafia, it would smack of a plot to bring down the US government. Why would they want to do this? What do they want? Are they doing this out of jealousy, or is it out of greed for riches? Is it because they want to show us, the United States, that we are not so invulnerable after all? No, there is something much greater at stake here."

Lee nodded, offering, "TJ, I think that you are on to something. As long as those missiles are still out there, we and the rest of the world are being held hostage. I think, in this case, technology and politics are simply enablers and whoever controls the munitions can drive, force, or yes, even blackmail the rest of the world to the goal line." After a brief pause for emphasis, Lee continued, "I ask you, what is the goal line here? Personally, I think it is economic gain. Global economic analysts and national intelligence estimates have been predicting for some time now that the nations that control the world's fossil fuel resources, clean water sources, and food-producing land space will 'rule,' so to speak."

Jerry slammed his hand down on the table. Nodding in agreement, he asserted, "I think you're right, Lee. On a near-term basis, I'm seriously concerned about inflamed emotions in the Middle East and the anti-American demonstrations that are occurring, which could grow to uncontrollable proportions very quickly. If there is indeed a politico-technical-economic conspiracy at work here, we need to separate the political parts from the technical and economic parts and deal with them separately. If we can neutralize any one of those, the other two components will be weakened and stalled. We need to put the persons behind this on notice that the Americans are on to them and they need to choose a side."

TJ again joined the exchange, offering, "We need a clearheaded political, diplomatic, technical, and economic assessment of all these factors. For my part, I want to address the political aspect of this with someone on the scene. I will leave the technical and economic assessments to you two. I plan to contact Ambassador Woodard and clue him in on what is happening, and maybe even tell him about our range of thoughts, suspicions, and the counter-options before we run out of creativity and time. I hear he may soon be on his way to DC for consultations, if he's not already here. You know, guys, there are a few other questions to be answered, but preeminent among all of them is, where are the other twenty-four cruise missiles? If we begin to expose any of the guilty parties, will there be a desperation launch of the rest of the missiles? You two need to reach some conclusions and a plan of action—soon."

As if prompted by some visionary, Admiral Manley reentered the conference room.

Smiling expectantly, he inquired, "Well, are we making any headway? I spoke to the president, and the demonstrations against US assets worldwide are becoming more intense. US forces have been alerted to increase their readiness to Defense Condition 3. They are making ready to defend and deploy as required. The National Guard Bureau has alerted each state's Guard units to begin recall plans and come to a standby alert status. Naval vessels have put to sea to insure their safety from shore-based attacks and to make ready to deploy if necessary. At the recommendation of the Joint Chiefs of Staff, the president has directed the secretary of homeland security to advise all state and city law enforcement agencies to implement increased internal security measures. We have indications that clandestine terrorist activities are underway. The president has activated hotline calls to all fifty state governors to fill them in on the status of events. She has also called the prime minister of Great Britain, the president of Russia, the premier of China, and others to implore them to stay calm until we get to the bottom of this mess. All of them have confirmed they are activating their own investigatory review groups. That's a good-news-bad-news action. Doing it buys time for them and us. Doing it also allows them to deduce what happened without all the facts and prematurely recommend sanctions against the US. Curiously, the Chinese put the vice president on the phone and he acted concerned but uninformed."

Admiral Manley surveyed the room, hitched up his trousers, and then continued. "Some other smaller governments are quietly undertaking their own review of events and, in some cases, are providing assistance to the CIA and covert US operatives in an attempt to get some answers. The people in countries all around the globe are nearly hysterical with this 'American atrocity,' as they are calling it. I take it that since you're all standing with your briefcases at the ready, that you have a plan and a course of action to share with me?"

TJ responded, "Yes, we are going back downtown to the NSC to start moving on our plans. In summary, we have found that the problem is political, technical, and economic. They are directly inter-twined. We are dividing the three tasks between the three of us. I am going to begin working on the political and diplomatic dilemma and will contact Dr. Woodard in Iran to seek his assistance. Dr. Grady is going to pursue the loss of the missiles and the probable espio-nage that resulted in them falling into the wrong hands. As long as the missiles are not under US control, the world remains hostage to those who have their fingers on the trigger. Mayhew is going to look at the adverse impacts that have occurred as a result of an apparent attack on US national infrastructure assets. We have no recommen-dations for actions at this moment. We will provide a recommended course of action when we have developed a fail-safe strategy."

"So you need a little more time? Well, I'll have Colonel Moyer escort you to a car to take you where you want to go. Keep me ap-prised of what you come up with, and call me if you need any help."

En route to the car, Lee turned to Mayhew and said, "Jerry, I need to talk to the Lambert, Richardson, and Hariston missile man-ufacturers to better understand what we're up against, technically speaking. I want to speak with them about the variety of warheads they can accommodate, the propellant capabilities, the guidance packages on board, and the means to program them. Can you set that up for me?

"Can do, Lee. I'll make a call from the car and have representa-tives ready to meet with you within the next two to three hours. For my part, I plan to make some calls to my French, Japanese, British, Israeli, and South African friends to collect on some overdue chits for information. TJ, if you get through to Ambassador Woodard, I'd like to be included in the meeting."

She nodded affirmatively.

Moments later, seated in a car en route back to the Old EOB, as if preprogrammed, they all reached for their cell phones to make calls, in order to begin closing in on a plan of action. Lee dialed Kathy's number at her office in Lake Oswego to determine the reason for her request for him to call her.

Later, on his flight back to Portland, Lee reflected upon the events and actions that day, but his subconscious mind was darting ahead to what might be awaiting him at home. Thoughts of Trish, Kathy, and the foreign "gentlemen" sighted in and around McMinnville raced through his mind. These were all curious but critical pieces of a complex tapestry.

Trish opened the door to showing me her new enterprise in McMinnville. I wonder...could it be that, perhaps, the missing missiles are there?

25

A DISCOVERY
OREGON CITY

A triangle is the strongest geometric figure known. It is also devastating in a relationship between men and women. Three sides aren't always congruent. Deception, part of another triangle, even when honed to a fine art, never yields a satisfying result.

THE sun was just rising over the mountains to the east in the lush, green Willamette Valley of Oregon as the big Boeing 777 touched down at Portland International Airport from Washington Dulles. Lee stirred in his seat, stretched, and raised his head to check the time on his wristwatch. Its digital display read 5:00 a.m.

I need to go home and get some rest before I talk with Mayhew at 1:30 today. I need to be sharp.

He reflected on his first meeting with Trish all those many years ago when he was in Navy OCS. He smiled reflectively.

We didn't have a very good introduction, but as I remember, the weekend ended up in a memorable embrace that lasted several hours.

Lee had no baggage to claim, so he went directly outside to the taxi stand to take a cab home. In a matter of thirty minutes he was unlocking the front door of his Oregon City residence. As the door latch clicked and he opened the door, he heard the rustle of linens or blankets. He instinctively reached for his belt, for the pistol holster that wasn't there. Instantaneously he was taken back to a time when he carried a 9mm pistol for just such moments as this. When he realized he had no weapon, two thoughts raced through his brain:

Damn, these last two days have been spooky and have made me suspicious about everyone; it's probably a good thing I don't have a gun or I might hurt myself.

He called out, "Who's there?"

Trish's sleepy voice called back, "Lee, it's me. Who did you expect? We have some unfinished business, remember?"

I hope I'm going to like this homecoming.

At noon, Lee awakened and enjoyed the view of the shapely body lying beside him. He noted the hush of silence that surrounded him. Trish was lying on her stomach, oblivious to the world awakening around her. Years ago, he would have extended his arm slowly, guiding his hand towards her slightly bared back. He probably would have slowly directed his fingers to trace an invisible trail upward across the soft skin on the back of her neck, moving ever so slowly and gently down her spine until they reached her shapely derriere. Her skin had always been so soft and smooth. The mild fragrance of her perfume suddenly invaded his senses. Nearly giving in to desire, he reconsidered and slowly got out of bed to head to the bathroom.

Alerted to the escape attempt, Trish began to stir, almost immediately awakening from a deep slumber. Slowly she raised her head, turned towards him, and frowned, "Where are you going? I'm not done with you yet. By the way, you were great this morning."

He nodded unemotionally. "You bring out the best in me."

"Is that it?"

"I, ah...."

"I know. You need to go to the bathroom. I suppose I should take care of business, too. Hurry back. We still have a little time before I have to leave."

As he cleared the threshold of the bathroom, he turned and mumbled over his shoulder, "Before I left, you said you would show me your new operation in McMinnville. When do I get to see this new enterprise of yours?"

She smiled. "Soon, ah, I think that I would like to show it to Kathy first because it's not quite up to speed yet. I need to see her about how to proceed with a new property value assessment. I still have a few expansion modifications to make before I show off my new prize." Trailing him into the bathroom, she shouted over the pelting din of the shower, "Lee, I have to go to Greece for a few days on business. Why don't you take some time off and go with me? I think that we could—"

"What? Wow, honey, that sounds very inviting, but this is pretty short notice. I'd love to, but I've got some consulting work to do for a client. Damn, I wish...."

With a little luck and a little cooperation from Kathy, after what she told me on the phone before I left DC, maybe I can find out what Trish is up to at Mountain View Aviation. Wait a minute! Why is she going to show Kathy the operation before me? She did say that she wanted to show me around the place. I wonder what's wrong with right now. It might be nice to see what's going on out there before she leaves for Greece.

Lee said, "When do you have to leave?"

Trish responded, "When do you have to begin the job for that client?"

"In reality, I've already begun," Lee said. "Yeah, you might say that I'm on the job as we speak. Actually, I'm going to catch up with him at 1:30 this afternoon. I have to get a move on."

"Could you put it off for a week or so? Are you sure you can't make it?"

Stepping out of the shower, he reached for a towel. "I'm positive. Besides, I don't want anything to distract me from being with you, or you showing me your new business."

"My, you are handsome without any clothes on."

"Don't get any ideas; I'm already behind schedule. You had best get dressed, Trish. We have to be out of here by 1:00 at the latest."

Smiling, she offered, "You don't give yourself much leeway, do you?"

Like the unwelcome knock from an uninvited visitor, Trish's cell phone started playing the Notre Dame fight song.

"I didn't know you were an Irish supporter."

"I'm not. I just like the song. Where in the hell is my purse?"

"It was beside you at the base of the nightstand."

She grunted, reaching for her handbag. "Someone sure as hell has terrible timing." She grabbed for the purse, lost her hold on it, and it fell to the floor, spilling its contents in several directions. "Fuck, I lost my grip on my purse and dumped all my junk on your carpet."

"Don't worry about the mess; just answer your phone. I'll help you retrieve your stuff after you take the call."

She frowned as she raised the phone to her ear. "Thanks a lot. My junk might be someone else's treasure. Ah, Yes. This is Trish. That would be Trish Knight." There was a moment of silence. "Yes… yes…yes… ah, I completely understand. Completely. No, no trouble. Thanks for calling."

After terminating the call, she paused for a moment as if collecting her thoughts. Nodding after a moment, she turned towards Lee to assist with the pickup of the spilled contents of her purse.

"I have to go. I'll call you."

"So I guess the tour of your facility with Kathy is being postponed?"

"You might say that. She sold it to me, so she knows the general configuration of things. She can wait."

After making sure that all the contents of her purse had been returned, she hurriedly began dressing, apparently overlooking the fact that she had trailed him into the bathroom.

"What is it, Trish? Your face is ashen. What's wrong? Tell me what's happened!"

Buttoning her slacks, she bent over to slip on her shoes.

"Lee, I said I have to go. I can't say why right now. I just have to go. I mean, I have to go right now! Thank God I had the presence of mind to drive my car."

"Okay, be that way. I guess that you'll call when you can. Oh, and Trish, I'll be available anytime you need me. Just call."

He smiled as she started to disappear through the bedroom door. "Drive safe. I'll be thinking of you."

Turning to acknowledge his comments, she smiled faintly. "I'll be in touch, Lee. I love you."

In what seemed like split seconds, Lee could hear the sound of her car coming to life. Shaking his head, he started buttoning his shirt as he walked towards what had previously been Trish's side of the bed. He absentmindedly began to straighten the articles resting on the night stand. Suddenly he felt something hard and cold, apparently nestled on the carpet under his sensitive left foot. Slowly he bent down to discover what it was. He frowned as he picked it up, carefully examining it.

Hmm, it sure as hell isn't mine. It must be some of the junk that fell out of Trish's purse.

He started to place it on the night stand, thought better of it, and again began to give it a thorough once-over.

Well, I'll be damned. It looks like a microchip. Yeah, sure as hell,

that's exactly what it is. Look at all the miniature circuits, the mini-tran-
sistors and the micro-soldered circuit connections. Shit, this could only
have been made by the most sophisticated chip manufacturing systems
available. I wonder. Could this have come from some aerospace industry
workshop? What in the hell is she doing with something like this? Nah!
She must have found it somewhere. Then again, that phone call, she re-
ally seemed to weird out when she received it. Hmm, she said that she has
to go to Greece. You don't suppose....

Lee put the chip down on the nightstand and went into the
bathroom to wash his face. Afterwards he shook his head, pondering
the significance of his discovery.

Yeah, it looks like Mayhew is going to get an earful when we get
together. If anyone will know about this, or want to know about this, it
will be him. Let me see, should I call him and alert him before we talk?
Nah, I'll tell him when we talk at 1:30. Yeah, and I will have the plea-
sure of getting together with Kathy. If I play my cards right, she could be
a link to help me uncover what is going on at Mountain View Aviation.

Damn, I have to get a move on. I have a conference call with Jerry
and TJ at 1:30. It's too bad that Trish seems to be tied up in all of the
international intrigue. It has a tendency to ruin what could be a terrific
permanent relationship. I sure wish that I didn't have to play this cloak
and dagger stuff with her, but the evidence of her involvement in all this
is too strong. When the conference call occurs with Jerry and TJ, I'm now
convinced that there is still a lot that I don't know about Trish; I have
a feeling I won't like what I'm going to find out. What's with this sud-
den crisis phone call this morning? Trish actually looked fearful. What a
fucking mess.

26

CHOCOLATE
CHIP COOKIES
OREGON CITY

ESP, the sense of anticipation without particular reason, is mind boggling. It often elicits comments such as, "How did he/she know that?" or "How does he/she do that?" At the very least, it gives cause to sit up and take notice and more profoundly view the person performing the feat.

AT 1:30 p.m. sharp, the report of Lee's telephone interrupted a lively thought process that found him trying to determine how to expand the information that Kathy had about his role, as well as his new knowledge of her involvement.

Mayhew had been very unwavering and insistent that he tell her. As he put it, "I know you are surprised to learn that Kathy is a CIA agent. I also know that it will be difficult to get used to viewing her as an agent, but understand that she can be of great assistance in helping us get to the bottom of this mess. She can use the woman's touch to help you get information from Trish Knight."

"Hello?"

"Eag, this is Jerry. This call is encrypted so we can talk freely. TJ will not be joining us now. I've already run a couple of thoughts by her. She's working with the State Department, trying to engage Ambassador Woodard in our planning process. I'll fill you in on it later."

"Okay, I understand. Thanks for setting up this call. I've spent the morning pondering how I could tactfully approach Kathy and what I was going to disclose to her. I could use some guidance."

"Yeah, I figured. That's why I set up this call. First, though, I needed to assure the agency was informed and that they could choose how and when to brief her on the next steps. As of now, they have connected with her and have provided instructions. So, that means you can just take the direct approach and just give her a call. I don't know everything she was briefed on, but I'm thinking that she probably now knows you have a role in all this activity. She may be genuinely surprised to learn that you are as deeply engaged in this as you are. We spooks don't always share all details with one another, so I suggest you test the waters with her first to see what she's been briefed on; then be as candid as you wish. At this point, given the short timeline we're on and the gravity of events, I suggest you tell her everything you know. Just be cautious about the environment in which you talk to her; the walls have ears."

"You're right. I understand. I'll give her a call as soon as we get off the phone. By the way, there are a couple of new, unexpected, and curious turns of events. Trish was in my place this morning when I returned and we, ah…talked. First, she said she wanted to take me on a tour of her new facility in McMinnville. I acted surprised and a bit aloof and said sure, anytime. She also said she wanted to take Kathy there as well. It may have to do with a legitimate realty activity such as a property appraisal in preparation for a sale, or it could be for something more nefarious. I couldn't read her invitation clearly, but Kathy sold her the property some time back and I understand it was in a degraded state of disrepair. Second, in her haste to take an incoming cell phone call, she spilled her purse on my floor. After the call, the mood took on a somber note. I don't know why. She wouldn't say more. She then had to make a quick exit to attend a meeting. She couldn't tell me where or with whom. Anyway, one of the items that fell from her purse was a computer chip. If I'm not mistaken, it looks like a memory chip from a sophisticated device I've seen before from my 'techie' background days. I think it needs to be analyzed."

"Okay, let's get it to Kathy, but don't just come out and tell her anything of these events on the phone. You need a face-to-face meeting with her and it needs to be soon. She'll be agreeable. You can pique her curiosity and her appetite if you use a code such as you would like to share a recipe for chocolate chip cookies with her. It's so far afield she'll know it's code."

"Hmm, that should be an interesting way to wrangle some private time with her. It's not that she's not interested, but wanting to give her a recipe for chocolate chip cookies? Come on, Jerry, we can do better than that, can't we?"

"Eag, I'll trust you to do it your way. Just be vague. You never know who might be listening in."

"Well, okay. Who knows, she just might be quite interested in the culinary arts, and who wouldn't just love to get a killer recipe for chocolate chip cookies?"

Mayhew chuckled, a prelude to a long, ensuing silence. Finally, Mayhew broke the silence. "Hmm, interesting! Three other things, Lee, all kidding aside. Query Kathy about a possible tour of the Mc-Minnville property. I know Kathy sold it to Anatolia Enterprises a few years ago. Before and just after she bought it, the condition of the property was all but useless, but in the last year there were some significant modifications and construction going on inside the hanger buildings, and security had tightened markedly. Also, significantly, the construction was conducted at night. Overhead imagery hasn't uncovered anything other than heavy-equipment tire tracks into and out of the buildings, and the tailings of some kind of ground excavation a hundred yards from the hangers. It appears as though things may have technically and markedly changed since then. Kathy may have some valuable insights into what Trish is really up to. Second, be careful, observant, and prepared for something unexpected from Trish or from those with whom she associates. I don't know what to tell you to watch out for, but someone may know you're a player in this activity and they may not want you to be. Just be sensitive to those well-known hairs on the back of your neck. Do you remember that little 9mm toy the agency issued you? You may want to put it and some spare ammo somewhere you can quickly get your hands on it. Finally, trust Kathy, but don't get any ideas that may cause you to lose your edge."

"Okay, I understand and appreciate the advice."

As soon as Lee hung up the phone, he started searching through the yellow pages for Windermere Realty.

Hmm, here it is. God, are there enough Windermere offices? Let's see, Lake Oswego. Yeah, that's the one.

After punching in the last number, Lee waited for what seemed like an eternity. Finally, a voice answered.

"Windermere Realty, how can I direct your call?"

"I would like to speak with Kathy Moen."

"Just one moment please."

A moment later, a familiar voice answered, "Hello, this is Kathy."

"Kathy, this is Lee. Are you busy? Better yet, did I catch you at a bad time?"

Kathy chuckled, "No, anytime you call is a good time. What's up?"

"I would like to discuss some business with you. How about having dinner with me tonight?"

"Is there anything that I need to know?"

"Yes, a mutual friend of ours suggested that I run a chocolate chip cookie recipe by you for your approval."

"I didn't know that you had an interest in baking and cooking." There was momentary silence on Kathy's end of the phone, as if she were distracted, or more realistically, recalibrating the conversation.

Could this be a code?

"Who is this special friend who wants me to try out a chocolate chip cookie recipe?"

"Jerry Mayhew, ah, it's a small world because he and I have been friends since our college days."

"You don't say."

"Yes, it is a small world."

"How about picking me up at my place?"

"Yeah, I think our minds are on the same wavelength. What time works for you?"

"How about 7:30?"

"I'll be there, but could we make it 7:00? I don't want some perishable ingredients to spoil."

"I'll see you at 7:00, Lee." Jokingly she added, "I promise not to start without you."

27

IT'S A SMALL WORLD
PORTLAND

Trust is difficult to establish, especially in a world where deception is commonplace and not unexpected. A friendship or a loving relationship can never develop without that elusive assurance.

LEE arrived at Kathy's home promptly at 7:00. Punctuality was a trait that he valued. Usually he would have even arrived a bit early, but he sensed that, on this occasion, early would not be appreciated. He mulled over all the last-minute advice Jerry had given him in the phone call. The only thing he didn't do was retrieve his 9mm Berretta from its hiding place. He wanted to read the situation that he and Kathy faced more clearly before he started "packing a weapon."

Greeting him at the entry to her condo, she said, "I'm glad you called me. If you hadn't called, I was going to call you."

"Before we go to dinner, do you suppose that we could talk about something—something rather important?"

"Sure, come on in. We can go into the living room and sit."

"That's perfect."

After showing him to the living room, she motioned towards the couch.

Nodding, Lee responded, "That will be fine. Are you going to join me or do you have a favorite chair?"

"No, the sofa is fine with me too."

Kathy took a seat on the couch near Lee and smiled. There was music playing in the background a little louder than would be normal for two people carrying on a conversation, but it was not overly loud. He could also just barely hear an audible hissing sound like radio static. He had heard it before and it sounded like white noise. Between the music and the white noise he knew the discussion they were about to have would be unintelligible if anyone were listening. "So, what's on your mind?" she said.

He began by somewhat nervously saying, "Ah, Kathy, we are not always who we appear to be. I mean, you are you, and I am me—"

Kathy interrupted, held up one hand, palm facing Lee, and said, "Lee, does this have anything to do with the chocolate chip cookies?"

With mild surprise, Lee answered, "Yes it does. Tell me, how do you know Jerry Mayhew?"

"Well, maybe I need to know how you came to know him."

"I thought I covered that earlier. Anyway, you probably already know the answer to that question. In fact, you have probably known the answer for some time."

"Okay, wise guy, so I know all about Jerry's and your background and how you are connected. Is that good enough?"

"Possibly, but before I get into sharing recipes that involve chocolate chip cookies, there are a couple things I'd like to know."

"Well, what are you waiting for? Why don't you just ask me and find out what you need to know?"

"Okay. If Mayhew contacted me by phone, and he wanted to make sure that he was talking to the right person, what would he do?"

"He probably would say, 'This is Phil.'"

"And then what would I say?"

Frowning, she replied, "You wouldn't say anything. Instead, he would continue, 'I hear there is no rain predicted in the Pacific Northwest for at least nine months.'"

Lee nodded. "What would happen then?"

Kathy smiled, apparently enjoying the back and forth game they were playing. "You would say, 'Yes, where I live, we either experience a drought or a flood.'"

She grinned. "There may be some slight variation to the sign and countersign, but that's essentially it. So, what happens now that I have passed your little test?"

"You passed, but…."

"Oh, so are you wondering why I didn't tell you sooner?"

"Yes."

"Think about it, Lee. This mess just broke. Before that damned missile attack in Iran, I was operating unattached. I was on a non-assigned status waiting for my sabbatical leave time to expire. Then there might be a new assignment."

"So when did you learn about my involvement?"

"Officially, I found out earlier today, before you called. My agency handler called early this morning with a lot of material about the meeting called by the president in the offices of the DNI that you tipped me off about. He, however, gave me a more detailed rundown on attendees, subjects discussed, and impressions from the directors that attended and actions they planned to take. Then Jerry called me from DC via an encrypted phone call. Unofficially, I suspected, but…. Anyway, now that you've decided to ruin a perfectly good evening with all of this business talk, ah, there's something I want to show you."

Kathy reached for a folder on the coffee table. Slowly she opened the folder and handed him what appeared to be a clipping from a newspaper.

Anatolia Enterprises Suspended from Government Arms Contract
by
Chip Walker

Anatolia Enterprises, Inc., has been suspended from supplying government-sponsored arms shipments, according to a posting on a General Services Administration website.

A June 20, 2017, posting on the GSA's Excluded Parties List System websites says that Anatolia Enterprises has been suspended for an unspecified reason and for an undetermined length of time.

The general description of the category of the suspension says that the action was taken "based on an indictment or other adequate evidence" that could lead to a debarment or "other causes" that could cause debarment.

Anatolia Enterprise's officials were not available for comment.

The McMinnville-Oregon-based company ranks No. 4 on Washington's Top 100 listing of key contract, federal government, small business prime suppliers.

Lee looked up from the clipping, cautiously searching for some clue to what Kathy was thinking about at that moment.

I wonder if I should tell her about my real relationship with Trish. Maybe she already knows. My sixth sense says, when in doubt, do nothing.

"This is good news if what we suspect about Anatolia is true, but either true or false, my sense is this may be premature and might cause Trish and her colleagues, whomever they are, to get suspicious and start hiding things or disposing of key evidence. If the suspension is for some innocuous reason, then maybe they won't be panicked."

"Look, Kathy, a lot of information has been revealed to selected people in the government in the last few days. First, I don't know the intention of this release. Second, since you know about this I hope it's not like some government operations where the right hand and the left hand are completely out of control, and third, I don't have a warm, comfortable feeling about who's in charge of clarifying the involvement of the US in the Iranian catastrophe. Until just recently, I didn't, uh…."

"I know. Mayhew has filled me in fairly completely." Smiling, she continued, "I even know all about your assignment to extract information from Trish."

"Kathy, that's strictly an operational task I have been assigned to. I'm to get up close and personal with Trish so that I can gain insight into her operation and her intent. So far, she has acted fairly uninvolved in any suspicious activity. But also, I know her well enough to detect possibly stress-related mood swings of anger, fear, aggression, and impatience. She can occasionally be very schizophrenic."

Kathy nodded thoughtfully. "Something like keeping your friends close, but your enemies closer, huh?"

"That's a very good way to put it."

"I suppose that includes intimate personal contact too, right?"

Lee's face flushed, his eyes not meeting her steady gaze.

"I'm sorry, Lee. You don't have to answer that. I know as well as anyone in this business that personal feelings can get in the way of doing our work, and sometimes personal contact can be a means to an end. What you do with Trish is your business. Just don't let it get in the way of—"

"I'd say that you have been perfectly clear," Lee interrupted, "but just so you know, I'll be scaling back a lot on the phase of the operation that involves Trish. A little less physicality, as it were." Grinning, he continued, "It's amazing what a little abstention can produce. Who knows? She might be moved to share more." Lee cleared his throat before proceeding. "So how much, exactly, do you know about Trish?"

"I know that she owns Mountain View Aviation, with a small fleet of three Chinook helicopters. When I sold the hanger and shop facilities to her it was a ghost town. Windows were broken out. Doors wouldn't open or close. The grounds and taxiways were overgrown. It was a mess. She got it for a very good price. Since that time, her company poured lots of money into it, financed by some obscure overseas bank. The modifications made it look operational but still unused. Very few people have seen much activity around the hangers. People have, however, heard things going on around there at night. I know that in the last eight months there has been some construction work going on inside the hangars. It looked like underground excavation based on the nighttime dump truck activity. I know, through Jerry, that she is the head of Anatolia Enterprises and that the plate they found in Iran after the attack makes her look…. Let's just say that she is a person of great interest to the CIA."

She paused, reflecting a moment, and then smiled. "I know that because of your connection to her, as well as the realtor-client trust that I have developed with her, you and I are going to be connected at the hip for some time—at least until we get this case solved."

Lee grinned. "How bad can that be? I've got the best of both worlds."

"You don't say, and what would you say if I told you that this girl's not for hire?"

"I never said you were."

Lee paused, nodding his head reflectively. "Yeah, I have a history with Trish, Kathy, but I can't just change directions all at once or she'll suspect that something is wrong and then this connection that you speak of will evaporate into thin air."

Kathy rose from the couch suddenly. "Just let me give you a little professional advice. Don't enjoy it too much, and please remember to be very careful. I have information that says she and some of her hired colleagues can be extremely ruthless to get what they want."

Lee grinned. "Isn't that true with most women?"

"Shit, Lee, I'm trying to be serious. I'm not real excited about giving everything I know to you only to see you run off to play house with her."

"So what am I supposed to do?"

"Just enjoy our professional relationship more. I know that this situation demands special actions. I just don't want you to…. I don't want you to put yourself in harm's way."

"Kathy, I promise to keep everything between Trish and me as professional as I can. In the meantime, I think that we had best head out for dinner or someone's going to have to ring up room service."

"Aye, aye, Captain. By the way, I have a meeting with Trish tomorrow at Mountain View Aviation. Anything in particular you want me to explore or look for?"

"Good! Excellent! She offered to give me a tour as well but indicated it won't be imminent. I didn't want to appear too interested, so I just left the thought out there for her to revisit."

"Did she say why she wanted you to see it?"

"Well she said she owned some industrial facilities and was

thinking she would be moving and expanding elsewhere and would like to sell what facilities she has here. She wants a realty assessment of value and potential alternative uses. She said she made some capital improvements to enhance the value and utility of the facilities, but she has not revealed the extent of what she has done. The only thing she has said is that the buildings are different now from what they were when she bought them. Now that the plot is thickening and she has become a person of interest, she may have ulterior motives that could range from efforts to find new and different allies to using it as a place to make people and things disappear."

"You're right. Her intentions are obscure right now. I guarantee you, however, knowing her as I do, that she has a definite plan in mind. I can't suggest anything that I think you haven't already thought of or have been instructed to watch for. I found a microchip that Trish dropped. I mentioned it to Mayhew and he said to give it to you so that you could get it analyzed. I think it may turn out to be a component for an avionics sensor."

"I'll take care of it."

"I don't need to say this, but just take in every detail. We already know the obvious. It's an aircraft hangar; it's on an airport; there are things known and unknown about the facility; there have been suspicious things going on at night in the buildings; and in a small town like McMinnville where everyone knows everyone else, some strangers have been randomly seen in town in the past few weeks."

"I'm very interested in the construction of the facility. If she, her company, and the facility were involved in the crisis, we may be able to hypothesize how she could perhaps ship missiles or the component parts from there. But if she's also going to run a legitimate aviation operation out there, while at the same time performing activities she doesn't want anyone to see, she has to have some way of concealing the merchandise. Also, keep your eyes peeled for people who seem out of place there, if you know what I mean."

"I do." Nodding, Kathy continued, "I can do that, and I have already been instructed to do just that."

"I know that you can, but be careful, and let me echo a piece of advice Jerry gave me earlier today. If you have any special toys to protect yourself in a compromising spot, can you get your hands on them in a hurry?"

Kathy smiled. "Not to worry. I've already given that some thought and action. After all, this is my line of work. I've survived my career by expecting a little adventure. By the way, where are you thinking about taking this famished lady to dinner?"

"How does the Rhinelander sound?"

"Do you have reservations?"

"I'm one step ahead of you."

"What makes you think that I want to go there?"

Lee grinned. "I studied your CIA profile."

"Get out of here! You didn't even know about me until—"

"Yeah, I know—today."

28

FROM THE MIDDLE EAST, LOOKING WEST
WASHINGTON, DC

*The briefing of a key player is essential
if the mission is to be accomplished.*

AMBASSADOR Woodard squirmed uncomfortably in his seat.

Damned government-issued furniture. Why is it never very comfortable?

Reading from the pages of a two-inch-thick, three-ring, hard-covered binder, he noted that the cover read in large, bold letters: FOR AMBASSADORIAL EYES ONLY. At the top and bottom of the cover page, as well as at the top and bottom of all the pages inside, were the words: TOP SECRET – BLACKTHORN. The book was a compilation of the briefings presented twenty-four hours earlier in the DNI's office by the directors of the NCIC, the NCTC, and the NCPC, but it had been expanded with updated intelligence on added items related to the world's current crisis. It was compiled by the National and International Intelligence Center, the NIIC. The center was made up of about one hundred highly trained analysts, strategists, and foreign weapons technical experts. This small, robust, classified unit had been highly successful and effective in the past because it served as a free-wheeling, think-tank fusion center for all data sources, all intelligence agency inputs, and all intelligence products. They made very accurate assessments and predictions about global events. In the past it had been extremely effective and accurate in identifying activities that led to catastrophic events. They were successful in predicting the Chinese government's reactions to the Tiananmen Square face-down; North Korean nuclear tests, and barrage missile firings into the Sea of Japan; the attack and sinking of a South Korean surveillance cutter by North Korean undersea assets; the Somali piracy of a Mearsk, Alabama, US cargo vessel; the Russian invasion of Georgia; the Chinese government's suppression of the Chinese Muslim Uighurs; the Iranian government suppression of student uprisings; and many other events that had impact on the international front. Perhaps their most accurate and relevant event was their prediction of a major attack against a highly visible domestic US target set for sometime in September 2001.

As Ambassador Woodard's eyes scanned the pages of data and discussion of events, he saw nothing new about the DNI briefings and findings that he had not already heard about or had been briefed on. He therefore quickly read the material presented by the principals at the briefing but focused more on the NIIC assessment at the end of each presentation. The NIIC assessment of the NCTC presentation was that the Chinese National Command Authority had apparently devised a secret strategy to disable and defeat elements of the US national infrastructure on a segment-by-segment, random and temporary basis. This would begin to introduce suspicion about the integrity and reliability of the central control centers that oversee and manage the banking, transportation, electrical grid, civil nuclear power, logistics movement, and communications sectors of the United States. If they could introduce mistrust of the continuity and reliability of these sectors, the entire nation would ultimately become vulnerable to massive system shutdowns, with no reliable backup capabilities.

The NIIC assessment of the NCTC presentation concluded a similar dire situation. The theft of crucial technical design data for national infrastructure systems had made hacking into sensitive country-wide control systems easy and would ultimately lead to access of classified national security networks and national command authority decision-making elements, as well as facilitate the further theft of more technical data and new, breakthrough technology still under confidential development.

The NIIC assessment of the NCPC presentation was equally dismal. The transshipment of sensitive nuclear systems parts to Taiwan, the movement of nuclear airborne weapons across the United States by Air Force B-52s, the loss of the forty-eight CALCMs aboard the USS *Salem*, the undetected launch of cruise missiles against Tehran, and the infiltration of secure US government facilities and select military units by subversives were all evidence that foreign nations and forces had already begun the subtle and deliberate disassembly of the United States' secure system of positive command and control of secret and top-secret processes and methodologies.

At this point, the Ambassador was in deep thought.

While the NIIC assessments don't blatantly come right out and say it, my God, we have been attacked too! Apparently we have been at war with the Chinese government and the People's Liberation Army without even knowing they were quietly destroying us. That could mean that the attack on Tehran is one of the final steps in the endgame of their ultimate strategy to discredit and bankrupt the US.

Before he closed the book, he saw one more note and a brief conclusion by the NIIC staff. It said the vice premier of China had placed a secure phone call to President Rashid Al Formadi of Iran offering economic, national defense, and petroleum industry technology assistance. The phone intercept revealed (and later overhead intelligence confirmed) that men and material were indeed marshaling at the western Chinese border areas. There were hundreds of trucks ready to roll and railroad sidings were already filled with railcar after railcar of food, medical material, heavy excavating equipment, and hundreds of military armored personnel carriers with the military markings painted over.

Holy shit! Those Chinese bastards are postured right now to move right in and conduct a bloodless and surreptitious invasion and takeover of Iran. They are using the United States as the reason to do so, without ever firing any shots, pointing any fingers, or issuing any allegations. All this seems to be an effort to systematically dismantle and destroy the United States.

John closed his eyes and leaned his head back for a moment to contemplate what he had just concluded.

Am I right? Has anyone else in the US or Iranian governments come to this same conclusion? I need Jane O'Donnell's input as soon as we arrive. I think I may need to see President Rashid Al Formadi sooner than anticipated.

When he reopened his eyes, he knew he had some other pressing issues to think through. He looked down at the tablet in front of him and picked up a stubby yellow pencil in one hand and a cup of decaf coffee in the other. He began to focus on the list of items he had placed on the tablet earlier and was obviously trying to make sense of it all. Number one on the list was the name **Brad Williams**.

He was a fine man, father, husband, and dedicated public servant. He was a longtime member of the Foreign Service, was respected and competent, had been trusted by two administrations before this one, and deserved more than an end to his life and career like this. I know his family will be taken care of, and they were reasonably well-off, so they won't be wanting for anything except the attention and love of a husband and father who worked many years for the point in his life when family was finally the number one priority. Now all of that has changed.

Number two on the list was an **Attack on Tehran**.

Why did it happen? Who would do such a barbaric thing? What could they possibly hope to gain with the indiscriminate nature of the detonations? The world is not at war. So far, we have been able to diplomatically work our way through our disagreements. What does the attacker want? There are those nations that would not do this. It's probably a lot longer than the list of those that would do this. I'm certain the country at the top of the list that has the capability to do this but certainly would not is the United States. I continue to believe in my heart of hearts that is true. So, what nations stand to gain with such an act of destruction? China? Russia? North Korea? Syria? Only two of those jump out at me as possible candidates who have the capability to do this; who have the capability to pull it off with anonymity; who have the clandestine resources to lie low for a while afterwards without fear of discovery; and who would have the assets to quietly infiltrate diplomatically, militarily, and peacefully, and worm their way into the Iranian government's confidence as a trusted and loyal friend who is just "here to help." That would be China and North Korea—maybe both in tandem.

Number three on the list was **Captain Aref.**

He is obviously not exactly who he says he is, but neither is he a traitor. He is also obviously gathering intelligence for the Iranian government, but he is not trying to work an under-the-table agreement for some nefarious cause. I don't need him as a conduit for information into the Iranian national government's thinking. My friend, the president, and the prime minister are trustworthy colleagues enough. I just need to be careful not to press too hard or attempt to extract too many internal thoughts from them lest they think they're giving more than they're getting. I need to carefully play Aref and feed him what I want to go through his channels, to match what is going through my channels. They need to know we are trusted friends and do not want to exploit their misfortune.

Number four on the list was **Injuries and Destruction.**

I have seen and attended to the injuries and wounds of Iranians, other Middle Easterners, and Americans alike who had the misfortune to get caught in the middle of this debacle. The injuries run the gamut from cuts and contusions to near-death or permanently debilitating wounds. The injuries are both physical and psychological. Both will require long-term attention. There will be demands on the medical and political assets of many nations for a long time to come.

Number five on the list was **The Weapons.**

It's been a long time since I've had any involvement with weapons that could wreak the kind of havoc we've seen here, and even then my knowledge was sketchy at best. But, I guess if I were trying to get the most advantage out of a surprise attack, a cruise missile attack might be the most effective. Cruise missiles have very definite payload-to-weight-to-thrust relationships. The destruction throughout Tehran is so devastating that the munitions had to be extremely powerful. If they were as powerful as I suspect, they had to be heavy with a fairly precise avionics guidance package on board. If they were that massive, they needed a lot of thrust and therefore couldn't have flown very far. That tells me they were air-launched, ground-launched, or sea-launched. Since there are no reports of unusual air traffic, either civilian or military, I would rule out air-launched. If the missiles were as heavy as I speculate, they wouldn't have the range to have flown from the Gulf of Hormuz to Tehran. If I'm right about this, I would rule out sea-launched. Besides, the sea-based platform would have to have been a missile-launching surface vessel or a submarine. What nation would want their good name attached to the ship that could do this kind of thing—rogue or not? It could be done but would have to be done with airtight, plausible deniability.

That leaves me with land-launched. With hundreds of miles of desert in all directions around Tehran, it would be fairly easy to pre-position several ground-launched cruise missile sites in the desert and then destroy or simply abandon the launcher rails. The evidence would then have to be buried to preclude leaving a data trail. After all, it's less important where they came from inside the Iranian borders than it is who put them there and who pulled the trigger.

Number six on the list was **What the US is preparing to do.**

I wish I had verification of what occurred leading up to all this. I can only trust that all sources and methods of extracting salient points of information are being exploited. The NIIC assessments in the BLACK-THORNE document appear to be well founded. Even though the evidence to support those assertions is still a little circumstantial, it all certainly sounds like a very elaborate scheme to reduce the US to third-world status. We don't have enough of a case yet to stand the scrutiny of a world court.

Before all this transpired I would have bet that our government's resources were in a defensive crouch and a mode of "every agency is in this for itself," and that there would have been a lot of finger pointing. That politics-as-usual attitude irks the hell out of me. Bureaucrats and politicians alike seldom step forward to say, "I should have seen this coming," or "Let me get involved to see if I can fix this," or "Let's collaborate and share what we know." I have to believe we'll come out of this as a nation, but I'm not so naïve as to think that all this will blow over in a month or so. If indeed the Chinese and/or North Koreans are behind this, we'll need incontrovertible evidence to prove they did it, and we'll need to build firewalls to distance and protect national US assets from further invasion and erosion. We have the power, will, and technology to gather all kinds of data from all kinds of sources, and we can defend ourselves if it should come to that. I also know we can deter a lot of different reprisal *actions but will leave a trail of unforgettable damage in our wake. We need to get to the bottom of this and discover who did it and why. If it was the Chinese, we need a reprisal plan that will deter any nation from ever trying such a plan again. The US response to this is a diplomatic, military, and intelligence imperative and I hope the leaders in those communities can be left alone long enough by the politicians to get us some answers. I pray to God we don't act precipitously and without a game plan or an exit strategy.*

Number seven on the list was **Anatolia Enterprises.**

What the hell are they doing in the middle of this mess? I have some knowledge of who they are and, in general, what they have represented in the past. They brought some kind of technical consulting business to the Willamette Valley even if it was somewhat nondescript and unfocused. There are some in the vicinity of McMinnville that obviously profited from Anatolia's work, but the source of the money and what it bought has always been impossible to trace. So, the people of the valley always said, "Let's not look this wealthy gift horse in the mouth," but if they are now involved in this debacle in some way, there are those in the world who will stop at nothing to get revenge—and there may be others in the world who pushed Anatolia out to the pointy end of the spear and will suddenly vanish when the shooting starts. All of that makes the McMinnville vicinity an international target. Based on what happened in Tehran, it means that whoever wants revenge will not stop at sending in a few hit men; they'll launch their own cruise missile raid and send the Valley back to the Stone Age.

Number eight on the list was **Restraining Impetuous Nations**.

I have been briefed on some of the diplomatic initiatives with some of the nations either directly or indirectly involved. I'm looking forward to hearing soon what we are doing with them and how we are proceeding. Jane O'Donnell is a thoughtful leader, skilled diplomat, and careful initiator. She has a competent staff around her, and they will have already put together some kind of game plan that will be our roadmap forward. I suspect she has long since alerted my counterparts stationed in other nations around the globe. I'm sure they have been cautioned to keep their eyes and ears peeled for any information that will show us a trail to follow, and to share anything and everything with their intelligence community analysts and agents. If there was something I thought I could do to help my old and newfound friends in Iran, I would certainly do it, but prudence says thus far I've done what I have been instructed to do and have not gotten out in front of Jane's diplomatic actions. She knows that if she wants me to take any added actions, that I would do it without question. I have some thoughts of my own on how to proceed and I'll certainly share them with her. Perhaps I can be most useful in interceding with President Rashid to dissuade him from taking any irreversible action with the Chinese. I'll just have to wait and see what she wants from me next.

Number nine on the list was **Restraining Our Own Politicians.**

I don't know what the political mood is in Washington or around the country, but I would be willing to bet it could be summed up in a word: FRANTIC. On a few occasions, members of the executive and legislative branches of government have cooperated for the common good. On many other occasions, however, they have become estranged bedfellows. Some members of congress who have illusions of grandeur want to leap out in front of our own leaders and "string up" anyone and everyone who knows anything at all about this. In the past, some elected and appointed members of government have been reticent to take initiatives—for fear of usurping someone else's responsibility—or have been fearful that they will get too much exposure and could be held accountable for actions that produce limited or no success. This situation is different now, but I don't have a sense that our political teammates share the same views as those who have been pushed to the front lines. I hope I'm wrong, but unless we all can be persuaded that we need to follow our elected leaders, and unless we all get in line behind them, this can be a defining moment in US history when we either transcend the confusion or we sink into the depths of a status of less than a third-world nation.

Number ten on the list was **What are we going to do about all this?**

The answer to this one lies in the call I received from Jane O'Donnell asking me to consider the risks in coming to Washington now at this crucial moment. My departure from Tehran could be regarded as abandonment of our interests in Iran and could be tantamount to an admission of guilt in the attack. The secure call from TJ Massadoti in the NSC was very persuasive. Her reassurance that she has the full cooperation of both department and agency resources and the collaboration of two very capable operatives who have been on the firing line before is comforting, but as she said, there is no limit to what needs to be done to find answers and take corrective actions.

Just then, Air Force Lieutenant Colonel Bill Hubbard, the co-pilot of the four-engine C-17, approached and broke the stream of conscious thought.

"Mr. Ambassador, we will be landing at Andrews Air Force Base in forty minutes. We have been cleared for a straight-in approach and landing at 1945 hours. Secretary of State Jane O'Donnell sent word that Deputy Secretary of State George Marshall will meet you on the ground. Your wife will also be there. I think we have been successful in maintaining the secrecy of your visit and the flight-line lights will be dimmed to protect your arrival. We have been instructed to stand by for thirty-six hours to pick you up here and return you directly to Baghdad for the chopper ride back to Tehran, just as we brought you out. We all hope you have a successful visit here, sir, and we will stand by for further orders from you."

"Thank you, Colonel. You have been very kind and very patient. I look forward to seeing you on the way back."

The colonel turned and went forward to the cockpit.

John felt the throttles to the engines being slowed and the slight pitch forward indicating a descent to the runway. Shortly thereafter he heard the first notch of landing flaps being extended. Moments later the dull roar of the landing gear doors opening could be heard and then the low whine of the hydraulic servos being activated to lower the landing gear. A second notch of flaps came on and the pitch forward became a little more pronounced. Moments later the big C-17 began the flaring maneuver and the throttles were reduced even more. Then the mild screech of tires on dry pavement could be heard along with the engine-reversal hissing that meant the aerodynamic thrusters were engaged, and the massive aircraft came to a taxiing speed. The pilots took the first taxiway they came to that would provide them the quickest access to the base terminal building. The giant aircraft stopped next to the building, all aircraft external lights were extinguished, and the engines were shut down. Air Force Master Sergeant Terry Tenpenny, the aircraft crew chief, entered the cabin where John was seated with his suitcase and led him to the stairwell leading to the tarmac. There were two people at the bottom of the stairway. John walked down the stairs to the waiting handshake of George Marshall and a welcoming hug from Rosemary. The three then quickly turned and walked to the open doors of a waiting, darkened limousine.

29

SETTING UP THE VISIT
PORTLAND

*Pop goes the weasel! Not a child's game, sometimes
international intrigue can be life threatening.*

AT a secluded Starbuck's coffee shop in an Oak Grove Mall, the
report of the cell phone interrupted a serious conversation between
Lee and Kathy.

Kathy frowned. "Damn, I wonder who that could be. You don't
suppose…?"

"Not even Trish could suspect that I'm here. It must be one of
your real estate clients."

As she reached for her cell phone, she noted that the time was
8:05 a.m. The digital readout on the phone identified the caller as
Trish. "It's Trish, be quiet." She cleared her throat and answered,

"Hello?"

"Kathy? This is Trish. Are you busy?"

"No, I just stopped for coffee. I am on my way to the office."

"I was thinking that today would be a good time to show you my facility with all the improvements I've made. It's either now, or I don't know when we can arrange it. Some business items have come up for me that have compressed my timetable. I have to make a quick trip out of the country."

"What time do you have in mind? I have a real estate showing today at 5:00 p.m."

"How about meeting me in an hour? We could meet at your office in Lake Oswego?"

"That's perfect."

After terminating the call, she looked at Lee. "Well, whatever plans we might have had for today have changed. Are you okay with that?"

Trying to decipher the bits and pieces of the phone conversation he had overheard, Lee said, "I'd say that depends on what you have to do."

"Trish wants to show me the operation at Mountain View Aviation. That is what we were hoping for."

"You're damned right that's what we wanted! What an opportunity!" He nodded while letting his mind drift idly for a moment. "Is there any chance that we can get together later today or this evening to discuss what you've seen or heard? We could do dinner?"

"Why don't I call you?"

"Maybe you could lay the groundwork for me to visit Mountain View."

"How would that work?"

"Well, you could ask Trish if she's had the opportunity to show her aviation center to me. It will encourage her to get that done. I also want to make sure that all suspicion is diverted from you. I don't want to do anything that might put you in jeopardy or put you at risk."

"Hmm, you don't really trust her, do you?"

"No, I can't say that I do. I think that she's out for number one, and number one in this case happens to be Trish Knight or whatever she is called by her inner circle of international thugs."

"Wow, all that in one short sentence. I guess that we're completely on the same page about who she is and what she does. Now all we have to do is connect the dots."

"Yeah, and in the process of connecting the dots, we have to ensure that it happens before there is another attack."

Kathy hesitated for a moment before speaking. "Lee, I am going to give you the name of a close associate of mine. She's also with the agency but is working another assignment. We back up one another on assignments when it's necessary."

Lee frowned, confusion etched on his face. "I don't understand. Why would you compromise another agent for no apparent reason, unless…."

Kathy nodded. "Yeah, in this game of intrigue, you never know. Uh, Arlene Lang will know exactly what to do and who to contact if…. I call her AJ."

"Now wait a minute, Kathy. All you are doing is making an innocent visit to Trish's operation. There's no way that she's gonna open Pandora's box for you."

"She may not, but who knows what I'm going to uncover on my own."

Lee nodded. "I suppose. Yeah, I guess that makes sense. I still think that you are overreacting." He hesitated for a moment, then, exhaled in resignation. "Where does the *AJ* come from?"

"Her full name is Arlene Judith Lang. Everyone calls her AJ, and about the overreacting, maybe I am and maybe I'm not. The way I look at it, why take chances? Besides, in this case, I'd kind of like for you to humor me. Her phone number is (503) 274-6491. Yeah, and her cell is (503) 970-5733. I'll write the numbers on one of my business cards.

"So, why does she go by AJ, and what does she do? Is she also in real estate?"

"She likes both of her names, so initials seem preferable, and no, she does something with career development for CPAs."

"Really, you mean sort of like the OEA for educators?"

"As far as I know; but I haven't really delved into her other professional life."

"What else do I get to know about her?"

"Hmm, all of a sudden the boy gets interested."

Ignoring her sarcastic probe, Lee inquired, "So if something happens, I just call this AJ gal and...."

"Yep, that just about covers it. AJ will know exactly what to do. When an agent goes down, the agency knows what to do. Someone will take his or her place until the mission is complete. If an agent goes down and survives, the agency likes to make sure that the agent continues to survive, heals, and is available later for new tasking. We don't want professional colleagues and next of kin to get unnecessarily spun up."

"And by that, you mean...?"

"You've heard of the Agent Protection Program, surely. Well, a surviving agent needs to go deep underground after an attack, for his or her own safety."

"I have heard of that. Hmm, okay, I understand. I must say I find this discussion about death, injury, and survival a little unsettling—especially if it's about someone I know or might care about."

Kathy exhaled slightly, indicating her mild exasperation with Lee's discomfort with the subject matter. She knew that as bright as he was, he had a habit of indicating he was finished with listening and talking, but the processing of information continued long after discussion ceased. "I will call you when I'm done out in McMin-nville."

Lee watched Kathy's exit from the coffee shop, while mulling over recent events and storing them in the recesses of his subconscious.

Kathy's down-to-business demeanor and her preoccupation with the bottom line serve her well in the service of our country, and in furthering her other career. Being with her professionally is stimulating because she's so observant, so quick to assess the surroundings, and so fast to decide a course of action. She's definitely many steps above Trish. I need to watch my step. I want to be respectful of Kathy—and do the job that I have been assigned.

30

THE DEBRIEFING
WASHINGTON, DC

Key players need to be included in the circle of transmitted
information if the mission is to be accomplished.

THREE thousand miles away, Ambassador John Woodard and
his wife, Rosemary, were sharing an early morning breakfast of orange
juice, coffee, scrambled eggs, crispy bacon, and homemade biscuits
with West Virginia apple butter. Located in the visiting ambassador's
quarters on the top floor of the US Department of State building, on
23rd and Constitution Avenue in downtown Washington, DC, was
almost like being in the penthouse of the very exclusive and expen-
sive Hay-Adams Hotel on H Street in downtown Washington, across
from the White House. They both had awakened early, knowing full
well that their time together would be short. They knew there were

meetings, plans to set in motion, an airplane waiting to fly back to the Middle East, and a terribly uncertain future lying ahead. They also knew several update meetings and strategy sessions were waiting two floors below them. "Rose," John said tenderly, yet confidently, as he had always done, "we've got some more bumpy roads ahead." These were the same words he uttered when they entered medical school, started his residency, began private practice, joined the Air Force as a flight surgeon in Vietnam, returned to enter graduate school in political science, accepted an appointment into the Foreign Service, and when his close friend and medical colleague Jane O'Donnell accepted her appointment as secretary of state and wanted him nearby. Somehow both John and Rosemary knew this was part of life's grand design: to place special people in special places at critical times. John took her hand across the breakfast table and said, "I know the US is right; our friends and allies will see the truth, and the people of that poor nation need our help. There are neighboring countries that are offering false hope and I really think I can help make a difference. Do you remember when Rashid and his wife, Aruba, came to our meager apartment in Washington, up near the National Cathedral in Woodley Park? After a great dinner you prepared, and after three bottles of Oregon pinot noir from the Willamette Valley, he said, 'One day when I am president of Iran, I will show my people civility, gentility, tolerance, and understanding. John, you, Rosemary, Aruba, and I will be friends internationally, as we now are personally. Call me, my friend, if you are ever in need, and I will respond, knowing you will be at my side.'"

John continued, "Little did we know at that moment his young daughter, Marisa, needed delicate eye surgery. Well, he called to ask my opinion and without him ever asking, I went to Tehran to assist in her surgery. I'm forever grateful that I went. Not just for her sake, but for the sake of the honest concern in the heart of Rashid that now may mean the difference between world peace and world war, which could be, maybe, just days away. I'm not going to hold my friendship for Rashid hostage to today's catastrophic circumstances, but I am going to offer him my assistance one more time in an unemotional review of all the facts about this holocaust, to assure we help him make the best choices for his country. I plan to offer Jane my best abilities in diplomacy and objectivity to help both our countries.

Over the years, John had looked to Rosemary for not only her love and understanding, but for her way of seeing the importance of each and every situation their lives had taken them through. Unlike John, she intuitively sifted through all the noise and emotion of events and could hone in on the real messages they each needed to hear. "John, I completely understand what must be done, and there are precious few people in this town, and indeed in the free world, who can do what you are best positioned to do. I just want you to know that no one expects you to be Rambo and singlehandedly deal with the bad guys all by yourself. I'm certain Jane knows the perilous steps that lie ahead and will assure you get all the right kind of support to solve this problem. You just need to know when to ask her for assistance."

John smiled wryly, as he often did when he fully understood the gravity of situations, and showed her that he had accepted her views by showing humor in the darkest of challenges. "You're right. There was a time not too many years ago I thought I was bulletproof and maybe a little Rambo-esque. But that little twinge of arthritic pain in my right knee occasionally reminds me I'm still a tough guy, but I'm older and wiser too."

Just then there was a soft knock at the door to the suite, and the steward opened the door to say, "Mr. Ambassador, the Madam Secretary would like to see you in her offices for a pre-brief in fifteen minutes."

"Thank you. I'll be there momentarily."

31

THE PLAN FORWARD
WASHINGTON, DC

When all parties are well informed of events and possible plans of actions, the possibilities of a plan coming together are enhanced.

JANE stood to greet John as he entered her office. "I hope you had a good night and found the accommodations much more comfortable than the cabin of that C-17."

"Yes, everything was perfect coming here. The ride back to Tehran will be a bit grueling, but hopefully I'll have enough new information to process that it will keep my mind occupied for several hours."

Jane then launched into the day's agenda, which would fill his morning and early afternoon with briefings on the status of warnings from Allied nations, data on offers of assistance to Iran and the US to provide humanitarian aid, and intelligence reports and backchannel communiqués from friends and competitors alike. Jane explained that all were intended to prepare him for his ambassadorial mission when back at the embassy.

Jane, John, the deputy secretary, and several desk officers from the Foreign Services Division then took seats around a large conference table in Jane's office suite. One by one, the briefers stood to make their presentations and field questions from John. The session was clearly keyed to John Woodard and the problems he had thus far encountered in Tehran, and to some potential challenges the staff believed he was going to confront when he returned. John listened intently and asked pointed questions dealing with the pros and cons of options. He knew that, at worst, the circumstances in Tehran could be a no-win situation for the United States since it was irrefutable that the missiles were manufactured in the States. At best, however, it was probable that John and his administration supporters could prove the United States had no role in the launch of the cruise missiles against Tehran.

John listened intently to each word from every briefer; he took notes and was provided status update books on each and every subject. Near the end of the afternoon session, before departing for Andrews, he was presented with a newly minted intelligence report from the NIIC. He found it most interesting and useful. It was a report jointly presented by TJ Massadoti from the NSC staff and Colonel Jerry Mayhew from the agency.

TJ began first. "Good morning, Mr. Ambassador. The state of US relations with most all the countries in the civilized world is worse today than it was yesterday, if that's possible. Editorials and articles in *The Times of London*, *The Paris Observer*, and the Moscow *Pravda Daily* all seem to be based on the same anonymous sources that point fingers of guilt at the US for the brutal attack on Iran. Countries that have been cautiously accusatory are the ones you might suspect:

Japan, South Korea, Saudi Arabia, Spain, Italy, Germany, the Baltic nations, and Central and South America, with the exception of Venezuela. The nations that have been most vitriolic are Venezuela, North Korea, Syria, Lebanon, Iraq, Afghanistan, and Somalia. You have heard reports here today about the views of each of these nations, and I'm sure have concluded there are very few chances you will receive open support from any of them. Backchannel messages, however, reveal most of our polite friends and allies are objective enough to also want to get to the bottom of this."

TJ continued, "On the other side of the coin, there are those who are ready to take the lead on seeking sanctions against the US, and who are unhinged enough to be teetering on the edge of declaring an all-out holy, diplomatic, and economic war on us. Most notable among these countries are Venezuela and North Korea. The Venezuelans are emboldened by their recent, secret acquisition of Russian and North Korean medium-range ballistic missiles. They are itching to launch against southern US cities, Columbia, Brazil, and anyone else whom they believe they can overpower. Curiously, China, India, and Pakistan have been subdued. We think India and Pakistan are preoccupied with watching each other. They each seem to believe the fever pitch of rhetoric, and the potential use of advanced weaponry could easily make one or the other suspect that an attack by the other is imminent. We have urged them to use restraint for now."

"China, on the other hand, bears watching," TJ went on to say. "A complete and detailed NIIC assessment is contained in a brief that will be packaged for you to read during your return flight. Their stated public commitments do not match their deeds. They have stated repeatedly that they have been unaware of weapons sales from North Korea to antagonist countries on China's western borders. It is well known that missiles, munitions, and weaponry have been transshipped across China from North Korea to southwestern Asian countries for more than two years. When confronted, the Chinese say they are unaware of any such activities. They react menacingly to political snubs and slights, regardless of how innocuous they may seem, and blackball countries they perceive as non-supportive."

"So," TJ said, "the following reviews will summarize what we know of the suspected role of the Chinese in this crisis. In fact, I can be more specific. At this time there is circumstantial evidence that China, with the assistance of a nongovernmental entity, could have been behind all the events that have occurred in the last thirty days. There are additional analyses currently underway of events that happened as long ago as last year at this time. Those events that went awry for various reasons were scrutinized under the control of very careful, technically skillful Americans who employed strict procedures with strict checklists. For multiple reasons, many of those events spun out of control, and it seemed to infer there was outside influence."

John interrupted, "It gives me no pleasure to say this, but I have done a cursory overview of some of these activities and have come to a similar conclusion. In fact, it appears as though some national entity has methodically attempted to dismantle much of the integrity of our US infrastructure to include financial, economic, power production, military command and control, and petroleum transport, in an attempt to weaken our ability to respond to crises." John, turning to Jane O'Donnell, said, "I hate to say this, Madam Secretary, but it appears as though some highly organized group, with the assistance of some nation, has declared war on the United States—without our knowing it. The attack on Tehran could have simply been a diversion and an enabler to weaken US influence and resolve around the globe."

"John, you have verbalized what several of us have believed but have been reluctant to say to the president. If what we think can be proven, it makes our tasks for the next week or so doubly difficult. We have to prove what we suspect, we have to prove the US did not launch those cruise missiles, and we have to avoid a global break-out of hostilities when we finally identify the real culprits. We've got one more report to give you, John, which seems to corroborate what many of us have thought for some time. China is working hard to develop and deploy resources to support their interests throughout the southeast and southwest Asian regions. Colonel Jerry Mayhew has a final report on some emerging military technology that supports a Chinese strategy in those regions, and undermines US capabilities and influence there."

Mayhew interjected, "Thank you, Madam Secretary. Ambassador Woodard, there have been some troubling developments in the last week involving Chinese citizens and the deployment of Chinese military assets. I am going to provide you with a summary and analysis here. A final report for you to read on your way back to Tehran will be on board the aircraft, so in the interest of saving time, let it suffice to say unidentified Asian personnel have been sighted performing suspicious activities in the Willamette Valley, and they appear to be employed by Anatolia Enterprises. Before the attack on Tehran, suspicious nighttime helicopter flights between McMinnville and a point off the Oregon Coast were detected. Return flights of the helicopters showed they were delivering large containers, coincidentally the same size as the AGM-86 cruise missiles. Ten days later those same crates were detected being airlifted out to sea. Intelligence reports show the Chinese nuclear-cruise-missile-launching *Chairman Mao-Tse-Tung* received the crates and disappeared. There is sufficient evidence to confirm that the missiles came from the USS *Salem*, were modified for submarine launch at McMinnville, and were launched by the *Chairman Mao* against Tehran. Do you have any questions?"

The administrative assistant to Jane O'Donnell quietly slipped into the room and handed her a note. Jane quickly read the note, turned to the group, and said, "Ladies and gentlemen, please excuse the ambassador and me. The president wishes to speak to the ambassador on the telephone."

John was on the phone a moment later. "Hello."

"Yes, I am standing by for the president."

"Hello, this is President Chenoa. Ambassador Woodard, good afternoon."

"Good afternoon."

"I want to express my gratitude for all of your fine work during this crisis. Your actions this week have been admirable and exemplary. I want you to not give up hope that we will find who did this. Please extend my sincere sympathy to President Ramadi for the damage and death that this crisis has created. When this is all over I look forward to visiting with you and your wife in the White House. Thank you again."

"Thank you, Madam President."

32

MOUNTAIN VIEW AVIATION
MCMINNVILLE

For some, touring an art museum is a rich experience. It allows the observer to discover the many moods and creative styles of the artists whose work is on display. For others, it can be nothing more than just a quick trip through rooms and halls lined with stuff hanging on the walls. To appreciate it, you have to have an appreciation for the unusual and for creations that are not always clear in their meaning. Curiosity and a desire to broaden horizons is the fuel, but beware that the curiosity doesn't do in the cat.

KATHY greeted Trish in the reception area of the realty office in Lake Oswego at exactly 9:00 a.m. Smiling, she nodded. "You're right on time, Trish. I like that quality in a person. Punctuality has always been important to me."

"In your business, it wouldn't pay to be late, would it? Let's take my car."

Kathy picked up her purse and her notepad binder from her desk, and they walked outside and got into Trish's 2017 Porsche Carrera S. She quickly glanced inside her purse to assure her cell phone and miniature camera were in there. The weather was mild and the windows of the small sports car were open. There was the scent of summer in the air. The combination of Trish's musky perfume and the relaxing smell of new leather upholstery in the Porsche made the day seem just right for a carefree drive in the countryside. But this would not be the day for a whimsical drive through the lush Willamette Valley. Kathy's senses were finely attuned to the moment.

Trish backed out of the parking spot in the realty agency's lot and headed west towards I-5, traveling along Cruise Way past the Mormon temple. She took the Tigard exit to Highway 99W (the South Pacific Highway) toward Newberg and McMinnville. Once on 99W, the traffic became snarled, lessening somewhat after leaving Tigard. Soon the green fields and hills of the farms and vineyards came into view. Nearing Newberg after casual conversation about Trish's new Lake Oswego home, Kathy said, "Well, what do you have in store for me today? I've looked forward to seeing the finished product ever since we consummated the sale."

Trish nodded. "There have not really been that many changes to the basic structure of the hangers and outbuildings. I have, however, added high-intensity internal lighting, air conditioning for steady environmental control, physical security control measures, and fire suppression systems, and I've updated the power and water systems. I've kept all of the helicopters and the hangars, as well as the operation, pretty much the same. I have created some storage space below a couple of the hangars. I think that is all that is different."

Pretending to show no particular interest in the changes mentioned, Kathy inquired, "So what exactly is your operation all about? Are you into providing helicopters for fighting forest fires and rescue missions?"

"That and much more. You might say that we generate technical solutions to move people, equipment, and resources, to solve problems."

"Hmm, that's impressive. Do you run the operation all by yourself?"

"I have been, but lately I've acquired some assistants. If you see some Asian gentlemen running about the facility, well, let's just say that they have the technical resources to help me broaden the capabilities of the operation and facilitate my ability to respond to situations."

Kathy looked out the window as Trish steered her Porsche towards the left fork that would take her towards the coast, bypassing McMinnville. This route was the most direct path to Mountain View Aviation and the site of the Spruce Goose, which was located directly across the highway from Trish's Mountain View hangars. Within moments Trish turned left into the Mountain View Aviation site.

"Are they helping you with the management of the operation?"

"No, they are more into the technical aspects. Anyway, chances are you won't even see them. I just wanted to alert you so that it wouldn't arouse your curiosity. Just focus on the facilities if you would, please."

Kathy took that abrupt response as a decree that that subject was about to be closed. Shrugging her shoulders to indicate that the appearance of the Chinese gentlemen that Trish mentioned was of no consequence to her. "Seriously, Trish, it sounds as if you're not all that excited about your new assistants?"

"Let's just say that I'm not used to yielding my authority. Ever since.... Well, that's another story."

Kathy interjected, "I have worked with other corporations, and their CEOs and senior executives have found it useful to shed some authority, but I doubt that you're likely to lose the control and responsibility for your own operation."

"You are so right. Yes, you can delegate or give away authority, but you never concede responsibility."

Kathy nodded, staring out the window as Trish's car approached Mountain View Aviation Hangar One. Visitors to the quiet Willamette Valley venue would normally pay scant attention to its existence, as the main thrust of their passage through that region would have been to visit one of the many wine tasting vineyards, visit the Spruce Goose, continue their travels westward toward Spirit Mountain for a little gambling, or go on to Lincoln City to enjoy a day at the beach. Nothing about the exterior of Mountain View Aviation would raise even the slightest suspicion of a trained sleuth. It was an unimpressive site, which most travelers would miss on their day's mission.

Trish brought the Porsche to a stop next to the entrance of Hangar One. Appearing completely inconspicuous, only a helicopter stationed in front of the offices and hangar gave insight to the operation of the facility.

"Isn't that an Apache helicopter sitting out front of the office area?"

"You have done your homework. Do you have any idea what their primary mission is?"

"Rescue or ground support operations, I suppose. Perhaps you are called on to provide assistance for fighting forest fires during the peak fire season?"

"Yes to all that. I have also broadened their use to help me with some of my important deliveries."

Looking up at the exterior of Hangar One, Kathy exclaimed, "My, it's amazing what a little paint and some refurbishing can do for industrial buildings. When I sold these to you, I expected you might have to demolish them and start all over again. This is very impressive." Then, remembering why she was there, she said, "I think the value of these facilities and the property may well be worth 40 percent to 50 percent more than your purchase price, but I need to see more. May I take a few pictures for my staff architect?"

Trish uncomfortably said, "Yes, a few."

The two women walked around the three hanger buildings and Kathy mentally counted the number of paces it took to circumnavigate the buildings. She suspected that the buildings were enlarged in length, but she wanted to confirm her thoughts. "I think I've got enough data about the outside. May we take a look inside?"

"Follow me."

They entered a door in the center hanger building leading to the interior, which, curiously, was a small ante room with sticky carpeting that seemed designed to gently pull debris from the shoes of people passing through the room. There was a strong air conditioned, forced-air system in the room that almost tore the pages from Kathy's notebook. Kathy thought back to her technical days with the agency when she was being introduced to new, leading-edge technology development systems.

Damn, this is a clean room used for high-tech systems development to prevent dust particles from getting into sensitive electronics. Why would anyone want to go to the expense of installing clean room capabilities, unless...."

They went through a door at the end of a short corridor, entering one of the massive hangers. There were three Chinook helicopters parked in the facility, untethered from the floor, with only wheel chocks in front of and behind one set of wheels. A small auxiliary power unit was plugged into the main power receptacle of each chopper. The aircraft were pointed toward the large, closed hanger exit doors, and the cockpit entry hatch on each chopper was opened as if ready for an emergency scramble order. Kathy walked closely by one of the helicopters and allowed her gaze to scan upward toward the rafters as if she were assessing the capabilities of the building. Her gaze lowered and she looked into one of the opened chopper hatches and into the cockpit. She saw a book that looked very much like a pilot's checklist or handbook. Without being too obvious, she looked at the book for as long as she dared.

My God, it's written in Chinese or some Asian tongue.

She kept walking a few paces behind Trish. "Would you object to me seeing the new storage that you've added under the hangars, Trish?"

Trish fidgeted nervously. "I don't know that we'll have that much time. Besides, everything down there is such a mess. It is still under construction."

"Hmm, I see. Well, I guess, I'll just have to imagine what it looks like. How do you access the storage areas?"

"We have hydraulically operated, sliding, reinforced aluminum floor panels."

"Do you mean that you have to open the entire floor every time you want to access the storage areas?"

"Heavens no, there is a stairway access as well as an elevator access. I did have to build it to code, and I wasn't prepared to use a parachute every time I went below."

"It is probably none of my business, but what sort of stuff would you contract to deliver?"

"Let us just say that I do some government work."

Kathy smiled. "That would be strictly a US-contract affiliation, right?"

"Primarily; I suppose that would be our primary contractual engagement."

At that moment a young Caucasian man in overhauls walked out of a nondescript door in the corner of the hanger and walked up to Trish, saying, "Ma'am, there are some gentlemen here to see you.

They say it's urgent."

"Tell them I'll be right there." She turned to Kathy. "This may take a few minutes. I'll point out a few improvement features you can evaluate while I take a few moments to meet with them. That will give you a little time to take a look through the other two hangars."

After a quick tour of the middle hangar, Trish excused herself and started to head in the direction of the offices.

"As you know, the other hangars are located on either side of this one. Feel free to go over there and, as I say, look over the property. When you're done, come on over to the offices. My meeting should be over by then and we can head back to Portland."

Kathy nodded.

This is too good to be true. She must not suspect a thing or she wouldn't leave me here where her new storage has been installed. I wonder where the stairs to the lower level are. Well, what do you know, I'll bet that door over there with the exit sign above it would be what I'm looking for, or she has a secret entry located somewhere else.

Kathy made a beeline for the exit door. Upon opening it, she noted a short hallway with an outside door leading to the next hangar and a second door located adjacent to it on the south hallway wall. When she opened it, she discovered a rectangular platform with what appeared to be an elevator, and a flight of stairs to its immediate left.

I think I'll take the stairs. I don't want to set off bells and whistles in case she has some sort of alarm or indicator attached to the elevator that she can monitor in her office.

She slowly and quietly descended the steel steps toward the floor some fifteen to eighteen feet below. The massive floor seemed to cover the full width and length of the hangar. The entire area was dimly lit and looked unoccupied. She reached the bottom two steps and stopped short when she spotted some long, winged vehicles that looked like twelve-foot-long airplanes with wingspans of approximately the same length.

Oh, my God, missiles! Let's see: one, two, three…uh, I count eight. I wonder if there are any identifying symbols or placards attached to them. Sure enough, there is a small plaque affixed to each one. Let me see what they say.

On a small, brass-like plaque was an inscription. It read:

**Components and sensors are provided by Lambert Aerospace Company, Richardson Corporation, and Hairston Airplane Company. Systems engineering and Integration supplied by Anatolia Enterprises, McMinnville, Oregon.
All parts made in the USA.**

Well, that just about clinches the deal. Lee will be very eager to hear about this. Now the question is: who in the world is responsible for launching these deadly little babies, and from where? I also wonder what the next target is and when it will be hit. I have to find a way to get hold of Lee, ASAP. I need to get pictures of these so that I can prove to my contacts what I've seen.

Taking her camera out of her purse and carefully setting her purse on the concrete floor, she started snapping photos of the impressive display before her. Suddenly she sensed that it was time to leave. Quickly stooping over to retrieve her purse, she stepped on the strap.

Damn, I'm getting so clumsy. If I'm not careful, I'm going to rip the strap off the purse or end up falling on my ass, or both. What's that?

Kathy wheeled around and started to head up the stairs. From somewhere above her, she heard the sound of voices. Quickly she mounted the stairs and exited the hangar through the west door. Outside again, she delayed a moment and then reached for the door to reenter.

"Ah, I see you are through with your assessment."

"Yes, I am. I took a quick look at the west hangar and was just about to come back to meet up with you over at the office. I suppose everything that I saw at the west hangar is duplicated in the east hangar."

"That is correct, Kathy." Trish turned towards the three Chinese men who accompanied her. "Kathy, these are the three gentlemen I told you about. I call them the Chinese generals who tell me what to do."

Smiling, Kathy nodded slightly to the men and returned her attention to Trish, who then said, "I'll be taking Ms. Moen back to Portland, but I should be able to return in two to three hours. Kathy, do you need to use the ladies room?"

Kathy checked her watch, and nodded affirmatively. "It's noon now, and I have to make a call to check in with my office. I'll tell them that I'll be back in plenty of time for my next appointment."

"Well, you know where the office is. Why don't you run over there to use the facility. That will give me a chance to show my colleagues what they can do to occupy themselves while I'm gone."

"Good. I'll make my calls and then meet you at the car?"

"Fine, I won't be but a minute."

Kathy headed in the direction of the offices while speed dialing Lee at his home.

His phone rang a few times and rolled over to voicemail. Lee picked it up and apologized for not being more prompt. "How did things go?"

"Meet me at my office at 2:00. I have something imperative to pass on to you. I'll give you details there."

"What happened? Anything interesting?"

"Do the names Wah Hu, Chung Mai, and Yee Hah mean anything to you?"

Before he could answer, she said, "I saw some missiles."

"Dammit, Kathy, you be careful."

"It's too late. The milk has already been spilled and I suspect that the cats are starting to gather."

Slowly she fingered the strap on her purse. Her face blanched when she discovered that the little trinket she had attached to it was gone. "Oh shit! I think that I just messed up big time."

"What happened? What did you do?"

"I think that I inadvertently left a trinket from my purse in the storage area where Trish has her missiles parked. Shit! Of all the dumb luck. I'll either have to come up with some pretext to go back and look for it, or I'll just have to hope that they don't spot it."

"You better get out of there. Should I alert AJ?"

"No, this is not that serious, yet. I'll be okay. You just make sure you're at my place at 2:00, okay?"

In the basement, the missing trinket had indeed been discovered. Wah Hu had found it next to one of the missiles. He held up the incriminating evidence for all to see.

"So, what now, Ms. Knight? What is your plan now? It appears your friend is either overly curious or is not who she seems. Regardless of who or what she is, she may now know too much for her own good."

Trish nodded. This was suddenly becoming more complicated than she had anticipated. "Yeah, I guess you're right. She just may, but I wonder why…. I've known her for some time and she has never done or said anything to arouse my suspicions. I will admit, however, she's been very curious about my affairs lately. So, we ought not to take any risks with what we're doing here."

Yee Hah said, "Wah Hu thinks that we need to find a way to take care of business before she reveals to anyone what she knows or suspects about what she has seen here."

"Well, I have to get her back to her office in Lake Oswego before 5:00. She has an appointment, or so she says."

Wah Hu checked his watch, nodding his head as he did so. "My watch indicates that it is 12:15. How long will it take you to drive your friend to her office?"

Trish shrugged her shoulders. "It shouldn't take more than an hour. Why?"

Wah Hu shook his head in exasperation, mumbling, "Not enough time to take care of business before her appointment."

"Besides, how would it look if something happened to her before the appointment and she does not appear for the meeting? It would arouse suspicion. So, if we're going to do something, it will have to be after she has that appointment."

Wah Hu nodded, and smiled. "If we could find a way to do it as soon as she is finished with her client.... We could stage an automobile accident. That way nobody would suspect foul play." Chuckling, he continued, "It is Chinese cure for what ails a snoopy cat."

Trish shook her head in exasperation. "That's all well and good, but how are we going to stage an automobile accident?"

Again, a sinister smile played over Wah Hu's face. "Chinese have way of making things happen. Not to worry, Ms. Knight. Wah Hu will take care of everything. You just get her to her office without causing her to be suspicious, and Wah Hu will do his part."

Trish glared at him, hissing as she responded, "You just remember that I'm driving Ms. Moen. Don't get any ideas about trying to kill two birds with one stone."

"Why, Ms. Knight, what would make you suspect me of doing something so evil?"

"Isn't getting rid of people your forte?"

"True, but Wah Hu never get rid of people that are of use to him, and at this moment you are still quite valuable to our cause."

"So, I take it that you will move to eliminate Kathy sometime after her real estate showing."

"Yes, I follow you to where you take Ms. Moen. From there,

Wah Hu will figure out what to do."

"Well okay, but just make sure that you don't do anything that will cause suspicion. I still suspect that Lee and Kathy are better acquainted than I had originally thought."

"Lee? Who is this Lee you speak of?"

"He's a personal friend, and no, we have nothing to worry about with him. He's about as dangerous as dynamite without a blasting cap."

Wah Hu smiled. "Hmm, why do you hold him in such high regard and describe him as being so inept?"

Trish smiled devilishly, mumbling, "Let's just say that he has other assets that more than make up for what he lacks in the hero category."

"Ah, so, Wah Hu understand perfectly."

"Hey, I just had an inspiration. I have some business to attend to in Lake Oswego regarding the new home I purchased there, so what if I were to arrange to meet Kathy after her appointment, for drinks and dinner?"

Wah Hu smiled, nodding his head. "Yes, and you could slip a little sleeping powder into her drink. When she leaves to go home, she'll be drowsy and…. My, my, Ms. Knight, we will have taken care of the problem and nobody will be the wiser."

"I'd best get a move on or she is going to suspect that something is up. You're going to follow me?"

Wah Hu nodded. "Yes, Wah Hu will be close at hand. It is always nice to confirm that a problem has been eliminated."

"So, when Kathy and I part company after dinner, my part is done, right?"

"Yes, Wah Hu will take over from there. All you have to do is pretend to be surprised when you learn of Ms. Moen's fatal accident."

33

AGENT BINGO
OREGON CITY

Suspicion is sometimes a good thing, as long as it is not accompanied by paranoia. Not taking the time to read between the lines is often the easiest way to miss the true meaning.

LEE was deep in thought and feeling like something was very wrong with the cavalier manner in which Kathy assessed her situation at Mountain View Aviation.

I don't like to feel this way about Trish, but right now I don't think that I can trust her any further than I could throw her. If she or her henchmen find that trinket from Kathy's purse, Kathy could very easily be in deep trouble. I think I should overrule Kathy on this one and get hold of AJ, although I'm not sure what good that's going to do.

After dialing AJ's cell phone number, Lee waited impatiently for her to answer. Finally a soft, melodic voice intoned, "Hello, this is AJ speaking."

"AJ, this is Lee Grady. I know the name isn't going to mean much to you, but—"

AJ interrupted, "Quite to the contrary, Lee. Kathy has spoken of you. Is the purpose of your call related to Kathy?"

"Yes it is. She has uncovered something out in McMinnville that I think could put her in harm's way."

"You mean that she finally made the connection to tour Mountain View Aviation?"

"She did—and more. I'm afraid she uncovered something that the people out there don't want out in the open."

"You mean something related to your trip out of town?"

"Something along that line, yeah, but that isn't the only issue here."

"I think you had better fill me in. Don't leave out one detail, Lee. Kathy's life might just depend on it."

"We need to meet."

"I could be available in less than an hour."

"Good! What place would work for you? I was coming towards Portland later today if that is any help."

"How about the Marriott Lounge on First Avenue?"

"I'll see you there in forty-five minutes to an hour."

Later at the Marriott Lounge, Lee related a chronology of what had been happening since he found the microchip on his floor. After telling AJ about Kathy discovering the cruise missiles in the storage area under Hangar One at Mountain View Aviation, he discussed Kathy's encounter with three Asian individuals who were known terrorists and were now in the employ of Anatolia Enterprises. The terrorists were named Wah Hu, Chung Mai, and Yee Hah. AJ started plotting her next move.

From what Lee told me, I would guess that one or more of those

Chinese bastards will probably try to do something to Kathy after she finishes with her real estate showing—to avoid arousing suspicion and to eliminate their problem on their terms. They always like to make their efforts to eliminate obstacles appear to stem from natural causes or at least unsuspicious accidents. I wonder what I would do if I were them. Kathy is in fantastic shape, so that probably rules out the use of Pentothal to induce what would appear to be a heart attack. The use of insulin to induce insulin shock would appear suspicious unless they planned to.... No, it can't be that obvious. I think that I need to call in a favor from my contact in the FBI. We need to be at Kathy's office prior to the time she has to take her client out on that real estate showing. It probably won't involve more than a couple of agents. Lee said that he was supposed to be at her office at 2:00 and she has a real estate showing at 5:00. So, if something is going to happen, it will occur after 5:00. I'd guess that it will be nearer to 6:00. Well, I'll just have to see what I can do to help turn this into a happy ending. I'd best be on the lookout for those Chinese assassins as well. This is going to be one time that they are not going to succeed in snuffing out some innocent soul. I have to be prepared to get her sequestered in a safe house so that we can put her in protective custody. Things are just a little too hot for Kathy at the present time, and may get hotter. It may be that Kathy will no longer be working with Lee on this case. He'll just have to get used to working with me.

34

SETTING THE TRAP
LAKE OSWEGO

Sometimes people make an appointment to drop in, while others just drop in. Hopefully the visit is not life threatening.

DURING the drive back to Lake Oswego, Trish broke the silence. "You know, Kathy, I have a little business to take care of in Lake Oswego. How would you like to meet for drinks and dinner after your real estate showing? I promise to not keep you out late."

Kathy nodded, somewhat taken aback by the suggestion.

I wonder what Trish has up her sleeve now. I wonder if she suspects that Lee and I are seeing each other. I doubt it, as I have made it very clear that Lee and I are just acquaintances. Still, a girl can't be too careful.

"That would be nice. I didn't have anything planned for this evening anyway. Do you think that we could just make it drinks? I'm not hungry, and besides, I have an early day tomorrow. I think that I'd like to head for the barn about 7:30."

"That would be just fine with me. I'm not hungry either. Come to think of it, I have an early day tomorrow as well. I have a lot of things to do before I take off for Greece in a couple of days."

"How long do you plan to be gone?"

"I should be able to take care of business in about a week, hopefully less."

"That's nice. Let's see, I should be done with my appointment about 6:00. Do you want to meet at my office?"

"Perfect, that was what I was about to suggest."

Kathy smiled. "It's a date then. I'll plan on being back in the office by 6:00. Besides, I don't think that my client is going to be too thrilled with the place I'm showing."

"What's the matter? Is it too pricy?"

"I'm afraid so, but sometimes you have to show the high-end stuff before you bring the buyer down to reality."

Trish nodded. "You seem to be able to read your clients very well."

Kathy smiled as she let her mind wander.

You are so right, Trish. If I didn't know you as well as I do, I could very easily be walking into a trap. I've had you figured out almost from the start. You are one self-centered witch, and you'd do in your mother to make a buck or two. What's more, you'd probably sacrifice the safety of the citizens of this great country to make that buck as well.

35

DAMAGE CONTROL IV
TEHRAN

Solving a puzzle often involves connecting the dots. In connecting the dots in an international puzzle, one has to rely upon the rumor mill, an abnormal occurrence someplace in the world, or unusual sightings. Some say that you need to look for something that doesn't belong.

AMBASSADOR Woodard was sitting at his desk when Captain Aref was announced. Casually he checked his watch.

Hmm, right on time. That Iranian son of a gun is punctual, concise in speech and manner, and provides what appears to be good insight as to what is going on. Above and beyond that, he appears to really want to help us solve this mystery. I wonder what he has for me today.

Rising to greet his visitor, the ambassador extended his hand. "Captain Aref, you are punctual as usual. That is a good quality."

"Thank you, Ambassador Woodard."

"So what do you have for me?"

Captain Aref smiled as he took a seat in front of Woodard's desk. "I wish that I could tell you some specifics such as who did it and why. All I can do is tell you what my sources tell me and let you try to make sense of it."

Ambassador Woodard nodded. "Anything that you can share will be appreciated."

"Well, first of all, when you want to solve a mystery, it is usually a good practice to follow the money. Following the money, in this case a quest for control of Middle Eastern oil, you have only to look at three major players."

Woodard nodded. "You must be referring to China, Russia, and the United States."

"That is correct, but you have to realize that my country's number one suspect would be China. Russia demonstrates its willingness to supply us with arms and ignores our efforts to become a major nuclear power. Your country would never, in my opinion, launch a missile unless it were a prelude to launching a full-scale attack on my country. Besides, the US isn't going to let that attack be a single probe. Considering the attack it launched on Iraq, twenty-four missiles would only be a drop in the bucket in terms of what it would hit us with before launching an invasion."

"So, in your opinion, that only leaves the Chinese. Would you mind sharing what might substantiate such a theory?"

"Well, for starters, the Chinese were very fearful that the Bush administration would invade Iran to control the oil. Additionally, a lot of activity was noted in Burma—activity that indicates, in retrospect, that the attack on Tehran might have been launched from there. There has also been a lot of talk out there pointing to Chinese involvement."

"Is that rumor or fact?"

"Again, this is only rumor, but there is also some credibility to suspect the involvement of an American corporation."

"This is only rumor, but the word on the street is that Anatolia Enterprises is up to its ass in this venture. Additionally, we have strong suspicion that the Chinese have an involvement, as you also suspect. It appears that the missiles are of American origin and those same missiles turned up missing from an American stockpile."

Woodard sat back in his chair, his hands clasped behind his head. "This is all very interesting, Captain Aref. I will pass along your thoughts. By the way, consider this as food for thought: did it ever occur to you that even if you hadn't found that little plate that pointed the finger directly at the United States as the culprit, the international community would already have suspected us of doing something like that because of your supposed nuclear presence and rumored buildup? In the meantime, please continue keeping your ear to the floor, so to speak, and feel free to meet with me anytime that anything significant comes your way. I will reciprocate when something comes my way. We don't have a huge amount of time to get to the bottom of this, do we?"

"You have my word, Ambassador Woodard. I have close personal ties to the United States and would do almost anything to help clear up this mess and find out who the real perpetrator is."

Woodard smiled, offering, "I appreciate those words, Captain. We're on the same page."

36

HELLO JANE
TEHRAN

Putting a puzzle together involves laying out all the pieces and then trying to figure out where the pieces fit so as to see the big picture.

CAPTAIN Aref had scarcely closed the door before Woodard's secure phone rang. He answered and heard the familiar, melodic voice of Jane O'Donnell on the other end. "John, this is Jane O'Donnell."

"Madam Secretary, I am so glad that you called."

"Why be so formal, John? Lighten up a little and let me have it. I assume that you have some news."

"I just finished meeting with Captain Aref, the Iranian captain I've told you about. He's the one who found the plate that ties the United States to this hideous attack."

"Yes, and what did he have to say?"

"I don't have verifiable proof, but the Iranian government believes that we both need to keep an eye on the Chinese. Who is it from the CIA you meet with in DC, who is involved with this matter?"

"That would be Mayhew, Jerry Mayhew. I believe that you know him."

"Hell yes, he's a longtime friend and fraternity brother of mine. We go back a long, long way. So, Jane, you might want to get hold of Mayhew and tell him to keep an eye out for a trail leading to the Chinese. If my informant is correct, we might be looking to thwart an attack on some major target on mainland USA. By the way, is Mayhew a direct contact or is he—"

"No, I have established contact with him through TJ…that would be Thelma Massadoti, at the NSC. I suppose you know her as well?"

"It's a small world, isn't it, Jane? Yes, I met her."

"She's very smart, too, John."

"So she is. Well, pass the word along and don't forget to keep me in the loop. I think something big is about to break."

"We're way ahead of you, John. Mayhew and Lee Grady, our agents working out of Portland, Oregon, are on top of it."

"You are kidding me. I personally know Lee Grady as well. I feel better now that I know we have people working on this who I would be willing to go to war with. Not to change the subject, Jane, but what sort of political implications are there?"

"Between you and me, John, there is a lot less saber rattling going on in Washington these days. I think that Bush was content to pass this mess on to Obama, who was unsuccessful solving it, and now it is a President Chenoa problem. Well, let's just say that she appears to have a much different agenda than previous administrations. It appears that business will be conducted far differently in the

Oval Office."

"I meant are there any political implications coming out of the election? It appears that the economy is suffering terribly."

"It's funny that you should ask. The economy is a real hot topic right now. As you might imagine, both parties are in a real dog fight to determine who has the best plan. I have been instructed to try to build bridges to 'our enemies.'"

"How is Paul Dryan, you know, the other candidate for president, reacting?"

"He appears to be supportive."

"That's a surprise. I thought Dryan would be willing to go to war over that issue."

"He is, if problems in Iran escalate. I don't think that he really believes that we'll be able to find a way to negotiate our way out of this mess, but he's willing to step aside and not make waves. Chenoa is going to get huge points for being perceived as a person who can bring people together to resolve a problem. Dryan doesn't seem to want to fight a war over trying to prove that rattling a few cages is the answer. I think he is tired of previous approaches, proving to the world that we go to the mat to stop terrorism."

"Well, no political point of view expressed here, but between you, me, and the fence post, I hope we can find a way to resolve all of this without having to create another front in the Middle East. We're already way overextended."

"Tell me something that any rational person doesn't know. Be safe and keep in touch."

37

SPRINGING THE TRAP
LAKE OSWEGO

*Only a watchful eye can keep an innocent victim from falling
prey to a carefully set trap. Once the trap has been sprung,
a decision has to be made as to what to do with the prey.
Do they run free or do you offer sanctuary?*

TRISH pulled up in front of Kathy's office in Lake Oswego at
2:00, giving Kathy ample time to prepare for her 5:00 p.m. appointment. A quick glance into the driver's side rearview mirror confirmed
what she would hope to see. She smiled.

*Good, Wah Hu is parking down the block behind me. He'll be able
to keep track of what is going on with no problem at all. Maybe I should
call him on his cell after Kathy gets out of the car and fill him in about
my plans to have a drink or two with her after she gets done with her*

client. Hmm, I would imagine that I should tell him that she'll probably be returning about 6:00 to meet me. I think that I'll suggest that Kathy and I go to Manzana. It's just down the street and has plenty of parking. Is there anything else I need to tell him? Nah, that little shit can figure it out.

Smiling at Kathy as she prepared to get out of the 2017 Porsche, Trish reminded Kathy of their rendezvous to have a couple of drinks after Kathy's appointment.

"So, I'm supposed to meet you here at 6:00, right?"

"That works for me, Trish. Any ideas about where we should go?"

"I was thinking about Manzana. There is ample parking there, the tariff for drinks is reasonable, and the ambiance is superior. What do you think?"

"That would have been my choice. Why don't I just meet you there? I'll have to stop by my office after the appointment, but I shouldn't arrive there any later than 6:05, um, 6:10 at the latest."

"That works for me. If I get there before you, I'll probably be at least one up on you."

"What do you like to drink?"

"I'm not too picky, but a good margarita always hits the spot."

"You're in luck. They serve damn good margaritas. Usually you have to go to a good Mexican restaurant to get a good margarita, but they do a decent job."

"Okay then, I'll see you at 6:00 or so."

As soon as Kathy left Trish's car, Trish hurriedly dialed the cell phone number of Wah Hu. After a brief report about the plans that she and Kathy had made, she pulled out of her parking spot and made her way towards her destination to see the loan office at Banner Bank.

Shit, I better get a move on. I sure as hell don't want to queer the deal for the temporary financing of my new home. I only have one more job to do, and that is to figure a way to slip Kathy the sleeping powder. Once that's been done, the rest is up to nature. Wah Hu will confirm that.... Hello, Grim Reaper. Getting rid of the competition and a fucking spy doesn't hurt my feelings one bit.

AJ drove slowly by Kathy's office. Arriving moments after Trish departed, she wanted to survey the landscape before settling on a parking spot. She quickly placed a call to Kathy's cell phone and received an abbreviated update on the visit to McMinnville—what she had seen and the follow-on meeting at Manzana's at 6:00 p.m. She informed Kathy that she would be close by and available for further talks after the meeting, and also informed her that plans were afoot to close in on Trish's empire. Scanning the street for a parking place, her eyes came to rest on a form sitting behind the wheel of a 2016 Honda Accord that was parked about a block from the front door of Kathy's real estate office.

It is a good thing that I told Lee not to keep his appointment with Kathy. We agreed that I would receive Kathy's update. No sense in muddying the waters with multiple reports.

That Honda parked over there, I wonder.... I think I'll drive by and check it out. Not fancy, but that Asian fellow sitting behind the wheel does have good taste. I've always liked Hondas. Trish has already been here and gone. I wonder what part she has to play in this little drama. I can't imagine that the Asian guy is going to be real overt about trying to get rid of Kathy. I'll bet that Trish has some sort of part to play. I'll just have to wait and see what unfolds.

Spotting a parking spot up ahead, she wheeled her BMW into the empty space. Once she was satisfied that she was parked so as to not get bumped when the cars in front and in back of her pulled out, she reached for her cell phone and pushed the ten keys that would connect her with Jack Maken, her FBI contact.

"Jack, this is AJ. Where are you?"

A deep, resonating voice at the other end replied, "I'm just about to pull into Lake Oswego. I'm coming from the north, from the Portland office."

"Good, do you have anyone with you?"

"Just as you requested, I brought Bill Vogt. You remember him, don't you?"

"Yes, I remember him. Wasn't he…?"

"Yes, he was with me when we brought down that interstate drug operation a couple of years ago."

"Yeah, I recall. What say that I brighten your day a tad bit?"

"Well, do I have to beg or are you going to fill me in before winter comes?"

"I think I've spotted a person of interest."

"And just who would that be, pray tell?"

"I've spotted an Asian fellow who might be from Anatolia Enterprises in McMinnville. Would you check a license plate number, FJQ 1432, for a 2016 Honda? Please get back to me as soon as possible."

"If the license checks out…it sure does! In fact, he's more than a person of interest. He has become a priority. So where is he now?"

"He's parked about a block from the front of Kathy Moen's office. I already told you where her office is, didn't I?"

"You did. If it's all the same to you, my partner and I are going to take care of the Asian guy. Suddenly this little adventure has turned into something more important than trying to keep some real estate agent from closing a bad deal. Are you going to be able to take care of the rest of the operation on your own if we bail on you?"

"No problem. I'm parked down the street from Kathy's office. As soon as she gets back from that real estate showing, things should start to hum. I'll be prepared for just about anything if you can get rid of the Asian connection."

"Consider it done."

"By the way, I have taken the liberty of contacting the agent protection program for agents that are in deep shit. I'll get back to you as soon as I see what unfolds here."

Jack chuckled. "You really like this Trish person, don't you?"

"I don't like anyone who goes after one of our agents. I'll talk to you in a few."

After AJ had concluded her meeting with Kathy, she dialed Lee's cell phone on her way back to her parked car. "Hello, Lee?"

"AJ, what's up?"

"Where are you?"

"I'm parked two blocks north of Kathy's office at the curb."

"Good, stand by. I got the debrief from Kathy. Lee, you were right. Stay right where you are. I might need your assistance. I think that Kathy is in big trouble. Kathy is meeting Trish at the Manzana at 6:00 or shortly after."

At 6:10 Kathy strolled into Manzana. Approaching the reception booth, she inquired, "Has Trish Knight shown up yet? I'm supposed to meet her for drinks."

The hostess nodded, responding cheerfully, "I just seated her. Please follow me and I'll take you to her table."

After being shown to Trish's table and exchanging a few pleasantries, Trish inquired, "So how did your appointment go? Are you headed for the million dollar club again?"

"No, just as I suspected, the price of the home was beyond their means. I managed to obtain another appointment with them, though. Now would be the time for me to wrap them up and put them into their affordable dream house. By the way, I've done a preliminary evaluation of the Mountain View Property and it appears that it is in fact going to be valued no less than 50 percent more than you paid. I also did a search of potential buyers for that kind of property. There are three corporations that are interested in facilities like yours. I will research them further."

For the next thirty minutes, Kathy and Trish discussed the real estate market while finishing off a couple of margaritas.

Suddenly, Kathy whispered, "Why don't you get me another one of those little devils while I hit the ladies room? This time get it on the rocks. I don't want to flirt with an ice headache. I'm buying, Trish. That's the least I can do for all that you've done today."

"So what was so special about what I did?"

"You provided the transportation, and with gas prices the way they are, that's not a small deal. Anyway, it's my treat and I won't take no for an answer."

Kathy had only been gone three minutes or so before the waitress brought the drinks. After the waitress had placed the drinks on the table, Trish casually opened a small paper bag, no larger than an Equal or Splenda packet, and poured the contents into Kathy's drink. Carefully she stirred the drink so that the sleeping powder would disappear as it dissolved into what Trish hoped would be a knockout punch.

There, that should take care of my end of the deal. In about thirty minutes, Kathy is going to be feeling very sleepy. I think I should suggest that we finish the drinks ASAP. I'll tell her that I have to get back to McMinnville for a meeting. I hope Wah Hu is in position.

Twenty minutes later, Kathy and Trish exited the lounge and headed for their cars.

"Are you okay, Kathy? You seem to be a bit unsteady."

"I'm okay. I'm just a bit tired. Shit, all of a sudden all I want to do is go to bed."

Trish smiled. "I hope you don't have plans for a romantic evening. Then again, what more could a guy want than a gal who wants to hit the sack."

"Well, you never know. As tired as I am, my guy should be able to just about have his way with me. Thanks for meeting me for drinks. I'll be in touch."

38

A LONG DRIVE HOME
LAKE OSWEGO

A meandering drive along the Willamette River through Lewis and Clark territory can be a pleasant entry into the throat of Portland's downtown high rises. Then again, it can be a short plunge into the abyss of unconsciousness.

BY the time Kathy had reached the intersection of SW Riverside Drive and SW Midvale Road, her white Mazda was weaving back and forth between the two northbound lanes. A continuation of Pacific Highway or Highway 43 from West Linn, the scenic artery that essentially connected Oregon City to Portland, meandered beside the Willamette River.

AJ had fallen in behind Kathy's car almost immediately after Kathy had bid Trish farewell in the parking garage across from Manzana. Now a scant three car lengths behind, she was too engrossed in a telephone conversation with FBI Agent Jack Maken to take immediate note of Kathy's erratic driving. A hundred yards behind AJ, Lee intently followed in his car.

"So, Jack, did you get our boy?"

"Yes we did. His name is Wah Hu and he'll be out of circulation for a long, long time. How are you doing?"

"Good, I'm following Kathy as we speak. Jack, she's all over the road. I've got to hang up. She could be in trouble."

Up ahead, just as Kathy's car passed Greenwood, an access street to the Lewis and Clark campus, it suddenly veered to the right. AJ watched in horror as Kathy's car plunged down an embankment towards the railroad tracks running beside the Willamette River.

Holy shit, what in the hell happened to Kathy? The way she was driving, it was almost like she was completely stoned or fell asleep at the wheel!

AJ brought her car to a stop at the point where Kathy's car seemed to disappear down the embankment, quickly dialing 911. Lee's car came to a screeching halt behind AJ's. He turned on his emergency flashers and leaped from his car, racing to AJ's car door. She was on the phone.

"We have an emergency here. Get your asses up the Pacific Highway ASAP. I'm parked just north of Greenwood. A car just disappeared down an embankment. I'm headed in that direction to see if I can help."

At that point, Lee spun around and raced down the embankment.

The operator answering the call commanded, "Stay on the line! You have to stay on the line!"

"I don't have time to talk to you. I'll put my cell in my pocket so that the line is open. The rest is up to you, and get that ambulance and the fire department out here as quickly as you can. If that car ruptured its gas tank going over the embankment, all hell is going to break loose any moment. There's not a second to waste."

AJ jammed her phone in her coat pocket as she peered over the embankment and followed Lee down the steep slope.

Her car went headlong into that pole below. Thank God the terrain isn't too rough. We should be able to get to her car without too much trouble. Oops, watch your step, AJ, or there will be two victims to take care of. Just a few more steps and I'll be there. Thank God Lee is already there. Shit, she appears to be unconscious. What's that smell? Damn, just as suspected, her gas tank must have ruptured. Well, no time to worry about that now. We have to get her out of her car before it blows.

By the time AJ and Lee had reached the car, a small fire had started. Grunting as he jerked on the driver's side door, he was able to pry it open wide enough to reach in and start to pull the inert body slumped over the steering wheel towards him. He detached the seat belt that probably saved her life—if she was still alive.

Christ, Kathy's unconscious and she has blood oozing from what appear to be lacerations on her forehead and scalp. My God, lady, it looks like you've also broken your nose, if all that blood running down your lip and chin is any indication. Let's see, my first aid training tells me that there's no need to worry about anything until I get you out of harm's way. I don't have time to worry about spinal injuries or blood loss. This may hurt and it may fuck you up for good, but I've got to get you out of here before this car of yours blows.

"AJ, give me a hand here."

Lee and AJ grunted as they started gently pulling Kathy backward through the small opening in the door by securing a hold under her armpits. After getting Kathy out of the car, they started to drag her up the hill, away from the burning car.

Kathy moaned.

"Thank God, you're not dead. You'll just have to bear with me, honey. We've got to get you out of here. Hold on, Kathy, here we go. Oomph…that's better. Now to drag you over there behind those trees and rocks so we can be protected from the blast and the fireball that's sure to come any second now."

Moments later, Lee and AJ, having carefully stretched Kathy out on the ground behind the only cover they could find nearby, knelt down to cover her from the explosion that they knew was coming.

Boom! Boom! The explosions from Kathy's car made the ground shake, the noise deafening, as a fireball engulfed Kathy's car.

I sure hope that ambulance is close. We don't have much time I'm afraid.

Hovering over Kathy, Lee and AJ went through the initial first aid steps for an accident victim. Lee applied pressure to the open wound and her nose while AJ instinctively bent over and checked for a pulse and made sure that she was still breathing.

Good, she has a good, steady pulse and her breathing pattern appears to be steady. Damn it to Hell, let's please let that ambulance get here so that we can get some assistance. This untrained medic needs some assistance very badly. This is one patient who I don't want to lose.

A voice shouted from somewhere above, "Hello down there. We're on our way with the gurney. Is the victim alive?"

"Yes, damn it, she's alive, but we're in need of some help ASAP."

"Hang on, we're coming."

Moments later the EMT duo arrived on the scene. "There are two guys up there directing traffic. They said something about being from the FBI."

Seeing that the EMT people were in charge, AJ turned and motioned to Lee to follow her.

Upon reaching a secluded point, AJ said, "I have to contact the Agent Protection people. Under no circumstances are you to say anything that might shed any light on Kathy's identity."

Returning to where Kathy was being attended to, Lee knelt down beside her and quietly said, "You did a great job. I'll stay with you as long as I'm needed."

Looking at the EMT, Lee inquired, "What hospital are you taking her to?"

"Providence. We will follow you."

AJ quickly interjected, "Make no calls about the identity of the victim. This is now a federal crime scene and you don't need to know anything more than you already know. Oh, by the way, as far as you are concerned, she is DOA."

Turning to Lee as they headed toward their cars, AJ said, "I'm going to call the APP to inform them of the accident. They will be at the hospital when we get here. Kathy will disappear."

39

A NEW PARTNER
PORTLAND

A partner is a complement to—or supplements—the efforts or performance of the other. Stated differently, a partner completes the other. A partnership is like a good marriage. Working harmoniously with each other, they anticipate and react without regard to their own personal well-being.

AT Providence hospital, after insuring that Kathy's injuries were not life threatening, Lee and AJ sat in a secluded waiting area. Lee inquired, "AJ, I need to know specifically what is going to become of Kathy now that she is in the custody of the Agent Protection Program."

AJ responded evasively, "That is for the agent protection people to know."

"Does that mean that I won't be able to see her?"

"That is about the size of it, Lee. In fact, I doubt that you'll be seeing anything of her for quite some time. Then again, that is somewhat up in the air."

"You say that she is in the Agent Protection Program. Will I be able to know where she is being kept?"

"You have a right to ask, but I, on the other hand, can only tell you that it is too hot for Kathy right now. Not even I know where she is going. With Wah Hu in custody and Trish and those other Chinese thugs running loose, her life isn't worth a plug nickel. Until we can nail them and put them away, she will have to remain in the Agent Protection Program so that we, I mean they, can keep a constant eye on her. The program is designed for her safety. No sense allowing her to be in harm's way."

Lee slammed his fist on the table. "Fuck! That fucking Trish struck again, huh?"

"Yeah, but with Wah Hu out of the equation, she's probably starting to hear footsteps."

"So, I guess that means that I'm working alone, huh?"

AJ smiled knowingly. "Not for long. I guess you'll just have to learn to get along with me."

Lee chuckled, "That won't be such a tough assignment." Studying her carefully, he cautiously inquired, "So does that mean that it's official?"

"If you mean that you and I are going to be working together, the answer is yes. Is that going to bother you?"

"No."

"Good. You and I should get along fine."

"I suppose you could put it that way."

"How else could I put it? Look, Lee, we have a job to do. The crisis still exists. I know that I am different than Kathy. However, I think that you will find that I am very good at what I do. You take my back, and I'll take yours."

AJ paused for a moment.

Lee studied AJ for a moment. "So where do we start, AJ?"

"We don't start anywhere until you get hold of Mayhew. You need to find out if it's time to take Trish down. If we don't do it now, we could be in for a long siege."

"I'll take care of that shortly, AJ, but for now, do you suppose that we can just sit back and reflect on where we are and where we are going?"

Maybe you should see what Mayhew has to say before I comment. We may have more important things to do than have a discussion. It's getting late. You should call Mayhew."

"Okay partner, you've got my attention. I'll make the call to Mayhew."

"Sounds good to me, and tell him while you're at it that old AJ would sure like to be a fly in the corner when Trish gets taken down. That bitch should have to swing from the highest rafters."

"That's a bit harsh, but I know where you're coming from. Would you like to be in on the conversation with Mayhew?"

"Absolutely. Tell me where and when."

40

TIME TO TAKE
HER DOWN
OREGON CITY

*What goes up will eventually come down—London
bridges, kingdoms, and even Humpty Dumpty.*

THIRTY minutes later, Lee depressed the final number of Jerry
Mayhew's cell phone number. After a brief pause, it rang once, twice,
three times.

"Hello, you, this is me. We're encrypted now." After pushing the
encryption button on their respective phones, Lee and Mayhew were
connected.

"Lee, how are you?"

"I'm okay. I'm here with AJ. You are on speaker phone and I
have an update for you. First, Wah Hu has been neutralized. Second,

Kathy has been in an accident and taken into the Agent Protection Program and has been reported as DOA to local authorities."

"Is she okay?"

"Yes. Third, we know that Trish is housing the missiles under Hangar One."

"Jerry, this is AJ. Lee and I are ready for our next task."

"Lee, I am so sorry about Kathy. As for the next task, I feel that we have to move to take down Trish."

"Jerry, that is a good idea, but I feel that you need to be here because we might have to do some negotiating to get Trish to cooperate so that we can fry the bigger fish."

"I like your idea, Lee. I might add that Trish has but two options. She either does our bidding or she could hang for treason. If I catch the redeye out of DC tonight, will that be soon enough?

"Jerry, is there anything that you want AJ and me to do?"

"Yes. First, you must contact Trish and let her know that Kathy is dead. Second, we have to have some story about Wah Hu so that Trish doesn't get suspicious. Third, we have established a definite Chinese conspiracy. We need Trish's cooperation for confirmation, then we need to use it as a lever to get her cooperation about a plan that I will discuss with you in private. Fourth, I have a plan developed by the aerospace industry that will absolve the United States of all culpability in this crisis—if it works."

"Jerry, AJ, again. Regarding the issue with Wah Hu, I think that I have a solution. I have a source inside the Oregon State Police who will contact Trish and tell her of Wah Hu's death."

"I like what I've heard. To conclude, you proceed with what you have to do, and I'll see you in the morning, in Portland."

After hanging up the phone, Lee turned to AJ. "I suppose that I had best make that call to Trish."

"Yes, and I have a call to make also."

41

AN IMPORTANT CALL
OREGON CITY

A probe for information and the receipt of the desired
information is the best way to anticipate outcomes.

AT 10:00 p.m., Lee dialed Trish's number. After the third ring, Trish answered, "Hi, Lee. Where are you? Can you come over? I miss you."

"Trish, I would really like to come, but quite frankly, I'm exhausted. It has been one hell of a day with my client."

"Damn, I was really hoping."

"Well, how about tomorrow? By the way, did you see the report on the TV news?"

"No, what happened?"

"Your friend, the realtor lady, Kathy, was killed in an accident."

"Are you shitting me?"

"Seriously, Trish, she is gone. It was an automobile accident near Lake Oswego."

"That is horrible. So, what time can we get together tomorrow? I would like to be with you before I have to go to Greece."

"Would 10:00 a.m. be too soon?"

A knock on the door of the motel room distracted Trish. "Lee, excuse me, but someone's at my door. Just a moment, please."

The muffled voices were all that Lee could hear. After a few moments, Trish was back on the phone. "Lee, something dreadful has happened. One of my employees was killed earlier this evening."

"So, who was at the door?"

"It was the state police. They couldn't find me at Mountain View, and a couple of my employees told them where they could find me."

"Trish, not to change the subject, but do you need anything?"

"I could use you."

"Trish, I am exhausted, but if that is what you want, I'll be there."

"Can you stay the night?"

"I will make a poor bed partner, but I want to make you happy. Trish, I will have to leave you about 7:00 a.m. because I have another meeting with my client."

"Just hurry. I need you."

Moments after concluding the call to Trish, Lee heard AJ's voice after the third ring, "Hello?"

"AJ, I have great news. Everything has gone according to plan. Trish has bought the story—hook, line, and sinker—I think. The Asian fellows who work for her also have been told. I pick up Mayhew at PDX at 0700. Would you like to meet there, or should I pick you up on the way to the airport? Tomorrow is going to be a big, big day."

"Please pick me up. I'll be ready by 0500."

42

DAMAGE CONTROL V
TEHRAN

Gathering the pieces of a puzzle and placing them into categories defined by shape, color, or special characteristics is a good way to put a complex puzzle together. Puzzles involving international intrigue often require the same sort of logic applied to the human element. In either case, the solution can bring about a feeling of great satisfaction.

UPON being summoned, Captain Aref strode smartly into Ambassador Woodard's office. Taking a cue to take a seat slightly to the right center of the ambassador's desk, Aref slowly sat in the soft, straight-backed chair. Nodding to acknowledge that he had very important news to share, he cleared his throat and began, "Ambassador, I think I have found an answer to the perplexing problem we face."

The ambassador responded, "Well, we now know who launched

the missile, who was behind the attack, and how to sooth the raw nerves that exist internationally. And I suspect you know how we can posture all of this in such a way that the United States is able to wipe the egg off its proverbial face. I am all ears. Please enlighten me and make my day." Dr. Woodard paused for a moment and then slowly lowered his head as if to express regret for what he had just said. "You'll have to excuse me, Captain. I hope that you will be kind enough to overlook my inappropriate remarks. I have really had a bad day. It seems that this entire matter has consumed me."

"Do not worry, Ambassador. I completely understand. When a person cares about something as much as I am sure you care about this issue, well…. In your previous statements, you gave me far too much credit. I have only come across some key bits of information that can, I feel, with almost 95 percent certainty, identify the source of the attack and the provider of the means to launch the horrendous assault on my country."

"Before you begin, please know that I too have some very interesting and important news to share with you. Please, enlighten me of the information you have. I need to know what you have learned, so that I can pass it along. I fear that this attack is only the first of what could be many."

"Well, you certainly have reason to fear future attacks because I have reason to suspect that the next targets are several sites within your country. As far as your country's involvement, well, I have every reason to believe that the perpetrator of the act was China—or a Chinese terrorist group that is working within China in concert with an American corporation."

"Now I have something to tell you that will confirm your suspicions. My country completely agrees with parts of your assessment. We have discovered that the cruise missile launch emanated from a Chinese cruise-missile-launching submarine. Every missile that is produced in the United States has an identifying plate attached to it. The plate you found identified a corporation in McMinnville, Oregon, as the originator. We have discovered that the missiles were altered by the Chinese to point the blame at the United States and the corporation in McMinnville. We are, as I speak, preparing to bring this traitorous corporation to justice. We have a plan to seek retribution on the People's Republic of China as well. As you know, there were twenty-four missiles launched against your country. There are still twenty-four missiles unaccounted for. As long as the Chinese have these missiles, as we have every reason to suspect, every nation in the world is at risk. We have no information to substantiate the rumor that our nation is at risk of being attacked. The Chinese would never be that blatant."

"Ah ha, so it was a plot hatched by the Chinese? Then the rumor that there are specific sites in your country targeted for missile attack doesn't have much credibility. I agree with you when you say that the Chinese would not be so blatant as to attack your country, so, what do the Chinese have up their sleeves instead?"

"I fear that their goal is to discredit our country and use their cunning ways to become the only superpower in the world to monopolize and control all oil-producing nations in the Middle East, first by annexing your country and turning it into a satellite of China. Again, we have a plan, which I can't divulge at this moment, to discredit the Chinese. Captain Aref, our relationship has been built upon trust. I implore you to not divulge anything you have learned from this meeting about the United States having a plan to discredit the Chinese. If we are to solve this problem, what has been said in this office has to remain between you and me, exclusively. I spoke with your president earlier this morning, and the information I have shared with you has been shared with your president."

Woodard rose from his desk and extended his hand to the captain. "It was so good of you to come in and share what you know with me, Captain. I believe that we have developed a sense of trust that will endure."

The captain smiled, responding, "I agree."

43

A NEW FLIGHT PLAN
PORTLAND

*A plan of attack is a prelude to a call to action. Once
the plan is in place, the wheels are set in motion.*

LEE roused to attention. Checking his cell phone to determine
the time, he noted that the digital display read 3:30.

*Shit, I better get my ass out of bed. I have to pick up AJ at 5:00 and
then pick up Jerry at the airport at 7:00. I should roust Trish, too. My
involvement with her is completely out of character for me. I am really
having problems with pretending to care for her while knowing what a
conniving bitch and traitor she is.*

Jabbing Trish gently in the ribs and then tenderly moving his
hand towards her breasts, he whispered, "Honey, I have to get up. I
have to be at the airport by 5:00 to meet my client."

Sleepily, Trish turned towards Lee. Taking his hand, she placed it on her breast. "Don't you have a little time to put the finishing touches on what we were doing last night?"

"I'm sorry, but I have to get a move on. How about us getting together later, after I am finished with my client?"

Disappointment was etched on Trish's face as she responded, "If we are going to get together it will have to be early this afternoon."

"Why?"

"I have to catch a flight out at 4:00. I am going to Greece, remember?"

"I didn't know it was going to be this soon."

Appearing to not hear Lee's comment, Trish asked, "What time do you think you'll be done with your client?"

"I should be able to wrap up everything by noon. If I were to be here at 1:00, would that work?"

"The time is perfect, but I won't be here. You'll have to come to my place out in McMinnville."

Rising from the bed, Lee paused and shook his head. "Hmm, perhaps we should plan on me being there at 1:30. Will that work?"

"That won't give us much time unless you plan to take me to the airport."

"Consider it done. I'll see you at 1:30. You'll have to excuse me. I have to dress and wash up before I leave." Smiling, he added, "I have to look professional for my meeting."

At precisely 5:00, Lee knocked on AJ's front door. Seconds later AJ opened the door. "Right on time; that's a good trait, as I've said before. So, do you have anything new to share with me?"

"Well, for starters, it appears that we have to get things moving. Trish is flying out at 4:00 this afternoon for Greece."

"Jesus, will we have enough time?"

"We'll have to make it work. Mayhew will figure it out if he hasn't already put all the pieces together. So, have you anything new?"

"I have some good news. Last night when the state police went out to McMinnville looking for Trish, they encountered Wah Hu and Chung Mai. After they were told where Trish was, the Chinese agents got real testy with the police."

"How so?"

"Well, when they were asked for identification and told about Yee Ha's death, the Chinese agents became very belligerent and exposed their weapons. The police had no choice. They had to take them down. So, our problem with the Chinese agents is over. All we have to do is take care of Trish."

"Hey, AJ, not to bring a halt to the good news, but don't you think that we should head for the Portland International Airport?"

"You're right. We can finish our discussion while we are driving."

At the Oregon City exit on I-84, Lee glanced towards AJ. "Have you heard anything more about Kathy?"

"All I know is that she is recovering and will be moved to a safe house within the next three or four days."

"Will I have an opportunity to see her?"

AJ smiled. "Lee, you are an open book. There is much more to this Kathy business than meets the eye, right?"

Lee blushed. "Well let's just say that I've known, or known of, Kathy for a while."

"You didn't answer my question."

"AJ, let's just say that if Kathy feels the way I do, well…. Let's get our thinking caps on. It won't be long before we meet Mayhew. I suspect we will get a grilling." Lee glanced at the clock in the car. It registered 6:45. Ahead, the control tower came into view. In the early morning light, the reflection of the sun made it appear much more majestic than it really was. Turning to AJ, Lee suggested, "AJ, why don't you call Mayhew to see if he is on the ground and where he wants us to meet him."

AJ dialed her phone.

Mayhew answered. "I am on the ground and will meet you at passenger pickup in about ten minutes."

AJ turned to Lee after terminating the call. "He'll meet us at passenger pickup in about ten minutes."

"Good. If he's not there when we arrive, we'll just go around and pick him up on our next drive by."

At precisely 7:02, Lee spotted Mayhew at the curb. He stopped the car and Mayhew got in. "Well, it is nice of you to pick me up, and it is good to see you both still intact. Do you have anything new that I need to know? How is Kathy? Where is Trish? What is the status of the Chinese agents? Are there any other collaborators? What is the status of the missiles in the hangar? What is our timeline to act?"

Lee smiled. "Just as I told you, AJ, we got the grilling that I spoke of. Well, Jerry, for starters, we don't have much time. Trish is scheduled to fly out of Portland at 4:00 p.m. today for Greece." In short staccato responses, Lee provided the rest of the information that Mayhew sought.

Mayhew inquired, "Where are we headed now?"

"We're headed for McMinnville. I know of a very nice place where we can talk to plot our strategy. It is in wine country."

Mayhew smiled. "I like the way you think, but let me be very clear: this is not a pleasure trip. International events are extremely tense. The UN Security Council meets today and may announce offensive actions against the US. The Middle East will impose sanctions against us later today. That means no oil. Our 'friends' are distancing themselves from us. President Chenoa says that we are out of time. By the way, Lee, the analysis of the chip you found on the floor came back. It's of recent Chinese manufacture and is part of a cruise missile guidance sensor." Mayhew paused for effect. "I have crafted a strategy to take care of our problem. Lee, you and AJ are going to be observers, and I will do all the talking when we meet with Trish. At this place in wine country you speak of, I will identify our strategy. I will disclose exactly how we are going to deal with Trish."

Lee asked, "Would it be appropriate to call Trish to suggest that I move our meeting up from 1:30 to 11:00?"

"Yes, call her and let her know. Let's see. How much longer before we get to your place in wine country?"

"We're about ninety minutes out. We should be there sometime around 9:00."

"Good, that will give us plenty of time to get our ducks in a row. By the way, where is this place in wine country?"

"Interestingly, we're going to a place called the Duck Pond Cellars in Dundee."

"Where we will not be partaking in the spirits, correct?"

"Correct. I'm going to call Trish now." He dialed Trish's number. A moment later a familiar voice answered.

"Hi, you, what's up?"

"I'm taking a short break from my meeting with my client. It appears that we're going to be done early. How would you feel about me arriving at Mountain View about 11:00?"

"Perfect. The more time I can have with you, the better."

"Okay, I'll see you then," Lee said, then disconnected the call.

AJ, Lee, and Jerry continued to drive south on highway US 99W through Newberg to a point just before the city limits of the small town of Dundee. On the right, as they were headed south, was a small blue sign that read *Duck Pond Winery, ¼ mile*. At 9:00 they turned into the long driveway leading to the cellars and tasting room. They parked on the south side of the parking lot and started to walk the short distance to the tasting room. The façade of the building was covered with a vine-and-flower-covered trellis supported by tall, graceful white pillars. To the right of the entrance there was a small pond with fresh water flowing into it. A dozen or so large, domesticated Koi fish were swimming among the lily pads. A Mallard duck decoy, the symbol of the winery, floated stoically at one end of the pond.

They walked in through the large, heavy, oaken front door to be greeted by Melissa, who came out from behind the tasting bar.

"Dr. Grady, how nice to see you again. Thank you for your call."

"Hello, Melissa," Lee replied. "Thanks for allowing us to meet here for a few minutes. We won't disrupt your business.

"It's no inconvenience at all. We're glad to be of help. Please follow me to the cask room here behind the gift shop. I've prepared a fresh pot of coffee and some finger sandwiches. Take as long as you want, and I'll ensure you are not disturbed."

The cask room was large and consisted of row upon row of large steel racks on which five levels of wooden casks filled with vintage wines in the aging process were stored. At one end of the room was a wine bar with four leather-covered bar stools. The coffee, cups, and sandwiches were arrayed at one end of the bar. Melissa left and closed the door behind her. They each poured a cup of coffee and took their seats.

Jerry, ever to the point, began, "Let's get started. I want to ensure that we know our strategy."

44

THE HAMMER FALLS
MCMINNVILLE

When a relationship ends, it is often painful. Often the question arises, "What could I have done differently?"

PRIOR to driving up to the office where he was supposed to meet Trish, Lee steered his car into the parking lot where the Spruce Goose was located. Almost directly across the highway from Mountain View Aviation, the hangar that housed the huge aircraft was an imposing sight. Lee glanced at the car clock. "We still have fifteen minutes. Have either of you seen the Spruce Goose before?"

AJ responded, "Yes, at least two or three times."

Mayhew exclaimed, "It has to be one big son of a bitch if it needs that hangar to house it. No, I've never seen it. Isn't the Goose the aircraft that Howard Hughes built during WWII?"

"Yes. Can you believe that it has only been flown once? Hughes took it out for its maiden flight just to show the government that it would actually fly."

"That's true, AJ. I understand it was only in the air for a matter of a few minutes."

"Yeah, just long enough for Howard to prove a point. So, how is this all going to play out, Lee? Trish is only expecting to see you."

"I suggest that you both get in the backseat and crouch down so that you are not visible when we drive in. Once I have parked the car, we can all get out and go into Trish's office. I can't wait to see the look on her face when she sees the three of us."

At precisely 11:00, Lee rolled his car to a stop about twenty-five yards to the left of the entry to Trish's office, turned off the ignition, and exited the car. Once outside, he waited for Jerry and AJ to also exit the car. "Jerry, from this point on, the ball is in your court. I will only speak to say hello when we walk into Trish's office."

"Good. This is going to be fun. I can't wait to watch the bitch squirm when I confront her with all that we know and what her options are."

A moment later, Lee entered Trish's office, followed by AJ and Mayhew. "Hello, Trish."

A look of surprise swept across her face. "What the fuck? Lee, what is going on? I wasn't expecting—"

Jerry interrupted, "You weren't expecting to see AJ and me, I presume. Well, now that the surprise factor has been eliminated, it is time to get down to business. I suggest that you sit down. What I have to say might be best taken while you are seated."

"What right do you have to come into my office and tell me what to do?"

"The proper response to that question, Trish, is what right do you have to conspire with the Chinese to discredit your nation? I suggest that you shut your mouth and listen for a change. Time is short, and what I have to say to you is that you don't have much time to make the most important decision of your life."

Trish's face blanched, and she gave Lee a quizzical look. "Lee, what is going on?"

Jerry quickly leaped to the attack. "We know about the inscribed tags that the Chinese placed on the stolen missiles that were launched on Iran. We know about the stolen missiles that you have housed in Hangar One. We know all about the role that Wah Hu, Yee Haw, and Chung Mai have in your sinister plot. In fact, Ms. Anatolia, we know everything about you and your dealings with the Chinese. In short, I must tell you that I am going to give you two options and tell you that you have exactly five minutes to make a decision." Turning to Lee and AJ, he revealed, "I haven't told you that I contacted the FBI and told them that they were to be on immediate standby, to be here to arrest Ms. Anatolia for treason. AJ, take my phone and push the number-three key. That will connect you with the agents. Tell them that we are ready for them to arrest Ms. Anatolia."

While AJ responded to Mayhew's directive, Jerry continued, "You see, Trish, time is running out on you. So, here are your options. First, you can choose to keep your mouth shut and be arrested for treason. I can promise you that choosing that option will cause you to make a visit to the Grim Reaper very soon. Second, you can choose to tell me where the remaining twenty-one missiles are located. We already have accounted for the three missiles that are housed in Hangar One and the twenty-four that were launched against Iran. So, what is it going to be? Do you want door number one or door number two?"

45

THE DECISION
MCMINNVILLE

*Yogi Berra put it very well: "When you
come to a fork in the road, take it."*

A black Honda pulled up in front of Trish's office. Taking note,
she petitioned for time. "Before I choose door number one or door
number two, I would like to make it clear that none of the charges
that you have made will hold water in a court of law. All you have
is an implication that I had something to do with the missile attack
on Iran. That is based on a plate that was found at the scene of the
bombing. Second, all you have is the word of a dead person, Kathy
Moen, about the supposed missiles in Hangar One. Third, Wah Hu,
Chung Mai, and Yee Hah have had no role in my operation that goes
beyond being employees."

Mayhew smiled. "Have it your way, Ms. Anatolia, but you should know that we have Wah Hu in custody and he is singing like a songbird. It also might interest you to know that Kathy Moen is alive and well. She has been placed in the Agent Protection Program and will testify against you, should that become necessary. Do I really have to make myself any clearer?"

Trish looked pleadingly at Lee. "Lee?"

"I'm sorry, Trish. We have you dead to rights. Your time is short. I suggest that you take door number two."

Trish's face contorted with rage. "You bastard, Lee. All the time you were fucking me, you were—"

Lee nodded. "Yeah, and the sex wasn't really even that good. You are a bitch—a despicable bitch—and your time has run out, Trish. What is it going to be?"

Shuddering, her shoulders sagging in resignation, she responded, "Okay, okay, you win. Tell me again what you want to know."

Mayhew replied, "For starters, where are the missing missiles?"

"Fifteen are located somewhere in China. The other six are on board a Chinese submarine operating somewhere in the Pacific, off the coast of Oregon."

"Okay, now why would you become involved in such a treasonous act?"

"Do you recall that the USSR boasted that they would bring us down economically? Well, during our last several administrations in the US, the former USSR's dirty work has been done for them because of all of the money poured down the toilet to restart our economy, support nations with no particular love for us under the guise of foreign aid to help cement relations, to support dictators who in the long run we have to end up deposing, by allowing 'aliens' to enter our country illegally to claim the rights that we Americans should have...the list goes on. Gentlemen and AJ, I am a patriot. I am a loyal and devoted conservative American. I was willing to do whatever it took to show the American public that we are not safe. We are giving our country away to those who hate us."

"And your solution is to discredit America to achieve this purpose? Come on, Trish, there has to be something much more sinister behind this than that."

"Okay, so I had a plan to march into Washington after Chenoa had been disgraced and take charge. I suppose you would call it a takeover."

With calm, measured restraint, and total disgust, Mayhew snorted, "That is one name for it. So, tell me why you were going to Greece."

"I wasn't going to Greece. Wah Hu, Chung Mai, Yee Hah and I have a rendezvous with the Chinese Mafia leaders in China—or at least we did."

Mayhew waved to the agents standing outside, motioning for them to come inside. "Gentlemen, take this woman into custody."

46

BEGINNING OF A NEW RELATIONSHIP
PORTLAND

Things aren't always what they seem. A house may look great from the outside but have many defects on the inside. This is also true with the human species. Character, unlike a wall that needs to be repainted or faulty plumbing that needs to be replaced, is more difficult to repair. Spotting character flaws can also be more challenging than determining the improvements needed for a home.

LEE walked into Kathy's hospital room.

"Right on time, just as you promised."

Lee smiled, an impish grin, his eyes foretelling a mischievous drama to follow. "Right, Charon. When someone special is waiting, it is easy to be punctual. So, is Tommy all hyped up for the game tonight?"

"All right already, that's enough of the coded messages! Do you play this game with all of your lady friends?"

"Actually, no. You're special. You require that extra touch."

Sliding into a chair near her bed, he shook his head in mild protest, or perhaps mild resignation. "Please don't make me out to be something I'm not. Actually, seeing you for the first time since your admission into the APP is a bit unsettling for me."

"How does that work? When I last spoke with you, you seemed quite your usual self. You're not just putting me on, are you?"

"Not at all. Actually, it's very easy and quite comfortable to carry on a professional conversation with you, Kathy. What I'm here for is a bit awkward for me. I never thought that I would ever be at this place in my life, if you know what I mean."

Kathy frowned. "I don't know what you mean."

"Maybe I'm just afraid of messing up things with you."

"Care to tell me what you mean by being afraid of messing up?"

He grinned sheepishly. "Kathy, I really like you. When you were in that accident and you were taken away by the APP, I was afraid that I had lost you. I...."

"Spit it out, Lee. What are you talking about? You might want to think of yourself sitting in the confessional."

"Are you a Catholic?"

"No. For Christ's sake, are you going to keep me waiting all night because you have a unique ability to change the subject?"

"No, I'm just stalling for time. Hmm, where to start?"

"Why not try the beginning. I'm in no hurry, and I sure as hell am not going anywhere. Besides, I find your company quite fascinating."

Lee's cheeks reddened as he slowly ducked his head. "Okay, you asked for it. Well, I met my deceased wife, Sandy, while I was in high school and she was a student at the University of Oregon. It seems...." His eyes started to mist. "I fell in love with her, eventually married her, and then she died...of cancer...." His eyes suddenly assumed a distant, empty glare. "Yeah, after seven years of agony, hope, promise, disappointment, and finally...the end."

"Oh, Lee, I'm so sorry."

Nodding, he slowly gathered himself. "No apology necessary. You had no way of knowing. Besides, I sort of set you up for this. Anyway, when I first met her, I thought it would never go anywhere. I guess eight years later, she proved me wrong."

"And Trish, where does she fit in?"

"In the middle, at the end, and now she's nothing. She is completely out of my life. Kathy, when you and I met, Trish was a person of interest that, well, she became nothing more than a job—a person who I had to deal with to accomplish an assigned mission."

"You are going to have to be a little more specific, Lee. When we first met, Trish seemed to be much more to you than that."

"Okay, a historical recap of my involvement with Trish would be, uh, I met her while I was in the service. It was supposed to be a weekend fling, but it turned into quite an adventure." He grinned. "It was a blind date that didn't start very well but ended up leading me almost to the altar."

"Wow! That is a bit impressive. Love at first sight?"

Lee stared at Kathy for a moment to weigh his response. Finally, shrugging, he nodded. "I suppose. Probably more so for her, but I wasn't exactly forced into submission."

"So, what happened?"

Lee grinned. "I hope you're ready for this."

"Try me."

"She died."

Kathy stared at him in animated disbelief. Finally, after the impact of his revelation had sunk in, she exclaimed, "Bullshit! She what? Oh come on, Lee. Who in the hell was I showing property to, a ghost?"

"No, and this is where it gets really weird. In a nutshell, that is what I was told by her father. He didn't want us to get married, so he concocted a story about her death in a car accident and forced his lieutenant, Vinnie Trabogo, to marry her."

"This sounds like something out of *The Godfather*."

Lee nodded. "Anyway, my wife, Sandy, put a case together against Trish's father, got Trish to testify, turn state's evidence, and put Trish in the witness protection program."

"So, she wasn't still in the program when I met her. How does that work? I thought that once you were in that program, you were there for life."

"That's probably true in most cases, but, well, let's just say for sake of avoiding an in-depth discussion, all the people that might have had an interest in seeing her dead had died. She came back into full view, running companies. I guess that T-Line, her old company, is now being run by her son, Truman."

Kathy smiled knowingly. "And her new operation in McMinnville turned out to be a cover for her involvement with the Chinese. Lee, cut to the chase and get down to what is important to me. Did you love her?"

Lee shook his head. "If you had asked if I used to love her before her faked death, I would have had to say that I probably did. Now, it's not the same. She isn't the same person who I thought I loved."

Looking intently into Kathy's eyes, he added, "I guess that brings us back to…. Well, now that this adventure is over, what am I going to do next? I suppose I thought of myself as a self-styled soldier of fortune. Maybe I saw or still do see myself as a cross between Rambo and Indiana Jones. Anyway, I guess my next pursuit is…it has to be you, if you'll agree."

Kathy's face reddened. "You mean to say that we finally get to concentrate on you and me? How refreshing. So what do you have in mind?"

"I resigned. I'm no longer doing the spook thing. I want to work on having a life with you. Maybe we can sell real estate together, travel, or...."

47

THE BEGINNING OF THE END

WASHINGTON, DC

Poker, at times, is a game of bluff. When you are sitting with a pat hand, it is time to raise the stakes and then smile as you rake in all the chips. Sometimes you have to know when to hold them and when to fold them.

PRESIDENT Chenoa sat at her desk in the Oval Office after a grueling two days of nonstop briefings in the Situation Room and one-on-one appointments in the office. She was waiting for the appointed time, in one hour, to make a phone call she hoped would be the most important communication ever initiated from the White House. Vice President Smith, Secretary of Defense Baker, and Speaker of the House of Representatives Billings had been deployed out of the Washington, DC, area to underground bunker facilities in the Central United States. If all went as planned, they would return tomorrow. If it didn't, they were prepared to exercise the succession of power plan developed years ago for use if Washington should be leveled.

The catastrophe in Iran had finally come to a head. United States relations with nearly every nation in the world, adversaries and friends alike, had reached a breaking point. The president had to be circumspect, vague, and evasive with all of them regarding a US explanation of why the country appeared to have attacked a Middle Eastern country. The intelligence assessments and evaluation of all bits and pieces of information had been so intense and so thorough that the United States even had to send undercover black ops operatives into several foreign nations to validate information given by their diplomats, because its veracity wasn't trusted. Under angry circumstances, meetings had to be conducted in Asia and Europe, and even American emissaries had been physically attacked in these overseas locations when they arrived. Diplomatic immunity for anyone associated with the Americans was nonexistent.

Every US administration department and agency had been involved in gathering information on how and why the attack occurred, and every intelligence community operative had gathered pertinent and extraneous data points. In spite of the difficulties of the last eight days in keeping the international community at bay and imploring them to show restraint, some nations took dramatic actions to punish the United States for what the world believed was an American plot to take control of oil assets in the Middle East, to blockade the Suez Canal, to annihilate the Muslim culture, and to exert its superpower status to become a dictatorial empire.

President Chenoa couldn't reveal to the world what US intelligence agents had found out about the attack as the investigation unfolded. To reveal findings prematurely, without verification, would not only make the information specious, but would tip off the real culprits whom we were trailing and drive them deeper underground. It would also disclose what the United States was going to do to retaliate. The United States was already considered guilty in the court of public opinion but was also thought to be like a wounded tiger; it was feared that it could lash out with nuclear claws to protect itself.

Soon the situation would be over. Technical assessments had revealed a nuclear submarine from the People's Republic of China had hijacked and sunk an American warship. It had stolen the warship's cargo of state-of-the-art cruise missiles and murdered the crew. It had done the same to an innocent civilian vessel and scuttled it to the bottom of the Pacific. It had co-opted an American aerospace corporation that performed certain sensitive defense projects and had enticed the management to collaborate in a treasonous activity. It had attacked an innocent neighboring Middle Eastern nation and created genocide, the results of which would last for decades to come. All these activities constituted acts of war.

Now the evidence was in. The proof was in hand. The truth was known and Chenoa's resolve was firm. US agents had achieved full disclosure from the treasonous leader of the Oregon Company that assisted the Chinese in their dastardly plan. The Mafioso connections in the United States and in China had been exposed for what they were and were forced to abandon all of their murder-for-hire, international extortion activities and clandestine weapons sales deals. The plan of retaliation and defense had been finalized. Chenoa believed with all her heart that once the *GO* code was given, such a holocaust would never occur again. If she was wrong, it could mean the end of the United States of America as it was known.

There was a soft knock at the door of the Oval Office. The chief of staff quietly entered and said, "Madam President, it is time to make the call to the president of China. The national security advisor, the deputy secretary of defense, the chairman of the joint chiefs, and the leaders of both houses of Congress are here."

She nodded affirmatively and the three men and two women filed quietly and somberly into her office. "Good morning, ladies and gentlemen. We sent a communiqué to the president of China two hours ago, alerting him that I needed to speak with him on the hotline, and we will initiate that call in fifteen minutes. Meanwhile, all of you have seen the same unequivocal evidence that I have seen and we have agreed on a course of action. I want to know now, from each of you, if you are still in agreement with all of the actions decided upon."

The national security advisor spoke for all of them and said, "We are in agreement, Madam President. We should move ahead."

"Good." Turning to her chief of staff, she said, "Bill, it's time. Place the call please and activate the recording equipment. I want a record of this call."

He placed the red telephone instrument in the middle of the Resolute desk and plugged it into the receptacle in the floor. The telephone was the only item on the desk. There was, after all, no other, more important matter to be managed there today.

A small green light on the front of the phone lit up, and President Chenoa picked up the receiver and pressed it to her ear. Each of her advisors in the room put the wireless earpieces into their ears so that they could listen but could not speak or be heard. Chenoa had met President Ming eight months earlier during her own presidential campaign as he stopped in San Francisco on his way to Venezuela for a state visit. She found, at the time, he spoke perfect English and seemed to be a very engaging man, but was a political realist as well—prone to grasp the realities of international relations. She also realized there was probably a bevy of advisors and translators on his end of the phone as well, one of whom was probably a speech and emotions interpreter who would judge her sincerity, level of insecurity, and intensity of resolve.

"Mr. President, thank you for taking my call. I wish we were talking under more pleasant circumstances. We are faced with a set of grave actions that have placed our two nations on a collision course that could result in more catastrophic events than have occurred in Iran."

"I am not certain what you are addressing, Madam President, but if there is a way we can resolve any differences between our two countries, I am willing to consider your thoughts."

That pompous bastard. He must think I don't know what he has done and I'm calling to surrender. I've been told he's arrogant but is a careful listener as well.

"Mr. President, my intention is not to assert there is no way to solve our differences, but first I wish to tell you what I know and have incontrovertible evidence of, which I have not yet shared with the leaders of any other nation. A month ago a US warship in transit across the Pacific, from the Pacific Northwest in the United States to Hawaii, was boarded, hijacked, and its cargo of cruise missiles stolen. The entire crew was murdered. A civilian vessel registered to the Canadian National Maritime Agency was also attacked and all on board were slaughtered. The missiles were delivered to an American company that it has been proven was engaged in espionage in concert with several People's Republic of China citizens. They modified those missiles with Chinese-originated parts and components. Twenty-four of those modified missiles were used in the raid on Tehran, which resulted in over thirteen thousand deaths. Mr. President, we have eyewitness accounts and evidence that these launches came from China's nuclear-powered cruise missile submarine, *Chairman Mao-Tse-Tung*, which at this time is in the western Pacific. All these actions are regarded by the international community as acts of war."

"Madam President, if you are accusing me and my country of atrocities, murder, hijacking, and an attack on a sovereign vessel of the United States, I assure you I am unaware of the details of such a fabrication and resent the accusation that my country would do such a thing."

"Mr. President, don't insult me by suggesting I would make this call without a strong wealth of information and absolute proof. There is a very unique and impenetrable software code imbedded into the onboard programs of each and every one of the remaining twenty-four cruise missiles that are now in your possession. Three of those modified missiles are located on US territory. Your worldwide, infrared surveillance system is as good as ours. So I direct your attention to the northwestern corner of the United States where there will be a large detonation that will be as a result of my order to destroy those three missiles."

She turned toward the chairman of the JCS, who was telephonically connected to Dr. Lee Grady, Colonel Jerry Mayhew, and their team of aerospace engineers at the Los Angeles satellite uplink-downlink site, and gave the first order to destruct. At that moment, a fireball erupted under Hanger One at the McMinnville airport in Western Oregon, totally consuming all the hangers and dwellings within a radius of three hundred yards.

"Now, Mr. President, let me give a second destruct order, which will tell us where a second group of missiles is located. Let me advise you, Mr. President, they are in the possession of a submarine belonging to the Peoples Liberation Navy, who are unfortunately in the wrong place at the wrong time and are guilty of doing the wrong thing."

President Chenoa turned to the chairman, who directed activation of the second destruct command. A moment later, all six missiles aboard the *Chairman Mao* exploded. The entire front half of the 550-foot-long, submerged submarine was obliterated. There was no time for Captain Chang to warn his crew, nor any time for there to be any warning issued from mainland China to take protective actions. Even if there had been time, there was nothing anyone could have done to save the *Mao*. A huge fireball erupted from the surface of the mid-Pacific. The submarine was completely destroyed and its debris began to sink to the bottom of the Pacific Ocean.

"Madam President, I don't know what kind of charade you are playing, but blackmail is also an act of war. If you think my country is in possession of US-government, war-making munitions you are sadly mistaken. We are a peace-loving nation and I will not stand for idle threats from you after you supposedly sent your missiles against Iran and are now out in search of a scapegoat."

"Mr. President, if you are the peace-loving nation you profess to be, then you'll welcome the opportunity to join with me in sponsoring an international peace treaty to be signed by you and me here in Washington to ban all nuclear weapons, author peaceful solutions to global conflicts, and stop selling weapons of mass destruction to poorer nations. You will also at least double your contribution to restore Tehran to habitable status again. For my part, no other nation must know exactly how this entire holocaust occurred, but they must know the United States was not responsible. Could it have been a rogue group of terrorists? Mr. President, I am now issuing the last missile destruct order for the remaining missiles that you say are not in your control."

"Wait, wait, Madam President, this is preposterous. I need a few moments to—"

Then, on the open telephone line, President Chenoa said, "General Gilmore, issue the third destruct order."

At the general's command, Grady was given the privilege of pushing the button. Thousands of miles away on mainland China, one hundred miles east of Beijing at a small, unobtrusive facility in the countryside, surrounded by high chain-link fences and concertina wire, a third massive explosion occurred, destroying everything within a radius of three fourths of a mile.

There was silence on the open telephone line for what seemed like an eternity but couldn't have been more than seconds. President Chenoa waited for President Ming to speak. There was the sound of an exhale in exasperation. Then he spoke.

"Madam President, it could be that criminal elements in my country may have been at work in this crisis, or someone in my government may have been negligent in maintaining proper surveillance of subversive activities. I will investigate. Also, perhaps there is good and justifiable reason for our two peace-loving nations to talk further about finding ways to work better together."

President Chenoa, who knew she clearly had the advantage, then said, "Thank you, Mr. President. I look forward to your call within twenty-four hours."

EPILOGUE

FORTY-EIGHT hours after the phone call President Chenoa made to President Ming of China, the Chinese president dispatched his vice president to Washington with a draft outline of a joint peace treaty in which the two presidents requested international political and economic participation. At the same time, a generous gift of one trillion dollars was given to the people of Iran from the people of China, along with massive amounts of medical and construction material aid.

Thirty-six hours after the phone call, a headline on the front page of the *Beijing People's Daily* newspaper announced that the People's Republic of China Security Service uncovered a multinational plot by international terrorists and underworld organizations. Leaders of the Mafia-style organization admitted responsibility for the recent launch of stolen submarine-launched cruise missiles against the Republic of Iran, which killed upwards of thirteen thousand Iranian and foreign citizens. The seven underworld leaders of this dastardly deed committed suicide to avoid prosecution and humiliation in a public trial for their crimes. A dozen other lesser criminal conspirators were incarcerated until their fate could be decided.

The news article went on to say that the rogue cruise-missile-launching submarine of uncertain nationality that launched the raid on Tehran met with a mysterious accident, which resulted in its total destruction at sea. There were no apparent survivors. The last line of the article noted that the citizens of the People's Republic of China and the United States of America had no role in this catastrophe and all citizens of these two great nations were outraged.

Dr. Lee Grady and Special Agent Kathy Moen remained close throughout her recuperation in the hospital and after she was released. Shortly after that they married, retired from active service to the federal government, and took a long overdue vacation. They bought a permanent home in Portland, Oregon, began touring the Western United States, and decided along the way to coauthor a travelogue for retired persons. During their travels, they encountered some unsolved mysteries that plagued small Oregon towns. With careers spent in helping solve mysteries, the temptation to assist local authorities was too strong to resist. So, they stepped forward to help bring wrongdoers to justice, and at the same time, continued to be a bridge for the three amigos.

Jerry Mayhew, Lee Grady, and John Woodard continued to stay in touch. They also agreed to get together someday to write a spy novel. Jerry and his wife, Joy, occasionally traveled with Kathy and Lee to vacation and lend support to the partnership that, jokingly among friends, came to be known as K&L Crime Solvers. Jerry continued to serve the agency and still received calls to assist in international terrorist tracking efforts.

Following the missile attack, John Woodard saved eighteen Iranian men, women, and children from life-threatening wounds. In one case, he performed emergency surgery in the embassy's infirmary on a ten-year-old child suffering from shrapnel wounds to her head and chest. He saved her from certain death. Dr. Woodard went on to serve as the American ambassador to Iran for nearly four more years and became a close confidante and advisor to the Iranian president. He was awarded the coveted Persian Palm Medallion award for his service to the people of the Republic of Iran. He returned to the United States in 2021 to become deputy secretary of state, where he served with distinction for two more years before retiring to the Willamette Valley of Oregon.

CAST OF CHARACTERS

Arlene Judith (AJ) Lang – CIA Special Agent
Dr. Lee Grady, PhD – Consultant Criminologist to the CIA and FBI
Jerry Mayhew – CIA Special Agent
Joy Mayhew – Jerry Mayhew's wife
Dr. John W. Woodard, MD, PhD – US Ambassador to Iran
Ms. Janice Strothers – Secretary to the Ambassador, US Embassy, Tehran
Rosemary Woodard – John Woodard's wife
Thelma J. Massadoti – Director of Middle Eastern Policy and Economic Support, NSC
Wah Hu, Chung Mai, and Yee Hah – Chinese Mafia terrorists and assassins
Nicole – Lee Grady's oldest daughter
Charon – Lee Grady's youngest daughter

Jason – Nicole Grady's husband
Vinnie Trabogo – Trish's late husband
Trush Anatolia – Trish's late father
Trish's mother – No name given
Trish Knight – a.k.a. Pat Brown and Trish Anatolia
Truman Trabogo – Trish's son
Deidra – Trish's good friend and confidante
US Vice President – Bill Richardson
US Secretary of State – Jane O'Donnell
US President – Sally Marie Chenoa
Kathy Moen – CIA Special Agent on sabbatical and real estate agent
Rashid Al Formadi – President of Iran
Ali Akbar Sanfezi – Foreign Minister of Iran
Captain Muhammad Hussein Aref – Iranian Army and Liaison to US Embassy
Colin Morris – Aide to Dr. Woodard and Station Chief
Ambassador Bradley Williams – Retiring US Ambassador to Iran
Vice Admiral Ellison Manley, USN Retired – Director of National Security
Lt. General John Laughlin, USAF Retired – National Security Advisor
Paul Dryan – Opposing party candidate for president in the November 2016 elections
Jack Makin – FBI Special Agent
Bill Vogt – FBI Special Agent

ABOUT THE AUTHORS

GARY L. HOLLEN

BORN in Bend, Oregon, Gary L. Hollen earned degrees and certificates from Willamette University, Western Oregon State College, and the University of Oregon. He served a tour of duty in the US Navy before beginning his thirty-seven-year career in the field of education. During that time he taught junior high and high school mathematics, coached basketball, served as a curriculum vice principal and principal, and supervised student teachers through Portland State University. He is a prolific writer and reader of novels. His recent literary ventures resulted in his novel *Surface Tension* being published in 2005.

Mr. Hollen is a fourth-generation Oregonian and the proud father of two beautiful daughters. His heart has been completely captured by his two lovely granddaughters and one all-boy grandson. He is widowed and is now retired and living in Portland Oregon.

JERRY MAY

JERRY May is a thirty-year veteran of the United States Air Force. He retired from the service in the rank of colonel after a variety of assignments in Europe, the Pacific, Greenland, the National Security Council in the White House and in the Office of the Secretary of Defense, and in the Headquarters, United States Air Force in the Pentagon. He also served in the North American Aerospace Defense Command Cheyenne Mountain Complex and the Air Force Space Command in Colorado. He is a graduate of Willamette University in Salem, Oregon, the University of Northern Colorado in Greeley, Colorado, the Kennedy School of Government at Harvard University, Cambridge, Massachusetts, and the Industrial College of the Armed Forces. He has two daughters, Tracey and Tricia, who are in government service. He currently resides with his wife, Joyce, in Melbourne Beach, Florida, where he continues to write and support the political initiatives of selected state and national candidates.

JOHN W. WOOD

JOHN W. Wood, MD, is a retired ophthalmologist and resides in Salem, Oregon, with his wife, Rosemary. He had a distinguished career in medicine and is a graduate of Willamette University, The Oregon Health & Science University School of Medicine. He completed his internship at Emanuel Hospital in Portland, Oregon, and performed his residency in ophthalmology at Vanderbilt University Medical Center in Nashville, Tennessee. He completed the School of Aerospace medicine primary course at Brooks Air Force Base in San Antonio, Texas, and the US Naval Medical School operational (tropical) medicine course at the National Naval Medical Center in Bethesda, Maryland. He served in the United States Air Force as a flight surgeon at McConnell Air Force Base, Wichita, Kansas, with extended duty at several Air Force bases in Southeast Asia during the Vietnam War. He is Board certified in ophthalmology by the American Board of Ophthalmology. He is a member of the American Medical Association and the Oregon Medical Association, received an executive appointment and served on the Oregon State Board of Medical Examiners, and is a member and former president of the Marion-Polk County Medical Society in Salem. He has served in various active surgical and consultative capacities in the specialty of ophthalmology and has been proactively supportive of the political objectives and goals of selected state and national political candidates. He is an avid reader and student of political science and national strategy development and a senior advisor to the goals of young men in the Sigma Alpha Epsilon fraternity.